blue
rider
press

K STREET

Also by M. A. Lawson

Rosarito Beach
Viking Bay

(writing as Mike Lawson)

The Inside Ring
The Second Perimeter
House Rules
House Secrets
House Justice
House Divided
House Blood
House Odds
House Reckoning
House Rivals
House Revenge

K STREET

[A KAY HAMILTON NOVEL]

M. A. LAWSON

BLUE RIDER PRESS
New York

blue
rider
press

An imprint of Penguin Random House LLC
375 Hudson Street
New York, New York 10014

Library of Congress Cataloging-in-Publication Data

Names: Lawson, M. A., author.
Title: K street : a Kay Hamilton Novel / M.A. Lawson.
Description: New York : Blue Rider Press, 2017.
Identifiers: LCCN 2016016473 (print) I LCCN 2016022501 (ebook)
I ISBN 9780399573842 (hardback) I ISBN 9780399575426 (ePub)
Subjects: LCSH: United States. Drug Enforcement Administration—Fiction.
I Undercover operations—Fiction. I Drug traffic—Fiction. I BISAC: FICTION
/ Suspense. I FICTION / Crime. I GSAFD: Mystery fiction.
Classification: LCC PS3612.A95423 K2 2016 (print) I LCC PS3612.A95423 (ebook)
I DDC 813/.6—dc23
LC record available at https://lccn.loc.gov/2016016473
p.   cm.

Printed in the United States of America
1 3 5 7 9 10 8 6 4 2

Book design by Lauren Kolm

For Gail.

For her love and support. This book, and all the others, would never have been written if she didn't do all the things she does for me.

K STREET

1

Simpson pulled the U-Haul into a loading zone in front of the build-ing on K Street. Otis nodded to Simpson—*You know what to do*—got out of the cab, and walked back to open the cargo door of the truck.

Otis was a little nervous about Simpson because he didn't know him all that well. When his previous wheelman, Connors, had been diagnosed with cancer, he'd recommended that Simpson replace him, and the one other time Otis had used him, he'd done okay. He didn't run his mouth, he stayed calm, and he followed orders without asking dumb questions, so he fit in with the rest of Otis's crew and should do all right today. All he had to do was drive; he wasn't going to be involved in the heavy shit. What Otis was really worried about was that he hadn't been given enough time to plan the heist.

In the back of the U-Haul were the three men Otis always worked with: Brown, McCabe, and Quinn. He had been lucky to get them all on such short notice. He knew none of them would be on another job because they'd each cleared almost fifty grand in Raleigh three months ago. He was also the only guy they ever worked with. Still, he'd been worried that one of them might have decided to take a vacation, particularly Brown, who liked to go on cruises with his sister. The idea of Brown and his loopy sister dining with the squares on a cruise ship always made Otis smile. But they'd all been at home or near their homes when he called. He wanted all the manpower he could get.

The U-Haul had a hydraulic lift platform, which was the only reason Otis was using it. He didn't know how much the safe weighed and he didn't want to try to manhandle four or five hundred pounds into the back of a van.

Brown placed a big toolbox on a hydraulic dolly rated for two thousand pounds and rolled it onto the platform, and Otis lowered the platform with Brown standing on it. The toolbox was aluminum, four feet long, two feet wide, and two feet deep. It held a lot of equipment and it was heavy. Quinn and McCabe jumped to the ground; Brown reached back into the truck and grabbed a large black gym bag, which he placed on top of the toolbox. Then they proceeded toward the entrance.

They were all wearing thin leather gloves, blue coveralls, and blue baseball caps. The coveralls were all size XL, except Brown's, which were XXL. They were also wearing sunglasses and fake mustaches. Otis had bought the mustaches for a racetrack job he'd planned two years ago but decided to drop when they changed security procedures at the track.

It was seven p.m. and still light outside, so the sunglasses weren't totally out of line, but four big guys, identically dressed, with sunglasses and big bushy mustaches . . . Hell, they *looked* like criminals. Otis could only hope that if there were cameras on the street, their features wouldn't be recognizable. If the guy wasn't paying them so damn much—Otis had never made this much on a single job in his life—he never would have agreed to do it.

Otis entered the building first, placing his right hand over the lower part of his face so only his sunglasses were visible. He glanced quickly around the lobby for surveillance cameras and didn't see any. He signaled to the three men waiting outside and they entered the building. Fortunately, there was no one in the lobby, which was what Otis had been hoping for. Otis pushed the button for the elevator and one of the three elevator doors opened immediately. Otis entered first, again keeping his hand over the lower part of his face. There wasn't a camera in the elevator, at least not that he could see. He noticed, as he always did, that the elevator had been manufactured by a company named Otis.

As soon as his crew was inside and the door was shut, Otis said, "Masks." They all took off the ball caps and the sunglasses and shoved them into the right rear pocket of their coveralls. From another pocket, they pulled out black ski masks and pulled them down over their heads. Otis pushed the button for the seventh floor.

As the elevator was ascending, Otis said, "Guns." Brown unzipped the black gym bag that was sitting on the toolbox, and Quinn and McCabe each removed MAC-10 machine pistols. Otis and Brown took out 9mm S&Ws. All the weapons had sound suppressors. Brown shoved his pistol into a pocket since he couldn't hold it and push the dolly at the same time.

They walked down the hall to room 711. Beside the door was a small brass plaque that read THE CALLAHAN GROUP; above the door Otis could see a surveillance camera looking down at him. There was nothing they could do about the camera except move quickly. He turned the doorknob but the door was locked. "Take it out," he said to Brown.

Brown removed the door-knocker from the toolbox: a four-foot-long, four-inch-diameter piece of carbon-steel pipe with two handles welded onto it. The pipe had come from Brown's garage and he'd welded the handles on himself two hours ago.

They were all big men—all over six feet tall and strong—but Brown was a monster: six-foot-six, over two hundred and fifty pounds. He swung the door-knocker, hitting the door just above the knob, and blew it open. They found themselves inside a small foyer, and behind an empty desk was another door. Otis turned the knob on the second door but it was also locked. "Shit," he said, and motioned at Brown, and Brown stepped forward with the door-knocker.

Gotta move, gotta move, Otis was thinking.

NORMALLY DAVID NORTON would have left the office at six but he was waiting for a call from Osaka, Japan, where it was eight a.m. It was a beautiful July evening, the temperature in the upper seventies. D.C. had been experiencing a brutal heat wave, but it finally broke and it was actually pleasant outside. Had he not been waiting for the Japanese lawyer to call, he would have been sitting on his deck at home, having a glass of wine. If he was lucky, he'd be sitting on the deck alone. If he wasn't so lucky, his wife would be having a drink with him, bitching about the seventh-grade morons she taught.

Jesus! What was that noise? Something had crashed into something. Then he heard the same sound, but closer this time. Maybe a bookcase in one of the offices had fallen over. He got up, went around his desk, and opened his door to investigate.

What the hell?

There were four guys coming down the hall toward him, pushing a dolly with a big metal box on it. It took a second for him to realize the guys were wearing ski masks, and about a millisecond later, he thought, *Oh shit, they've got guns*—which was the last thought David Norton ever had.

QUINN DIDN'T HESITATE. As soon as the short, bald guy stepped into the hallway, he raised the MAC-10 and squeezed the trigger. A three-round burst. All three bullets hit the bald guy in the chest.

. . .

PHIL KLEIN WAS an accountant; he'd been one all his life and, without a doubt, this was the most interesting job he'd ever had. He just hoped that he didn't end up in jail one day. His job was to create a completely fictitious financial life for the Callahan Group. A small part of the income received by the Group was legitimate. A large part of the Group's income, however, came from mysterious sources—at least they were mysterious to Klein—and he created a financial portrait of a company that, at least to the IRS, appeared to be very successful.

And this was what made the job so unique. Normally what companies tried to do was juggle the numbers to make a company look *less* successful, like it had experienced enormous losses and had so many expenses that there was no profit to pay taxes on. But that's not what Callahan wanted. He wanted Klein to make it appear as if the Callahan Group was one of the more successful lobbying firms on K Street. Callahan had also told Klein to never try to slip one past the IRS—which, as a tax accountant, went against Klein's nature. Callahan said he wanted Klein to do absolutely nothing that might trigger an IRS audit.

Like David Norton, Phil Klein's brain couldn't immediately comprehend what his ears were hearing. The first thing he thought of was the time his eighteen-year-old daughter ran her Mazda into the garage door. Then he heard the sound again. He got up from his desk and flexed his right knee, which always locked up when he sat too long, and heard the spitting sounds, three quick *pffts*. And like Norton, Klein opened his door to investigate.

He immediately saw Norton, on his back, his white shirt looking as if he'd spilled cranberry juice down the front. He looked down the hallway next and saw men in ski masks coming rapidly toward him. Two of the men were holding what looked like machine guns. Klein jumped back into his office just as one of the men fired half a dozen shots at him—and he realized the spitting sounds he'd heard were bullets being fired from a silenced weapon, a sound he'd only heard in movies. The bullets made grooves in the wall outside his office and dug chunks of wood out of the doorframe. He slammed the door shut, locked it, and ran for the phone.

"GET HIM," OTIS SAID, "before he calls the cops." Quinn ran down the hall to the office of the man who had just stuck his head out. He tried the doorknob, but it was locked. He stepped back and fired six shots directly through the door—the .45 caliber bullets tore through the door like it was crepe paper—then motioned for Brown, and Brown swung the door-knocker and the door flew open. Quinn entered the room prepared to shoot again but saw the man lying behind his desk. At least three of the bullets he'd fired through the door had hit the guy. He appeared to be dead but Quinn's orders were to make sure, so he fired a round into the man's head. Quinn figured if the guy wasn't dead now, he was fucking immortal.

THOMAS CALLAHAN NOT only heard the doors being bashed open but could actually see what was happening because there was a security camera above the door to his office pointing down the hallway.

Callahan's door was always kept locked, and he would check to see who was in the hall before he admitted anyone. The security camera fed directly into a small monitor on his desk. So he could see the men coming; he saw one of them kill Norton; he saw the same man fire half a dozen rounds at Klein's door. Klein was most likely dead now, too, and Callahan figured that he was going to be dead himself in the next couple of minutes.

The first thing he did was take the document he'd been given by Sally Ann Danzinger and put it in his safe. Seven hours earlier, she had given him a sealed envelope and told him to place it in his safe, unopened. And Callahan did. But after Danzinger left, and when he could no longer control his curiosity, he'd removed the envelope and opened it. Inside he found a document that meant absolutely nothing to him: It was a single short paragraph that was just numbers and symbols. So he put it into a new white envelope and sealed it, but when his people started getting killed, the envelope was still on his desk. His safe was open and he ran to it, tossed the envelope inside, slammed the door shut, and spun the combination dial to lock the safe.

The only other thing inside the safe was fifty grand in cash—petty cash he kept on hand for emergencies. He was religious about destroying paperwork after missions were completed, so there wasn't anything else in his office that might reveal the true nature of the Callahan Group.

He had no idea, however, who the masked men were or why they were there. Callahan had done things over the years that could cause several entities—foreign and domestic—to want him dead, but there wasn't anything he'd done lately that seemed a likely cause for what was happening. He couldn't help but wonder if his people were dying because of the document Sally Ann Danzinger had given him.

Callahan glanced at the monitor on his desk and could see that all four men were now outside his office. He opened the center drawer of his desk and took out an old .45 that he'd been given when he was a lieutenant in the army, over thirty years ago. He was supposed to have given the gun back when he gave up his commission and returned to civilian life, but he lied and said it had been stolen. The army didn't believe him, of course, but what could they do?

Callahan couldn't remember the last time he'd fired the .45. When he first joined the CIA, right after he got out of the army, there'd been a few years where he'd been required to qualify with a sidearm, but that had been almost twenty years ago. And that was probably the last time he'd fired the weapon. He wondered if the bullets were still good. Probably. Bullets didn't spoil like milk, he hoped.

Callahan figured he would be able to kill at least one of them before they killed him. If he got lucky, he might be able to get two. He smiled. There were a lot of ways a man could leave this earth, and considering his lifestyle—he smoked, he drank too much, he was overweight—he'd always figured that he'd be attacked by his own overworked heart. Dying with a gun in his hand wasn't the worst way to go; he just wished he knew why he was going to die.

He took up a position on the right side of his door. A second later, the door blew open and a big guy followed the door-knocker partway through the door and into his office—and Callahan shot him in the head. He started to shoot again but one of the guys with a MAC-10 let out a burst, shooting right through the wall where Callahan was standing next to the doorframe. Drywall and paint couldn't stop the bullets.

He wasn't sure how many times he was hit—he knew he'd been hit at least once, but he didn't feel any pain. He staggered backward, almost falling, just as a man stepped into his office holding a pistol.

Callahan raised his hand to shoot the guy, but he was too slow.

"GODDAMNIT," OTIS SAID SOFTLY, looking down at Brown's body. He'd known Brown for almost twenty years. He'd been one of his best friends, and Otis didn't have that many friends. And Brown's sister . . . She was going to fall apart when she learned her brother had been killed. He'd never expected, in a damn office building, that anyone would have a weapon.

OTIS LOOKED OVER at the man he'd shot: an overweight, gray-haired guy in his sixties. Otis had hit him once in the chest and he could see blood oozing out of another wound in his side where Quinn had shot him. He didn't seem to be breathing. Otis pulled the picture he'd been given out of his pocket and looked at it. Yeah, the guy was Callahan, and there was the safe in the wall, just like he'd been told. He hadn't planned to kill Callahan right away; he'd been planning to force him to open the safe so he wouldn't have to steal it—but now that wasn't going to happen.

The big, loud .45 that Callahan had used to kill Brown was on the floor near Callahan's right hand. Otis kicked the gun away. He turned and said to Quinn, "Make sure nobody else is here. Take the door-knocker in case the offices are locked."

Quinn nodded and picked up the door-knocker, which Brown was still clutching in one dead hand.

"Get the safe out of the wall," Otis said to McCabe.

McCabe was looking down at Brown, holding his MAC-10 down by the side of his leg. "Jesus, I can't believe he got Ray," McCabe said.

"Goddamnit! Get moving!" Otis said.

McCabe pulled Brown's body out of the doorway and pushed the dolly and toolbox into the office. He opened the box and removed a battery-powered DeWalt Sawzall—and attacked the wall surrounding the safe. The Sawzall had blades that could cut through metal, and he'd brought plenty of extra blades. In the toolbox was also a portable acetylene torch kit and a canister of gas, which meant that McCabe would be able to cut through any metal he couldn't saw through. Otis really hoped they didn't have to use the torch because then he'd have to figure out how to disable the smoke detectors.

Unless there were other people on this floor, Otis wasn't too worried about anyone calling the cops. They'd used weapons with silencers and the round Callahan had fired had been loud, but he'd only fired once. He figured that if there were still people in the building on the floors above and below them, they might have heard the shot, but when they only heard one, they would have dismissed it as some sort of urban anomaly.

Otis couldn't help but think that he'd been a fool to take the job, no matter how much the damn guy was paying them. He never, ever worked this way: with no planning, no reconnaissance. And now Brown was dead and he had no idea how long it was going to take McCabe to chop the safe out of the wall.

Otis had one cardinal rule, a rule he'd lived by since he was seventeen: Don't let greed get you jailed or killed—and he'd broken his own rule.

While the Sawzall was chewing through the wood and aluminum frame holding the safe into the wall, Otis opened the bag that had contained the weapons and started dumping everything on Callahan's desk into it. He'd been told to take all the papers in the office, as well as any computers, flash drives, or disks.

Quinn was back. "There's nobody else here," he said.

"Get his phone," Otis said to Quinn, pointing at Callahan. He could see the phone on Callahan's belt, an old-fashioned clamshell phone, not a smartphone.

Otis placed Callahan's laptop and phone in the gym bag along with all the papers. He opened the drawers of the desk but didn't see any disks or flash drives. Based on the type of phone Callahan used, Otis got the impression that Callahan wasn't a high-tech type. He was surprised when he opened one large drawer and found it filled with bottles of booze and a carton of cigarettes. Then all he could do was wait for McCabe to finish with the safe.

Fifteen long minutes later, McCabe was done. Fortunately, he hadn't had to use the torch. McCabe pulled two three-foot-long crowbars out of the toolbox and handed one to Quinn, then he and Quinn jacked the safe out of the wall and let it crash to the floor. If there was anyone on the floor below, they definitely would have heard that. The good news was that the safe wasn't that big. It didn't look like it weighed more than a hundred and fifty pounds. "See if you can pick it up," Otis said, and McCabe and Quinn easily moved the safe onto the dolly.

From the beginning, Otis had planned to leave all the tools and the toolbox, and he'd told McCabe to wipe the tools of prints. All he could do was hope McCabe had done a good job, and if there were any fingerprints, he hoped they were Brown's, because he was going to have to leave Brown, too.

"Let's get out of here," Otis said.

"What are we going to do about Ray?" McCabe said.

"What the hell do you think we're going to do?" Otis said. They weren't Marines. They didn't take their dead with them.

"Jesus," McCabe said, "his sister is gonna go batshit."

That was the same thing Otis had thought, but he'd worry about Brown's crazy sister later.

Otis handed Quinn the bag containing the papers and the laptop. McCabe pushed the dolly out of the office with Quinn following. Otis would make one more sweep to make sure he hadn't missed anything. And he'd put a couple of bullets into Callahan's face just to make sure he was dead—and as a little payback for Ray. Callahan was going to have a closed-casket funeral.

2

Kay Hamilton rode the Farragut North Metro station escalator all the way to street level, letting the escalator do the work. Normally she was too impatient, and would have walked up the moving stairs, passing people too old, tired, lazy, or infirm to walk. She was taking her time today because of what she was about to do: She was on her way to Callahan's office to tell him she was quitting.

A year ago, Kay had been employed by the Drug Enforcement Administration.

She'd been a good agent—hell, she'd been a *great* agent—but the DEA fired her. She had to admit that she hadn't been an ideal employee—she didn't play well with others—but when she broke a drug dealer out of jail to exchange him for her daughter, who'd been kidnapped by a Mexican drug cartel, and then went to Mexico and killed the leader of the cartel . . . well, she couldn't really blame the DEA for handing her a pink slip. In fact, she could have gone to jail for some of the things she'd done, but fortunately the bureaucrats didn't want the media heat that would accompany a trial.

She ended up with the Callahan Group when her best friend in the

DEA—who was, incidentally, the woman who fired her—told her that there was a certain organization in Washington that valued her talents and wanted to hire her. Kay had assumed that this organization would be one of the intelligence agencies, as she had the ideal skill set for intelligence work—and it turned out she was right. Except for one small thing. The Callahan Group was not a legitimate government agency.

Fifteen minutes after leaving the Metro stop, Kay reached the Group's building on K Street. When she'd told Callahan she needed to speak with him—she didn't want to tell him on the phone that she was quitting—he'd said to come to his office after seven, that he'd be there until at least nine. Callahan often stayed late, maybe because he didn't want to go home to his shitty, empty apartment.

Kay noticed the U-Haul parked in the loading zone but didn't think anything of it; she figured someone was moving into or out of the building. She even noticed the driver sitting in the truck: a guy with a thick mustache wearing blue coveralls, a blue baseball cap, and sunglasses. It was odd that he was just sitting there with the truck idling and not helping the crew who was doing the moving. Then she was through the door and didn't give him another thought.

When the elevator reached the seventh floor, the first thing Kay noticed was the smell: The corridor smelled like a shooting range. But before she could process what her nose was telling her, she saw two men walking toward her, one guy pushing a dolly supporting a safe, the other man holding a black gym bag. What she noticed most, however, was that both men had MAC-10s. The one pushing the dolly had his weapon on a sling over his shoulder so he could push the dolly with both hands; the one holding the gym bag was holding his MAC in his right hand, the bag in his left.

As soon as the man holding the bag saw Kay, he dropped the bag and started to raise his weapon—and she immediately reached for the Glock she wore under her blazer. She realized later that the thing that saved her was that the man was left-handed; after he dropped the bag, he wasted a millisecond or two transferring the weapon from his right hand to his left, and fired before he could really aim. As the bullets from the MAC-10 flew past her head like a formation of pissed-off hornets, Kay shot the guy twice in the chest.

By now the other man had unslung his MAC from his shoulder and was in a position to fire, and Kay thought: *Gotta find cover!* The elevator door had closed behind her, but just down the hall from her and to her right—away from the man with the MAC—was an alcove with vending machines. Without really aiming, Kay fired four times at the second man as she ran for the alcove; she didn't expect to hit him, she just wanted to distract him—and she did. He returned fire as he was simultaneously dropping to his belly and attempting to use the safe on the dolly for cover. His bullets chopped up the walls and the ceiling of the corridor, and before he could aim more accurately, Kay dove into the alcove.

OTIS HAD JUST finished his sweep of Callahan's office and was taking a stride toward Callahan to shoot him a couple more times when he heard shots coming from what sounded like a handgun. Since Quinn's and McCabe's MAC-10s had suppressors, he knew it wasn't his guys firing. *Son of a bitch!* He sprinted out of Callahan's office to see what was happening. His men weren't in the hallway, which meant they were in the corridor heading toward the elevator. As he entered the corridor, he caught just a glimpse of a woman with a long blond ponytail firing at McCabe from a room farther down the hall.

Then Otis saw Quinn lying on his back.

KAY WAS THINKING, *SHIT!* Not only was the guy firing a machine gun, the vending machine alcove was on the right-hand side of the hallway, which was a problem because she was right-handed. In order for her to shoot accurately, she'd have to step partway out of the alcove. She transferred her Glock to her left hand and dropped to one knee. She planned to poke her head out, but she didn't want it to be at the height the shooter would expect.

She stuck her head out—like a really fast turtle poking its head from its shell—and fired a three-round burst from the Glock left-handed. As she was firing, she saw another masked man—how many of them were there, for Christ's sake!—running toward her. Fortunately, he was holding a pistol and not a machine gun. As soon as she fired—all three of her shots went high and to the left, not even coming close to the man hiding behind the safe—both men fired at her, the guy with the machine gun just holding down the trigger, emptying the magazine and chewing up the wall near the alcove.

Kay pulled her head back into the alcove before it was blown off. She had another problem: Her Glock held thirteen bullets—and she'd already fired nine.

OTIS REACHED MCCABE AND QUINN. "Goddamnit," he said. "Who is she?" But he was really wondering why the woman was armed, just like Callahan. Who were these fucking people?

"I don't know," McCabe said, answering his question. "She just stepped out of the elevator."

"Gotta keep her pinned down."

Otis looked down at Quinn: His eyes were wide open. He looked dead. It appeared that the woman had put two bullets right into his heart. Although he knew it was a waste of time, he touched Quinn's throat and felt for a pulse. There wasn't one.

"We need to get out of here," McCabe said. "She could be calling the cops right now."

Otis shoved his 9mm into a pocket and picked up Quinn's MAC-10; he wanted all the firepower he could get. "Give me a clip," he said to

McCabe, and McCabe handed him a fully loaded magazine. Otis ejected the magazine from Quinn's weapon and inserted the full one.

"You push the dolly," he said to McCabe, and he picked up the gym bag with his left hand. He could fire the MAC with one hand while holding the bag in his other hand.

Otis pulled the trigger as he and McCabe started moving toward the elevator, sending a dozen bullets ripping down the hall. But because of the angle, he couldn't shoot *into* the alcove. They reached the elevator a few seconds later, and the door immediately opened. It hadn't moved since the woman had stepped out of it.

Otis fired another long burst at the alcove. Because he was farther down the hall, he hoped some of his bullets might actually enter the alcove and ricochet off something and hit the woman. He heard her cry out in alarm or pain. As he fired, McCabe pushed the dolly inside the elevator. Otis fired off one last burst and joined McCabe—and just as the doors were closing, the damn woman fired three shots into the elevator. It was a fucking miracle that none of the ricochets hit him or McCabe.

KAY COULDN'T DO a thing but crouch in the alcove as one of the men fired two dozen rounds at her; the wall around the alcove now looked like it had been attacked by a demented woodpecker.

She heard the elevator ding and she knew that the men were about to escape. Then the guy ripped off another volley; some of the bullets struck the Coke machine and fragments peppered the walls around her, scaring the shit out of her. But she wasn't hit, and she wasn't finished. She guessed at the position of the elevator and fired three more shots.

A moment later there was complete silence.

AS THE ELEVATOR DESCENDED, Otis said to McCabe, "Take off the ski mask."

K STREET   I   17

"I can't believe Quinn and Brown are—"

"Goddamnit, get your head on straight! Take off the ski mask."

It wouldn't do to have people see them walking out of the building wearing masks and pushing a safe.

McCabe removed his mask, as did Otis, and they put the MAC-10s into the bag containing all the items Otis had removed from Callahan's office. They then put on the baseball caps and sunglasses they'd worn when they'd entered the building. Otis noticed that the fake mustache McCabe was wearing was slightly askew, but he let it go.

McCabe pushed the dolly out of the elevator and Otis held the door open as he rolled it out of the building. McCabe positioned the dolly and himself on the hydraulic lift platform of the U-Haul; the platform ascended and McCabe pulled the dolly into the back of the truck. Otis shut the door and joined Simpson in the cab.

"Go," Otis said.

"Where are Brown and Quinn?" Simpson said.

"They're dead. Now drive."

They needed to dump the U-Haul as soon as possible. By now the woman must have called the police and she might have seen the U-Haul sitting in front of the building. He noticed a parking lot on the street they were on. He told Simpson, "Circle around the block and go back to that parking lot."

Since the safe wasn't as heavy as Otis had expected, he and McCabe could easily transfer it to the trunk of a car. Simpson pulled into the parking lot and said, "What are we doing?"

"Look for a car you can boost. I want to dump this truck. We'll leave it here in the lot." Otis knew Simpson had used a fake ID to rent the truck; he also knew that Simpson could steal anything with wheels.

KAY STAYED WHERE she was for a moment after the elevator descended. Judging by the silence, she was sure they'd gone and she was alone.

Holding the Glock, she stepped out of the alcove, ready to jump back in if she was wrong.

She had three options. Option One: Run down the stairs and try to catch up with the men before they escaped and maybe kill another one with the last bullet she had. But by now it was probably too late for that. Option Two: Call 911 right away and let the cops take over. Option Three: See if anyone was still alive on the seventh floor before she called the cops.

She selected Option Three. Because of the nature of the work performed by the Callahan Group, she'd just as soon not get the cops involved until she had a better understanding of the situation. And she needed to know if Callahan was still alive—although she was pretty sure he wasn't.

Kay proceeded down the hallway until she reached the door that led to the Callahan Group's suite of offices. It had been battered open. She passed through it and entered the reception area. During normal business hours, a man name Henry—an Iraq war veteran with a prosthetic right leg—sat at the desk in the reception area. Henry wasn't your normal greeter; he carried a .44 Magnum revolver. Kay had feared that she might find Henry's body, but she didn't. He might have gone home before the men with the MAC-10s arrived.

Behind Henry's desk was a second door that was always kept locked; it had also been battered open. Kay stepped through and looked down the interior hallway. At the end was Callahan's office and along the way were half a dozen smaller offices. Kay could also see a man's legs sticking out of a doorway.

It turned out the legs didn't belong to Callahan but to a man Kay barely knew. His name was David Norton and his white shirt was soaked red with blood. She'd only met Norton once but knew he was a lawyer. She felt for a pulse and confirmed that he was dead.

She took another couple of steps and came to another door that had been bashed open. As well as almost tearing the door off the hinges, somebody had fired shots through the door. She looked into the office and saw another body. She didn't know the man. Again, she confirmed that he was dead before proceeding.

She finally reached Callahan's office. His door had been knocked open like the others, and she could see the instrument that had been used to open the doors on the floor: a piece of pipe with handles welded on top. The wall next to Callahan's door had also been perforated by bullets.

The first thing she saw in Callahan's office was a big man lying on the floor, dressed in blue coveralls and wearing a ski mask. He'd been shot in the head. She then briefly took in the condition of the office: a raw hole in the wall where Callahan's safe had been, tools all over the floor—a Sawzall, crowbars, sledgehammers, a large toolbox—whoever these guys were, they'd come prepared—and then she saw Callahan sitting on the floor, his back against the wall.

Callahan's blue shirt, like Norton's, was crimson with blood. She was certain he was dead, and she felt tears well up in her eyes. Callahan had been a deceitful, manipulative bastard—but an extremely likeable one. She stepped over to him and felt for a pulse—and, remarkably, found one. His heart was barely beating—but it was beating.

Without thinking about what the consequences might be, she pulled her phone out of a pocket and called 911. "I need an ambulance here right away," she said to the operator, trying not to scream into the phone. "A man has been shot at least twice and he's going to die if you don't get the medics here." She gave the operator the address and the location of Callahan's office and hung up before the operator could say anything. She then ripped Callahan's shirt open to see if she could stem the bleeding.

3

Two and a half hours after calling 911, Kay was sitting in an interview room at the D.C. Metro Police Department on Indiana Avenue. Across the table from her was a detective named Mary Platt, a stout, mannish-looking woman in her forties with big hands and short dark hair that was streaked with gray. Kay thought Platt looked like an older, tougher version of the girl who used to play goalie on her high school soccer team.

Kay's clothes were covered with Callahan's blood; Platt had been kind enough to let her wash the blood off her hands. Well, maybe not so kind; they'd let her wash the blood off so they could fingerprint her. As Kay sat there, she couldn't help but recall one of Callahan's favorite sayings: *Tell the truth as often as you can, because that way it's easier to keep track of the lies you tell.* And that's what Kay was doing: trying to keep track of the lies she was telling Detective Mary Platt.

The cops had arrived at Callahan's office—with guns drawn—before the medics did and found Kay kneeling, pressing a handkerchief against a wound that was stubbornly seeping blood. When they saw Kay's Glock on the floor, they started screaming at her to stand up and back away from the gun, probably assuming that she was the one responsible for the four dead bodies.

Kay started screaming back. She said that she wasn't going to stop pressing on Callahan's wound until the medics got there and for them to quit fucking around before Callahan died. Eventually, they all stopped screaming, and the medics loaded Callahan onto a gurney and hauled him away. Kay's gun was confiscated and she was led away in handcuffs; maybe she shouldn't have sworn at the cops.

Kay figured that there was now a large crime scene crew poring over the carnage in Callahan's building. TV trucks would be parked outside on K Street, screwing up traffic, because some cop, to make a few extra bucks, would have told the media that there were dead bodies inside. Kay also figured that whomever Callahan worked for—if he, she, or they owned a television set—must be aware that the Callahan Group had been attacked.

Kay started with the truth, telling Platt everything that occurred after she stepped off the elevator. It was when the detective asked her why she happened to be packing a .40 caliber Glock that she began lying.

The cover story for the Callahan Group was that it helped U.S. companies do business overseas. This mission was clearly stated on the Group's website, www.CallahanGroup.com. They showed companies how to avoid paying taxes on income earned overseas; they helped in negotiations with foreign regulators—meaning Callahan knew who to bribe. Like many other firms on K Street, the Group also lobbied Congress to create a favorable business environment for its clients. And Callahan actually did employ a number of people, like David Norton, the dead lawyer, who really did those sorts of jobs.

The reality—which Kay wasn't about to tell Mary Platt—was that the Callahan Group was also a covert intelligence organization that was brought into play when the U.S. government didn't want to use the nation's legitimate intelligence agencies.

It was after Kay had explained the Callahan Group's cover story that Mary Platt asked why she was carrying a weapon.

"I'm basically a security guard," Kay said.

"Why would a lobbyist need armed security?" Platt asked.

"I don't really know, to tell you the truth. All I know is that I was hired to provide security, and I'm used as a courier to shuttle documents to people. And when rich big shots visit Callahan, I drive them around and they like that I'm armed. I got the impression that a lot of what Callahan did was pretty sensitive stuff involving big financial deals, and that's why he needed security."

"Why would someone steal the safe from his office?"

"I don't know," Kay said. "I know he sometimes kept cash in it—that was another reason he needed security—and I'm guessing he kept important documents in there, too. But I don't know for sure."

"Come on," Platt said. "You provide security but you don't know why?"

"Hey," Kay said. "Why don't you go down to a Chase bank and ask the guard in the lobby what Jamie Dimon is doing today? He'd have just as good an idea about Jamie as I do about Callahan. I'm telling you, I'm a grunt. I'm not management."

"You're a little overqualified to be a security guard, aren't you?" Platt said.

"What do you mean?"

"What do you think I was doing while you were sitting here? I was checking you out. You're ex-DEA."

"Yeah, well, if you really checked me out, then you'd know that I got fired."

"The records don't say that."

"I know. They say I resigned. But the truth is, I was told to either resign or they were going to fire me and maybe throw me in jail."

"Why?" Platt asked.

"I'm not going to tell you that. Maybe the DEA will, but I doubt it. What I can tell you is that the DEA wasn't willing to give me a good recommendation, which is why I'm now doing security work. I gotta pay the rent, you know."

"I think you're lying to me."

"Hey, think what you want but—"

"One thing I do know is that you've killed quite a few people," Platt said. "You killed four in Miami when you worked there—that was on the Internet—and just a few months ago you were in this police station after you killed a guy you claimed was trying to rape you."

"He *was* trying to rape me and he had a knife. I wasn't charged with anything," Kay said. The real reason Kay had killed the man had to do with a Callahan Group mission in Afghanistan—but she wasn't about to tell Platt that either.

"Yeah, I know you weren't charged," Platt said, "but the fact remains that you've killed a lot of people."

Kay felt like saying, *And a couple more you don't know about.* But she didn't. Instead she said, "What's your point, Detective? Are you accusing me of killing all those people in Callahan's building?"

"No, not yet," Platt said. "After I get back results from ballistics and start matching bullets to bodies, then maybe I will."

"I only shot one guy," Kay said, "and ballistics will confirm that. You didn't find any MAC-10s at the scene because the killers, the robbers, whoever they are, took their weapons with them, but ballistics will show that Callahan's people were killed with MACs. There are also security cameras all over the place in Callahan's office. The cameras will back up my story."

"A funny thing about those cameras," Platt said. "My technician said they don't record anything. What they do is give you a real-time picture of people walking down the hall or entering Callahan's office."

"Well, I didn't know that," Kay said.

"You're in charge of security and you don't know how the cameras work?"

"I never said I was in charge of security."

Kay knew that in reality the cameras did record a twenty-four-hour period of footage, but the recording went to someplace in cyberspace, like the Cloud, and Platt's technicians hadn't been smart enough to figure that out. Yet.

"And you seem to forget," Kay said, "that I'm the one who called 911 and I was trying to save Callahan's life when your guys arrived on scene."

"That's true," Platt said, "but something screwy is going on here and I think you're lying to me. I don't buy that a hotshot ex-DEA agent was working as a low-level security drone."

"Okay, that's it," Kay said. "I'm leaving now, unless you're arresting me."

"If you don't come straight with me, I will."

"Bullshit."

"Hey, you admitted you killed a guy. I can keep you in a cage for at least twenty-four hours. So you got anything else you want to say to me?"

"No."

Platt stared at her for a long moment, probably trying to decide if it was worth the hassle to arrest her, then said, "Go on. Get out of here. But you better stay in town, and you better answer your phone when I call."

"Sure," Kay said. What did one more lie matter? "Do you know if Callahan made it?"

"No," Platt said, "but I'm guessing he's still alive or somebody would have called and told me that I've got five homicides to solve instead of four."

"Do you know the name of the man I killed?"

"Not yet, and if I did, I wouldn't tell you. You're not part of this investigation. You're a suspect."

Kay could tell that she and Mary Platt were not going to become close friends.

4

K ay went to her apartment on Connecticut Avenue, took a quick
shower, and changed out of her bloodstained clothes. She put on
a clean white T-shirt, jeans, and running shoes—clothes she could
fight in if necessary. She also put on a lightweight blazer and under the
blazer was the empty holster that had contained her Glock—the Glock
the D.C. cops had confiscated and were holding as evidence.

She was going to go see Callahan next, but before she did she
wanted a gun.

That is, she wanted a *bigger* gun. She had a little five-shot .32 she
could wear in an ankle holster—sort of a lethal fashion accessory—but
the problem with the .32 was that it was only accurate from very close
range and it didn't have the kind of stopping power she wanted. She
wanted a *lot* of stopping power in case the guys with the MACs showed
up again.

On the floor below her lived a gray-haired lady in her seventies
named Eloise Voss. Voss had introduced herself to Kay one time when
they were both standing in the lobby waiting for an elevator. Voss was
slim, in great shape for her age, and as tall as Kay, and Kay was

five-foot-eight. Voss had no doubt been a real looker when she was younger and she seemed friendly—smile lines radiating from bright blue eyes—but the main thing that Kay had noticed was that the woman was *very* observant.

Kay usually hid her Glock under a blazer or a jacket, but every once in a while someone would spot it. When that happened, and if the person seemed alarmed, she'd say she was an off-duty cop or a security guard or whatever came to mind.

The day she met Voss, when they were alone in the elevator together, the woman got just the briefest glimpse of Kay's weapon, but instead of going all big-eyed with shock, she said, "Never liked Glocks myself. They just never felt right in my hand. I use a Beretta." Then she got off the elevator, leaving Kay standing there with her mouth open. The woman had barely seen the Glock, yet had been able to immediately identify it.

Kay now took the stairs down to Voss's apartment on the seventh floor. Because of the hour, Kay was afraid Voss might be sleeping, but she could hear the television playing on the other side of the door. Voss might have sharp eyes but her hearing wasn't perfect. Kay hesitated for just a moment, then knocked.

Voss answered the door wearing a bathrobe and holding a brandy snifter in her hand. She smiled when she saw Kay.

"Ms. Voss, I'm Kay Hamilton, your neighbor from upstairs," Kay said. "We've met before." Kay said this thinking that someone Voss's age might not be able to recall her name.

"Yeah, I know," the old woman said. "You're the gal with the Glock and the cute daughter."

There was nothing wrong with Voss's memory.

"Look, I know you don't really know me, but you mentioned you had a Beretta, and I want to borrow it. I lost my Glock tonight and the only other gun I have is a .32. I'm involved in something . . . something very serious. I can't tell you exactly what, but I want a bigger gun. You can keep my .32 for protection until I can return your Beretta."

"Actually, I do know you," the woman said. "Well, sort of. You're ex-DEA. You had quite a career with those cowboys." When Voss saw the look of surprise on Kay's face, she added, "When I saw you packing, I checked you out."

"How did you . . ."

"Come on in. I'll get the Beretta." She said this like Kay was borrowing a cup of sugar. A minute later she handed Kay a plastic Walgreens bag containing the gun and two full magazines. "And I don't need your .32. I've got a .38 around here somewhere in the unlikely event I need a gun."

"I'm just curious," Kay said. "I'm guessing you're retired now, but what did you use to do for a living?"

"Secret Service. And boy, do I ever miss it."

Ah. That explained it. "You know," Kay said, "when things settle down a bit, you and I need to go have a drink together."

Voss smiled. "I'd really like that," she said.

KAY HAD ASKED one of the medics where they were taking Callahan as they were loading him onto the gurney. They told her that they were going to the George Washington University Hospital trauma center, a place used to dealing with gunshot victims. When she arrived, Kay told the lady at the information desk that she was Callahan's daughter and had driven up from Richmond after learning that he'd been shot. She said that she lived in Richmond to explain why a dutiful daughter would have taken so long to arrive at the hospital to check on her dear old dad.

She was passed around to a few people until a nurse finally told her that Callahan was in surgery. The nurse, a middle-aged woman with a face that radiated compassion, took Kay's hands into her own and said, "He was really in bad shape when they brought him in here, honey. He'd lost a lot of blood. But we've got good docs working on him and they're doing everything they can to save him. You're just going to have to pray that he makes it. Do you want me to show you where the chapel is?"

Kay doubted prayer would help—particularly in Callahan's case—so she found an area with a couple of sofas, and because it was almost midnight, she had the space to herself. She wasn't tired. She was still too wound up from what had happened and she needed to figure out what to do next.

She had no idea why a team of professionals would be willing to risk breaking into Callahan's office while it was still light outside. And she knew they were pros because of how they'd been armed and because of the tools they'd brought with them. She didn't know, however, why these men would be willing to kill for whatever was in the safe. The team looked to be the kind that did bank robberies or armored car heists—heists that would net hundreds of thousands of dollars. She knew that Callahan kept quite a bit of cash in his safe, but not *millions*. So she guessed that the robbers had been after something other than money—but because Callahan had refused to tell her the whole truth about the Callahan Group, Kay didn't have any idea who could tell her what that might be.

BARB REYNOLDS was the woman who'd fired Kay from the DEA, and she had also been Kay's mentor. Barb was an old D.C. hand, high up in the Drug Enforcement Administration, and a lot like Kay when it came to her personality. Barb knew about the Callahan Group because Callahan had once tried to recruit her, but Barb had turned him down. But it was Barb who recommended Kay for the job because she knew Kay would be perfect for covert operations: She was smart, she was brave, she had a gift for learning languages, and she'd proven more than once that she could be lethal when necessary. Callahan's people did background checks on Kay, then after she'd signed a bulletproof nondisclosure agreement, Callahan interviewed her and told her the supposedly true story about the Group.

According to Callahan, he worked directly for the President of the United States. Callahan had spent twenty years at the CIA, had worked at the Pentagon, and had ended his civil service career as a deputy to George W. Bush's national security advisor. In other words, he was qualified to manage intelligence operations—or to perform any other sort of skullduggery a president might want done.

Callahan had said that it was Bush, via an unnamed intermediary, who'd asked him to form the Group. Callahan admitted that he never spoke to the president directly. He said his conversation with Bush's guy happened not long after 9/11, and the president wanted a private-sector company—an entity not subject to congressional oversight—that he could personally deploy if he felt the need. And the beauty of the Callahan Group, from the president's perspective, was that the president could—and would—deny any involvement with it, if it screwed up in any way.

In the past year, Kay had been part of a team who overcame the security forces guarding a North Korean physicist so the physicist could defect to the United States. She'd also been involved in another operation involving a Russian who'd been brought secretly to the U.S. by the CIA as part of their program to prevent proliferation of nuclear materials. In both these operations, the Callahan Group was called in to help because there would have been a political firestorm if the CIA had been officially involved. But the biggest operation Kay had been part of had been a complex job in Afghanistan that had resulted in a number of people getting blown to pieces by a bomb—and Kay was almost among them. It was after the Afghan op that she began to have doubts about working for Callahan.

Kay had known from the beginning that working for Callahan was legally problematic, but she rationalized her participation by believing that the president, as commander in chief, actually did have the authority to form an organization like Callahan's. She also figured that if the Callahan Group was ever exposed, it would be Callahan and the president who would be held responsible, not her. She was just too low on the totem pole. The main thing was, Kay loved being part of an organization that dealt directly with national security issues but wasn't hobbled by the federal bureaucracy.

But after Afghanistan, Kay began to suspect that Callahan had lied to her about working for the president. She met with her friend Barb to talk about her concern, and Barb surprised her by saying that no president—and certainly not Bush or Obama—would take the risk of running a group like Callahan's. (Which rather irritated Kay, that Barb hadn't told her this *before* she accepted the job with Callahan.)

Barb said that Callahan was most likely working with some rogue group connected to the intelligence community. That is, someone with ties to the CIA, the NSA, the DIA, or maybe Homeland Security. That would explain—as Kay had observed many times—why Callahan seemed to have such ready access to classified information. It would also explain how Callahan received the funds needed to run his operations: The money was being funneled to him through the massive secret coffers of the intelligence community. But when Kay demanded that Callahan tell her the complete truth about the Group, the stubborn bastard refused—and that's why Kay had decided to quit. She wasn't going to continue to put her life at risk when she couldn't trust the man she worked for.

But now whoever was running Callahan had a major problem. A safe had been stolen and its contents could possibly endanger national security. There was also a team of D.C. cops and forensic weenies rummaging through Callahan's offices, and who knew what they might stumble across? But most important, someone had tried to kill Callahan. Kay was not going to quit until she found out who tried to kill him and why.

. . .

KAY FELT A FINGER poke her shoulder. It was the nurse with the kind face who'd told her that Callahan was in surgery.

"I'm sorry to wake you, honey," the nurse said, "but I thought you'd want to know that your dad just got out of surgery." Kay looked at her watch; it was almost six a.m. Callahan had been in surgery for over ten hours.

"Thank God," Kay said. "Is he going to be all right?"

"I'm sorry, but it's really too early to say. He made it through the surgery okay, and for the time being he's stable, but we're going to have to watch him closely."

"Can I talk to him?"

"No. He's in the recovery room right now and still unconscious. We'll move him into ICU in about an hour, but I doubt he'll be able to talk. You can at least go in and hold his hand for a bit, then you'll have to leave so he can rest. Oh, and the people in the business office want to see you. They need his insurance information."

"Yeah, sure," Kay said. She had no idea who insured Callahan or if he even had insurance. She wasn't going anywhere near the business office.

Kay found the hospital cafeteria and had a breakfast of fake scrambled eggs and sausages made out of vegetables that tasted only vaguely like real sausages. The breakfast was advertised as "heart-healthy." She was glad it was good for her heart because her taste buds certainly didn't like it.

She checked her watch. Only half an hour had passed since she'd spoken to the nurse, and she imagined Callahan would still be out cold. To kill some time, she left the hospital and walked around the block, stopping at a Starbucks for an apple fritter loaded with fat and cholesterol.

She went back to the hospital and up to the floor where the intensive care unit was located. She lied to the nurses at the nursing station, saying again that she was Callahan's daughter and just wanted to sit with her dad for a while. "Because, you know," she said, "I was told he might not make it." Kay had always found that nurses, in general, were the nicest people on the planet. They naturally sympathized with her and told her it was okay for her to see her "dad."

Bandages covered Callahan's gray-haired chest. Fluids were flowing into him, a tube fed oxygen to his nose, and he was connected to a machine monitoring his vital signs. He looked like a man on the verge of death—and Callahan hadn't been particularly healthy looking *before* he'd been shot. He was overweight and pale because he rarely ventured out into the sun. He smoked and the only exercise he got was doing one-arm curls: lifting tumblers filled with alcohol to his lips.

But Kay needed him awake; she needed some answers.

She walked to the side of the bed and said, "Callahan." He didn't stir. She prodded his shoulder gently and again said, "Callahan." Nothing. Not knowing what else to do, she sat down in the visitor's chair. She'd wait a while and see if he came to.

An hour later, Kay sensed a change in the way he was breathing and went to stand by the bed. "Callahan," she said. "Can you hear me?"

Callahan's eyes opened slowly. Kay could actually *see* the pain in his eyes. He was really hurting. "Can you tell me anything about what happened? Why did those guys take your safe?"

Callahan's lips moved but no sound came out. There was a sink in the room but Kay was afraid to give him water because he might start choking. And for all she knew, maybe he wasn't supposed to be given fluids orally. She went over to the sink and wetted a paper towel and pressed the damp towel gently against his lips.

"Callahan, give me something. Anything."

Again his lips moved and this time he croaked, "Press."

"Press?" Kay said. "What do you mean? The press knows something? Don't talk to the press?"

His lips moved again, barely opening and closing, and he said, "Press. Cot."

"Prescott? A person named Prescott?" Kay said.

"Olivia." This was followed by a long pause—Callahan was battling the pain—then he said, "N."

"Olivia Prescott?" Kay said. "Olivia *N.* Prescott?"

But Callahan was gone. He wasn't dead, but he was either asleep or in a coma. She poked his shoulder a couple more times, and when he didn't respond, she gave his hand a light squeeze and said, "God be with you, Callahan."

She said this knowing it was extremely unlikely that God and Thomas Callahan were on speaking terms.

5

K ay didn't know what Callahan had been trying to tell her. She didn't know if he meant Prescott, Olivia N., and "N" was Prescott's middle initial, or if Callahan had said "N" as the beginning of another word. Or maybe he didn't say "N" at all; the way he'd been slurring his words it was impossible for her to be sure.

She wondered if Prescott could be Callahan's girlfriend or one of his ex-wives. He had four ex-wives. Callahan, at the age of sixty, wasn't all that physically appealing, but he was charming and likeable and seemed to have no problem attracting women. Why they didn't stay married to him, as near as Kay could tell, was that he would fall in love with the next Mrs. Callahan while still married to the current Mrs. Callahan. It seemed unlikely, however, that Callahan had given her the name of an old flame because he wanted the woman at his bedside as he lay dying.

The other thought that occurred to her was that maybe Callahan had been trying to tell her that Prescott was the person responsible for the attack. The guys with the MAC-10s had been *guys*—at least Kay didn't think any of them were women—but that didn't exclude the possibility that a woman was their boss. Then she thought, no. If Callahan had known that someone—Prescott or anyone else—might attack his office and kill his people, he would have been prepared for it and would have dealt with the threat.

The last possibility—and the one that Kay thought most likely—was that Prescott was a person who would have answers, a person who would know why Callahan had been shot and why his safe had been stolen.

KAY RETURNED TO HER APARTMENT, poured a Coke for the caffeine, and booted up her laptop. There was only one thing she could think to do to find Prescott on her own: She did an Internet search using one of those people-finder search engines.

She was surprised to learn that, in the entire United States of America, only seven Olivia or O. Prescotts were listed. Sometimes, it was a good thing no one could protect their privacy.

Five of the seven Prescotts were located in Lake Placid, Florida; Schenectady, New York; Las Vegas, Nevada; Greenville, Texas (wherever the hell that was); and Hurst, Texas (wherever the hell that was). The sixth Prescott lived in Indio, California, and her name was Olivia M. Prescott, making Kay wonder if Callahan had said "M," not "N." But it was the seventh Olivia Prescott who interested Kay. The seventh Prescott lived in Laurel, Maryland, which was only twenty-five miles from D.C., practically in Callahan's backyard. And Laurel, Maryland, was located even closer to another place: Fort Meade—home to the National Security Agency.

And maybe that's what Callahan had been trying to say: Olivia Prescott, NSA.

Kay entered NSA and Prescott into Google and came up blank. She then entered just NSA, and there was the NSA's website, www.nsa.gov, as if it were a normal government organization, like the IRS or the

Social Security Administration. On the website was a little box titled: *Leadership*. Kay figured that if Callahan knew anybody at the NSA, it would be one of the top dogs.

When she clicked on the *Leadership* button, however, it showed only two people: a U.S. Army general who was the current director, and his deputy, a sneaky-looking guy—at least Kay thought he looked sneaky—named Paul S. Scranton. And that was it. Of the approximately thirty thousand people employed by the country's largest, most well-funded, most secretive intelligence service, only two employees were identified on the website.

She went back to the people-finder engine. An address was given for the Olivia Prescott who lived in Laurel, Maryland, but her phone number was unlisted. Even though she knew she might be wasting her time, the only thing Kay could think to do was go to the address in Laurel. It was a long shot, but a long shot was better than no shot at all.

But before driving to Laurel, Kay decided to call two people. One of those people was Henry Sill, the Group's "receptionist." The other was her lover.

Because he'd spent twenty years at the CIA, Callahan was a big believer in compartmentalization. This meant that the people who participated in his operations were only told as much as Callahan believed they needed to know. He also compartmentalized the Callahan Group: Those folks who worked the legitimate side didn't know the folks on the covert side, and not even the folks on the covert side knew who everyone was. Callahan, like the NSA, also didn't have a directory with a neat alphabetical list of his employees.

While Kay had been working for Callahan, she'd met a few other people. Sometimes all she was given was a first or a last name and it wasn't always clear if the name was real or fake. Like Morgan. Kay had worked with him twice—he was one of Callahan's top operatives—but she had no idea how to contact him.

One of the people she knew how to contact, however, was Henry

Sill. Henry was an ex-Marine. He survived three tours in Iraq without getting so much as a scratch, then came to work for Callahan, and somehow got his left leg blown off below the knee. Kay didn't know why or how.

Henry, unlike Kay, actually did provide security for Callahan, and his prosthesis didn't make him any less lethal. Henry sat at the front desk, armed, and he didn't allow people into the main office unless he knew who they were or unless Callahan gave him permission. Kay also wanted to know where Henry was yesterday and why he hadn't been at his post. If Callahan had known that he had something worth killing for in his safe, Henry would definitely have been standing guard.

SHE CALLED HENRY, and the first thing he said was, "Kay, did you hear what happened?"

"Yeah. I was there."

"You were?"

"I don't want to talk on the phone, Henry. Where do you live?"

Henry didn't answer.

"Look," Kay said, "I don't want your home address, I just want to know where you are relative to where I am so we can meet at a place that's convenient for both of us. Right now I'm on Connecticut, a couple of miles from the zoo."

"Let's meet at Dupont Circle," Henry said. "The Starbucks by the Metro station."

"Okay," Kay said. "How fast can you get there?"

Henry paused before he said, "Half an hour."

Cautious bastard. She wondered if he was lying about how close he was to Dupont Circle so he could get there before her or if he really was half an hour away.

Henry wasn't in the Starbucks when Kay arrived. She bet he was outside, lurking, watching to see if she'd been followed and if she was alone. That is, Henry was lurking as well as a six-foot-five, two-hundred-and-thirty-pound black man with a shaved head can lurk. He wasn't the inconspicuous type. Ten minutes later he walked into the coffee shop. If you didn't know that one of his legs wasn't flesh and bone, you'd never guess by the way he walked.

He took a seat across from her. "Is Callahan alive?" he said.

"Barely," Kay said. "He was shot at least twice. They got him to the hospital in time to stabilize him, but I'm not sure he's going to make it. I went to check on him but he wasn't conscious."

"So what happened?"

Instead of answering his question, she said, "Where were you yesterday, Henry?"

"One of my kids had a baseball game."

Kay hadn't known that Henry had children. She didn't even know if he was married or not.

"I told Callahan I wanted to leave early," Henry said, "and he said go ahead. He said there wasn't anything going on—I guess he meant that he didn't have some operation underway—and that I didn't need to be there. I left at four. If I hadn't . . ."

He didn't finish the sentence, but she could tell he was sick with remorse and guilt, thinking that he could have prevented Callahan from getting shot if he had been there.

"So what happened, Kay?"

Kay told him how four masked men had battered down the doors, shot David Norton and another man she didn't know, and ripped the safe out of Callahan's wall. She concluded by saying, "Callahan killed one of them before they shot him. I arrived just as they were leaving, and I killed one, too."

Before Henry could ask another question, she said, "How many people were there when you left?"

"Five. Norton, Phil Klein, Kathy Matthews, and Stew Unger. And Callahan, of course."

"The only one I know is Norton," Kay said. "What do Klein and Unger look like?"

"Unger is tall, almost as tall as me. And in good shape. He rides a bike to work."

"Then the other guy they killed must have been Klein. The man I saw wasn't in any better shape than Callahan. What did these people do?"

"They all worked the straight side. Matthews is a lawyer, like Norton. Klein's an accountant. I don't know what Unger does; he spends a lot of time on the Hill and overseas."

"The break-in happened around seven," Kay said. "Unger and Matthews must have left before then or they'd probably be dead, too. Do you have any idea why someone would want Callahan's safe?"

"No. I know he kept cash in it, but I don't know how much or how anyone else would know."

"I don't think this was about the cash," Kay said. "This is about something else. Do you have any idea who Callahan really works for, Henry?"

"What do you mean?" Henry said, acting as if the question shocked him. "He works for the president. You know that."

"I think Callahan lied about that. I've thought that for some time. But *someone* was working with him, and I think it was someone in the intelligence community."

"Why would Callahan lie?"

Kay almost said: *Come on, Henry. Callahan lied about everything.* Instead, she said, "He lied because he's trying to conceal and protect whoever his real boss is. And if you have any idea who that person could be, you need to tell me. I need to know in order to find out why Callahan was shot."

"He worked for the president," Henry stubbornly said—and Kay could see she wasn't going to shake his faith in Callahan.

"Did anything unusual happen yesterday before you left?" Kay asked. "Anything out of the ordinary?"

"No. The office was really quiet, and a bunch of folks are on leave since it's July. And like I already told you, I'm pretty sure Callahan didn't have any sort of operation going on." Henry paused. "Well, there was one thing. A woman came to see him."

Kay immediately thought that Henry was about to tell her that the woman was the mysterious Olivia Prescott. But instead he said, "Her name was Sally Ann Danzinger. She showed up unexpectedly and said she wanted to see Callahan. She's some sort of political activist."

"What kind of activist?"

"Left-wing. Anything the Democrats favor. Environmental stuff, pro choice, minimum wage. That sort of thing. When she came to see him, I had her show me her ID then looked her up online. But I don't know why she came to see him, and she was only there a couple of minutes, and Callahan didn't say anything to me about her after she left."

"Huh," Kay said. She couldn't imagine why a liberal political activist would come to see Callahan unless maybe it was to complain about something the straight side of the Callahan Group was doing.

"Have you ever heard the name Olivia Prescott, Henry?"

"No. Who is she?"

"She's . . . Aw, never mind. It's not important."

Before Henry could ask more questions about Prescott, Kay said, "You need to call everyone you know who works for Callahan—you know a lot more of his people than I do—and tell them to stay away from K Street. We don't want to give the cops a bunch of people to question until we know what's going on. Even the people on the cover side. They've seen people like me coming and going. And they're not stupid. I'm sure at least some of them suspect that Callahan was playing another game."

"Okay," he said. Then he looked away from her and she thought for a minute he was going to cry. "If only I'd been there. I could have—"

"This wasn't your fault, Henry."

"Maybe not, but . . ."

Kay didn't have time to make Henry feel better. "After you call everybody, we need to get the identities of the two men who were killed. That might give us a lead to whoever planned this."

"Do you think the cops will tell us?"

"No way. Right now the detective in charge is treating me like I'm a suspect. Do you have any contacts on the force?"

Henry nodded. "Two guys I served with in Iraq."

This didn't surprise Kay. If Henry's friends were hometown boys and veterans, they'd be at the top of Metro P.D.'s hiring list.

"But my buddies work patrol," Henry said. "They're not detectives. They're not big shots."

"Talk to them anyway, and ask them to help. We need those guys' names and we need them fast."

"Okay. What are you going to do?"

"I'm going to do the same thing, try to identify the men who were killed. I'll call some of my old DEA pals to see if they can help."

That was a lie. Kay was going to go see Olivia Prescott. Maybe she should have told Henry about her, but she wanted to know more about Prescott before she shared the information.

KAY LEFT THE STARBUCKS but didn't return to her car. Instead, she walked around trying to find a quiet place that had a pay phone. It's easier to find unicorns than pay phones these days, and it's even harder to find one in a place that's quiet. She finally found one in the Dupont Circle Hotel. She wanted to talk to her lover—who also worked for Callahan. He was in New York.

She called Eli Dolan's cell phone. "It's me," she said.

"Have you heard what happened?"

"Yeah, I was there."

"You were?"

"Look, I'm calling from a pay phone. Go find one near you and call me back." She gave him the number of the phone she was using. Kay didn't like to talk about anything important on cell phones; they're basically radios.

As she waited in the phone booth for Eli to return her call, a fat guy in a suit walked up looking sweaty and flustered. "Hey," he said, "I gotta use the phone. My cell's dead and I gotta check in with my office right away. It's a big deal."

Kay opened her blazer and showed him Eloise Voss's Beretta. "Go away before I shoot you," she said, and the fat man left.

A moment later the phone rang. "What happened?" Eli said.

She told Eli the same things she'd told Henry. "Do you have any idea what Callahan could have had in his safe that would be a motive for this? I mean, I know he kept cash in there, but unless he kept millions, I don't think this was about money."

"I don't know what was in his safe. I do know he was ultracareful about not keeping paperwork about missions in his office. Maybe there was something in there about an op he was planning, but I don't know how anyone else would have known. I mean anyone outside the Group."

But *someone* had known. And one possibility was the people who were really controlling Callahan—and maybe they had shared the information with the wrong people.

"Eli, if you know who Callahan really works for, this is the time to tell me."

Eli, sounding exasperated—because Kay had asked this question before—said, "Kay, I'm telling you, I don't know who he works for. He's always denied working for anyone other than the president."

"But the way Callahan gets the money to finance his operations must give you *some* idea," Kay said.

"Kay, I'm going to tell you something now that will make you an accessory to a crime. Are you okay with that?"

Kay didn't hesitate. "Yeah, I'm okay with that. Now quit stalling."

"The government buys services from many private-sector companies. And I'm talking about *services* as opposed to *goods*. Goods are tangible. For example, tires for military vehicles. If you buy tires, then somebody should be able to find those tires.

"Services are different and, as I said, the government buys services from many different outfits. It hires experts and lawyers and consultants. It hires scientists and professors and engineers. It hires researchers and pollsters and—"

"Yeah, yeah, I get it," Kay said. "It hires people who don't produce anything but a pile of paper."

"That's right. And what I do for Callahan is set up dummy corporations that provide nonexistent services. These companies often have strange names that don't tell you what they really do, and someone in the government funnels money to these companies. A portion of the money is then funneled back to the government in the form of taxes to make the companies appear legitimate. But I don't know who is moving the money into the accounts. Somewhere, in some computer, are phony contracts with my phony companies to justify the money being spent. And whoever controls the money is able to keep folks like the GAO from auditing these contracts."

"Could it be someone like the NSA?"

"Why do you ask that?"

"I don't mean the NSA specifically," Kay said, rapidly backtracking, "but any intelligence agency. Could the intelligence community be the source of Callahan's money?"

"I suppose. The NSA has a massive budget and is continually buying private-sector services for encryption and eavesdropping technology. But since the intelligence agencies are part of the executive branch, the White House could also be involved in some way, as Callahan claims. Plus, the operating budget for the White House is about one and a half billion a year, and some of that money could be vectored Callahan's way."

Kay still didn't believe the White House was involved—but there was no point continuing to debate this with Eli. Not now. She started to ask him if he'd ever heard of an Olivia Prescott associated in any way with the Callahan Group—then stopped. She trusted Eli, but knowing Prescott's name could put him in danger.

There was also another reason she didn't tell him, one not quite so noble. If she told him, he would try to interfere with whatever she might do next. Eli would want to deliberate, consider the upside and the downside, do background research, develop contingency plans, and so forth—and Kay didn't operate that way. She followed her instincts, and when her instincts told her it was time to act, she acted. She wasn't exactly reckless but . . . Okay, she could be reckless, but Eli's tendency for moving slowly and cautiously usually frustrated her.

She'd tell him about Prescott later, when she knew more. Maybe.

"What are you planning to do?" Eli asked.

"Try to get the names of the guys Callahan and I shot." That wasn't a lie—it just wasn't the complete truth. "If I can get their names, it'll give me a starting point for finding who was behind the attack."

"Is that all you're planning to do?" he said—and she could tell he was suspicious that she wasn't telling him everything. Sheesh. You'd think a girl's boyfriend would be more trusting. She was glad she wasn't in the same room with him so he could study her face, like a poker player looking for an opponent's tells.

"Yeah, that's all," she said. Then she added, "For now."

He was silent for a moment, apparently still thinking she was holding out on him. "Kay, whoever is behind this is obviously willing to kill. You need to be very careful because you have no idea where the threat could be coming from."

"I'll be careful," she said. And that wasn't a lie.

AS KAY DROVE TOWARD LAUREL, MARYLAND, she thought about Eli. She'd been thinking about him a lot lately, wondering what was going to happen to their relationship if she moved out of D.C. after she parted ways with Callahan. He knew she was dissatisfied with Callahan, but she hadn't told Eli she was quitting; maybe she should have, but she wanted to tell Callahan first. All she knew was that, after she quit, there was a good chance things wouldn't stay the same.

She met Eli two months after she came to work for Callahan because Eli was involved in the disastrous Afghan op—and it was a case of lust at first sight. He was almost forty, had a slim yet muscular build, sandy-brown hair, blue-gray eyes, and was as handsome as any man Kay had ever known. He had a subtle sense of humor and, in spite of his accomplishments, didn't take himself too seriously. He was generous and fun to be with—and he was filthy rich. Like Kay, he'd been married once and was now divorced. Unlike Kay, he had no children.

It sometimes seemed as if they had very little in common, other than the Callahan Group and sex, that is. Kay came from a middle-class family. Her father had been a cop, which was one of the reasons why Kay had gone to work for the DEA: Having a job where you packed a weapon was part of her DNA. Eli, on the other hand, was born to a couple of trust fund babies with a silver spoon in his mouth, and thanks to intelligence and hard work, he increased the size of the spoon. His net worth was in the millions.

Before going to work for Thomas Callahan, he'd worked for Goldman Sachs—that's where some of his millions came from—and during the financial meltdown in 2008, he migrated to D.C. with a few other Goldman people and took a low-paying job at the Treasury Department. In other words, he came to Treasury to help the country recover from all the things that Goldman Sachs and similar institutions had done to create the financial meltdown. Someplace along the way, he crossed paths with Thomas Callahan and became Callahan's money guy—but that was a part of his past he refused to share with Kay.

Eli spent more than half his time in New York, not only because he preferred to live there, but because New York was where he had to be to do his job, New York being the financial center of the universe.

He had a penthouse apartment in Manhattan with a view of skyscrapers and polluted rivers, but because he spent so much time in D.C., he also owned a small town house in Georgetown—*small* meaning it was only worth a couple of million. Kay was currently living in a two-bedroom apartment on Connecticut Avenue near the National Zoo and the only view she had was the apartment building across the street. Kay's idea of a home was a place with a backyard where you had to mow the grass on Sundays. Eli Dolan had never owned, much less operated, a lawn mower.

Their roles in the Callahan Group were also completely different. In addition to managing—and hiding—the money Callahan needed to fund his covert operations, Eli also identified individuals who were financially supporting terrorists or otherwise engaged in enterprises that were a threat to the United States. With the help of a couple of handpicked hackers, he sometimes intercepted money going to the bad actors and diverted it into Callahan's coffers. Almost everything he did was done with a computer and a telephone. Kay, by comparison, was one of the people Callahan sent into the field to deal with people face-to-face. Eli was a financial assassin; Kay was the real thing.

But there was one thing they had in common. They both liked playing dangerous, high-risk games. When Kay had worked for the DEA, the game had been catching drug dealers—and she'd enjoyed it immensely. The rules of the game—meaning the law—was something you either had to work with or work around. Working for Callahan was a different kind of game and the stakes were considerably higher—and no one worried about the rules. Kay liked that there was no net to catch you if you fell, and Eli was the same way. He liked the intellectual challenge of outwitting the government's bean counters, and he liked even more the challenge of beating the money guys who played for the other team. He also knew that if he was caught, he might go to jail or become a target for those he was playing against. He once told Kay that, because he'd never served in the military and had spent most of his adult life selfishly making money, working for Callahan was his idea of a public service. He wasn't being facetious.

As for their personal relationship, the word *marriage* had never come up—and Kay wasn't sure what she'd do if it did. They were monogamous—at least as far as Kay knew—but at this point in her life, she wasn't sure she was ready for another marriage. She liked having her own space and didn't want a full-time, live-in partner. Maybe one day she would, but not now. And the arrangement they had seemed to suit Eli as well.

When they were together, they enjoyed each other's company and had a marvelous time. Sometimes they'd just spend a quiet weekend sitting around Eli's town house, reading and watching movies when they weren't in bed. Other times, they sampled more exotic locales, like the week they spent in Paris and another in Jamaica, just because Eli had an urge for sunshine in January. It was nice having a rich lover.

But she didn't know what was going to happen after she quit working for Callahan. She had no intention of moving to New York unless someone—and she couldn't imagine who—offered her a job there. And since Eli appeared to have no desire to leave the Big Apple . . .

Aw, enough. This wasn't the time to worry about the future. After this was all over, she'd figure out what to do.

6

Olivia Prescott lived in a sand-colored high-rise. The apartments had large balconies and the grounds were manicured. It looked expensive. Not a place where multimillionaires would live, but the condos were probably in the six-to-eight-hundred-thousand-dollar range, which made Kay wonder if she had the right Olivia Prescott. If Prescott worked at the NSA as Kay was guessing—or hoping—she probably couldn't afford the place on a civil servant's salary. Well, maybe that wasn't true. If Prescott had some rank—if she was a GS-15 or higher—and had held that rank for a long time, then maybe she could afford it.

Kay walked up to the front door, which was locked of course. But outside, in a covered recess, were doorbell buttons and an intercom screen. O. Prescott lived in 5A. There was an S. Terrance in 5B. But there was no 5C or 5D or 5E, which Kay assumed meant Prescott occupied half the fifth floor. She pressed the doorbell button but no one answered, which didn't surprise her. It was only noon; if Prescott worked, she probably wouldn't be home for at least another five or six hours.

She went back to her car to wait—and Kay hated waiting. She'd hated stakeouts when she was with the DEA; she hated any situation where she was forced to sit and do nothing. But what other option did she have?

She called the hospital to check on Callahan's condition, but the nurse said she wasn't permitted to divulge any information over the phone and that Kay would have to talk to her in person and prove that she was related to Callahan. Kay pointed out that she'd been to see Callahan earlier, and at that time she hadn't been required to show ID or any other document proving she was his daughter. The nurse said, "Well, things have changed." Kay thanked the unhelpful nurse and hung up. She figured the cops had probably told the nurses not to talk about Callahan to anyone they didn't know, as they might be talking to the people who shot him—and who might come back and try to finish the job.

Kay was hungry. She hadn't eaten since six that morning, but there weren't any convenience stores or restaurants near Prescott's apartment. She thought about driving somewhere and stocking up on Coke and sandwiches, but before she could make a decision, her phone rang. She didn't recognize the number on her caller ID, just that it was a 202 area code.

"Hamilton," she said.

"This is Detective Mary Platt. I want to see you in my office. Immediately."

Kay restrained herself from telling Platt the many reasons why she didn't give a shit what she wanted.

"Why do you want to see me?" Kay said.

"Because I have more questions."

"I'm sorry, but this isn't a good time for me."

"Where are you?"

"I'm not going to tell you. I don't want you to send a couple cops over to pick me up."

"You don't seem to understand the seriousness of this situation. I can arrest you for homicide."

"Oh, bullshit. By now you've gotten back ballistic results, and you know that the only guy who had a bullet from my gun in him was wearing a ski mask."

"Be that as it may," Platt said, "I don't really know that you didn't shoot those other people. What I do know is that I can arrest you and keep you in a cell until some smart-ass attorney is able to get you out. And that might not be as easy as you think. A *massacre* occurred in that building and you're withholding information. I think the DA might even be able to convince a judge that you shouldn't be granted bail. I want you in my office now."

The Big Bad Wolf was huffing and puffing, but Kay had dealt with much bigger bad wolves. "Sorry," she said. "Not now. I'm busy. But I can spare you a few minutes. So if you have questions, ask them."

Platt didn't say anything and Kay could imagine her squeezing her phone with one of her big hands, stopping herself from screaming into it.

"We can't figure out who else works for Callahan except for you and the two dead guys," Platt said. "We can't find a personnel directory and we can't get into any of Callahan's computers. They're protected by a system that's too good for our geeks to crack. So far."

"Well, I can't help you with that," Kay said. "I don't know anything about computers."

"I need the names of Callahan's employees. Maybe one of them will know what was in his safe that was so important to these people."

"Let me think about that," Kay said.

"What the hell do you mean, *Let me think about that?*" Platt said.

"It means I need to decide if it's smart to give you people's names. Giving you their names could put them in danger."

"Goddamnit, if you don't—"

"I'll tell you what. You give me the name of the guy I shot, and I'll give you the name of a guy who is, like, Callahan's office manager. Okay?"

"You're *bargaining* with me?" Platt said.

"Calm down before you have a stroke. I just want to know who I shot. That doesn't seem unreasonable to me. And if you arrest me, my lawyer will get his name anyway."

Platt again hesitated. "His name was Jack Quinn. He served time for armed robbery twelve years ago, an armored-car heist in Ohio. He hasn't been convicted since then."

"How 'bout the other guy, the one Callahan killed?"

"I gave you all I'm going to give. Now tell me the name of this office manager."

"Okay. A deal's a deal," Kay said, as if she wouldn't break a deal with Platt whenever it suited her. She gave her Eli Dolan's name and cell phone number.

As soon as she ended the call with Platt, she called Eli. "I'm sorry I had to do this to you, but I gave your name to the D.C. Metro detective who's investigating the attack. Right now cops are roaming all over Callahan's office, pawing through desks and trying to get into the computers, and you're the best person to stop them."

She thought Eli would get pissed at her for giving Platt his name, but he didn't. Instead he said, "I already concluded the same thing. I'm on my way to LaGuardia right now. I'll deal with the detective."

"Thanks. And see if you can get the cops to give you the name of the man Callahan shot. The man I shot was named Quinn and—"

"How did you find that out?"

"I traded your name to the detective."

Eli laughed.

"Anyway," Kay continued, "Quinn was a convicted armed robber. But I still can't figure out why a robbery crew would hit Callahan's office."

"So what are you doing now?" Eli said.

"I'm waiting for somebody who might have some information."

"Who?"

She ignored the question. "Eli, the other thing we need to do, and I should have thought of this earlier, is get Henry over to watch Callahan. Whoever did this might try again."

"You think they would try to kill him in a hospital?"

"I don't know. But then, I never would have dreamed that guys with machine guns would attack the office in broad daylight."

"Okay, I'll call Henry. Who are you waiting to see?"

"A DEA guy I used to work with who has contacts in D.C. Metro. I'm hoping he might know someone who can give me the name of the other man who was killed."

She didn't know why, but like a little kid, she crossed her fingers when she told this lie. She told Eli good-bye and said she'd call him later.

SHE LOOKED AT HER WATCH: five p.m. She'd wasted the entire afternoon sitting in front of Prescott's place. For the third time that afternoon, she walked up to the apartment building entrance and leaned on Prescott's bell. No answer.

She returned to her car and called her daughter at Duke, but the call went to voice mail. Jessica was most likely still in class or maybe sitting in the library, cramming anatomy or physiology into her brain—subjects that Kay wouldn't have been able to pass if someone had been holding a gun to her head. The fact that it was July made no difference to her daughter, who seemed determined to set a record for becoming an M.D. Kay left a message saying she missed her and to give her a call when she had a chance.

Kay didn't have what would be considered a normal relationship with her daughter—Jessica called her *Kay*, not *Mom*—because Kay had really only known Jessica for two years. Kay was fifteen when she'd given birth to Jessica and had allowed the girl to be adopted by a married cousin who was dying to have a kid. But when Jessica was fifteen, after her adoptive parents died, she appeared back in Kay's life. She—reluctantly—asked Kay to become her guardian so she wouldn't have to go into the foster care system, and so Kay—also reluctantly—became her mother again.

They'd gotten off to a rocky start, as might be expected. For one thing, Jessica thought that because Kay had given her up for adoption, she obviously didn't want to be a mom. They also had nothing in common. When Kay was in high school, she cared mostly about sports and boys—which explains how she got pregnant—and after graduation she went into law enforcement. Jessica, on the other hand, was a straight-A student, excelled in math and science, and was now taking premed courses at Duke. Jessica, in fact, was so bright that she'd skipped her senior year in high school to attend college, and Kay had no doubt that she would one day become a brilliant doctor.

They were brought closer together when Jessica was kidnapped in San Diego while Kay was working for the DEA. Now they got along well. Even though they still didn't have much of anything in common, they talked frequently on the phone, Kay making sure that Jessica had everything she needed and was doing all right, and driving down to Duke some weekends to see her. The truth was that Kay was a lousy mother, but she was trying to become a better one. It was fortunate that Jessica was very mature and away at college, so when Kay left the Callahan Group, her daughter's life wouldn't be affected. She would make sure it wasn't affected.

After she left the message for Jessica, she decided to get something to eat before she passed out. She'd find a fast food place, get something to go, and come back to Prescott's place. She was just about to pull away from the curb when a cab stopped in front of the apartment building. A tall, thin woman got out of the rear seat. The cabbie opened the trunk and handed her a rolling suitcase, and the woman headed for the door of the building.

Could this be Prescott? Kay wondered. There was no reason to think it was. It could be any one of the other tenants. But why not check? Kay allowed enough time to pass for the woman to collect her mail and reach her apartment, then walked up to the doorbells again.

"Yes? Who is it?" a woman said through the intercom.

"I'm here to see you about Thomas Callahan."

The woman immediately said, "I don't know what you're talking about. You've buzzed the wrong unit."

"Fine," Kay said. "In that case, you won't care if I give your name to the D.C. cops."

"Who are you?"

"My name's Kay Hamilton. I work for Callahan."

"Well, I still don't know what you're talking about."

"After Callahan came out of surgery, he said one thing to me. He said 'Olivia Prescott'—and I think you're the Prescott he was talking about. But since you're acting like you don't know Callahan, I'm going to pass your name on to the cops and let them figure out if you're telling the truth."

Kay figured that if this Olivia Prescott was connected in any way to the covert side of Callahan's operation, the last thing she would want is the D.C. cops knowing her name. On the other hand, if Prescott was the one responsible for the attack on Callahan's office, the same would be true.

Whatever the case, after a long moment of silence, Prescott said, "I'll buzz you in so we can sort out this nonsense."

"Thanks," Kay said. But she was thinking: *Gotcha*.

7

Prescott was in her sixties, lean, flat-chested, no hips to speak of. She had thin lips, a bony nose, and her eyes were pale blue and seemingly lifeless. She was wearing a short-sleeved white blouse, black slacks, and low-heeled black loafers, and, except for one thing, she fit Kay's image of a cranky spinster librarian. The one thing was her hair, which was cut in a short, wavy bob and dyed platinum blond, reminding Kay of a 1920s flapper. She couldn't imagine why a woman Prescott's age—and with Prescott's seemingly no-nonsense demeanor—would dye her hair that color.

"Now what's this all about? Why are you here?" Prescott said.

"I told you. When Callahan came out of surgery, he gave me the name Olivia Prescott. Your name."

"There must be dozens of Olivia Prescotts in this country," Prescott said.

Kay noticed that Prescott didn't ask who Callahan was or why he'd been in surgery, but didn't bother to point this out. "Actually, there are only seven Olivia Prescotts," she said, "and you're the only one who lives a short distance from D.C."

"But why are you here?" Prescott asked again.

"I need your help. Since you didn't ask why Callahan was in surgery, I'm assuming you know what happened to him. Anyone with access to a television or a radio knows what happened on K Street. I'm also assuming you're one of the people who's been running Callahan. I'm trying to find out who shot him and why, and I need your help."

"I don't know what you mean about me *running* Callahan."

"I think you do. And think about this, Olivia. Right now a bunch of cops are inside Callahan's office, rooting through all the paperwork and trying to get into the computers."

Prescott shook her head, but before she could say anything, Kay said, "I'm not bluffing. I'll give your name to the cops and let them take it from here. And if I give the cops your name, the media will most likely get it, too. Do you really want the press digging into your relationship with Callahan?"

Prescott stared at her for a moment, her lips compressed into an unyielding line. Again she started to say something, but then turned her back on Kay and walked over to stand in front of a window. The only thing Kay could see out the window were trees and other apartment buildings. She knew Prescott wasn't taking in the view; she was trying to decide if it really mattered if Kay gave her name to the police.

As Kay waited for Prescott to make up her mind, she looked around the apartment. It was nicely decorated but cold, like Prescott. Lots of stainless steel and the furniture was mostly white, beige, or black. There were no knickknacks on shelves, no family photos, and there was hardly a primary color in sight. On one wall were two photos of trees taken in winter, snow on the ground, the trees leafless. Kay found them depressing. On a coffee table were magazines that Kay couldn't imagine a normal person reading: *Scientific American, Mathematics Magazine, American Journal of Physics.* Who the hell reads shit like that? A college professor—or maybe someone who works for the NSA?

Prescott turned back to face her. "Sit down," she ordered and Kay could tell she was a woman used to giving orders. "This is going to take some time."

Kay took a seat in a chair that had been built for aesthetic appeal, not comfort. Prescott dropped into a couch directly across from her and crossed her long legs. Kay could see the fatigue in Prescott's face.

"Do you know who Sally Ann Danzinger is?" Prescott said.

Danzinger. That was the woman Henry said had been to see Callahan yesterday, the political activist. But Kay wasn't there to share information with Prescott. "No. Never heard of her."

"What about the Layman brothers?"

"Yeah, I've heard of them. Rich guys involved in Republican politics."

"That's correct. And Sally Ann Danzinger, I guess you'd say, was their Democratic counterpart."

"Was?" Kay said.

Prescott ignored the question. "Sally Ann hated the Laymans. She accused them of using their wealth to achieve the goals of the ultraconservative right. The fact that Sally Ann was doing the same thing for liberal causes was irrelevant to her."

"What does this have to do with Callahan?"

"Just shut up and listen. Sally Ann was convinced that the Laymans were bribing politicians and violating campaign finance laws. Her lawyers have filed dozens of lawsuits hoping to gain access to documents that would prove the Laymans had committed crimes. She hired private detectives to follow them, and her detectives allegedly monitored the Laymans' phone calls, made attempts to get listening devices into their offices, and bribed employees to provide incriminating evidence."

"How do you know all this?"

"A lot of what she did is a matter of public record or speculation reported by the media. The Laymans have also filed their share of lawsuits against her. But the point I'm making is that Sally would do *anything* to get the Laymans. She was obsessed with bringing them down. Anyway, she called me yesterday when I was in London. She—"

"Wait a minute. Why would she call you?"

"Because I've known her since college. We were in the same sorority at Princeton. We were close when we were young but grew apart when she became so radical. One of the things that strained our friendship was her strong objection to the NSA monitoring the communications of American citizens. I tried to explain to her that what the NSA does is both legal and necessary, but she wouldn't listen to reason, and the last time I saw her she called me a Nazi. Until yesterday, I hadn't spoken to her in three years."

Prescott had just admitted she worked for the NSA. She probably thought that, since Kay had her name, Kay already knew who employed her or would find out soon.

"As I was saying, Sally Ann called me yesterday while I was in London. She—"

"What time did she call you?" Kay asked.

"It was after two in London, so it would have been around nine a.m. here. Now quit interrupting and pay attention. Sally Ann told me an employee of Zytek Systems had given classified information to a foreign government. Zytek is heavily involved in submarine sonar systems, the Laymans are majority shareholders, and one of the Layman brothers' sons is the CEO. When I asked her how she knew this, she told me that someone who works for the NSA had intercepted an e-mail from Zytek to an operative of a foreign government. Do you understand what all this means?"

"No," Kay said. She was still reeling from the words *operative of a foreign government.*

"It means that Sally Ann had somehow managed to convince an NSA employee to monitor communications related to the Laymans. But Sally Ann refused to tell me the man's name when I spoke with her."

"How do you know it's a man?"

"Because he was killed yesterday."

"What?"

As Kay was trying to absorb this revelation, Prescott said, "Sally Ann had a copy of the e-mail the NSA man had intercepted. Actually, she had a copy of an *attachment* to the e-mail. But she didn't know who sent it, she didn't know who the recipient was, and, like I said, she refused to tell me the name of the man who gave it to her.

"I told her to take the copy of the e-mail attachment and deliver it to Callahan and that I would pick it up when I got back from London. When I got off the plane, I learned about the attack on Callahan's office. That's when I also learned about the NSA man who was killed."

"Why did you tell her to take it to Callahan? You said you didn't know him."

"I never said that I didn't know him. I said I wasn't *running* him, whatever the hell that means. I knew Callahan when he worked at the CIA and I told Sally Ann to take the copy to him because, at the time, I didn't know who in the NSA I could trust or who was leaking information to Sally Ann. My plan had been to get the document from Callahan today and begin an investigation, but by then Callahan had been shot."

"Have you spoken to Danzinger since you got back?"

"No. Sally Ann was also killed yesterday."

"Jesus Christ!" Kay said. "And they killed all these people to get their hands on an attachment to an e-mail? It's that important?"

"The answer to your question is no," Prescott said. "They didn't kill to obtain the copy of the e-mail attachment. Whomever the e-mail was sent to *already* had the attachment. They killed them to hide the identity of the government who received the e-mail and to protect their spy at Zytek."

"Did you warn Callahan that what Danzinger was bringing him was dangerous?"

"No. I never talked to Callahan and I had no idea someone would do this. I just wanted the document out of Sally Ann's hands so she wouldn't give it to someone else."

"How did you find out that Danzinger had been killed? It wasn't reported on the news."

"As I said, I learned about the massacre in Callahan's office when I got off the plane. I had no specific reason to believe that it happened because of the information Sally Ann had given him, but obviously the thought occurred to me. It also occurred to me that if Callahan had been attacked because of what she had given him, then she could be in danger, too. I sent men to her home to bring her to a safe house, but when they arrived, the police were already there.

"And Sally Ann's death was on the news but her name wasn't mentioned, as they hadn't notified her next of kin. The police told the media that a home invasion had occurred and the homeowner and her companion were killed."

"And the NSA man you said was killed. Who was he and how was he killed?"

"His name was James Parker and his body was found in a park in Anacostia yesterday afternoon. He shot himself in the head—or so the cops think. I think he was killed, because I don't buy the coincidence of Sally Ann being killed and Callahan being attacked the same day an NSA technician decides to commit suicide."

"Are you sure Parker's the one who gave Danzinger the attachment?"

"No, not one hundred percent. But Parker was in a position at the NSA to have intercepted the e-mail. He was also not an ideal employee. He was one of those people who thought he was brighter than he really was and that the agency didn't appreciate his value. He was also politically active. The agency discourages political activism but, unfortunately, we can't stop it. So I suspect that Parker worked with Sally Ann because he shared her political views. Or maybe she paid him. I don't know. I already have a team tearing Parker's life apart.

"So now do you understand what happened, Ms. Hamilton, and why it happened?"

"No," Kay said. "I don't understand how the killers, or whoever hired them, knew about the e-mail in the first place. Parker gave the attachment to Danzinger and Danzinger told you about it. But how did the killers find out about it?"

"I don't know," Prescott said.

Kay suspected that Prescott wasn't telling her everything she knew. But what Kay really didn't understand was how anyone could have pulled this off so fast. In a ten-hour period, someone had found out about the e-mail intercepted by the NSA, killed an NSA employee, killed Sally Ann Danzinger, learned that Callahan had the e-mail attachment, and then stole the safe from Callahan's office, killing two of Callahan's people along the way. Who the hell were these people?

34 HOURS EARLIER

8

The National Security Agency's headquarters are at Fort Meade, Maryland, in two box-shaped high-rise structures that appear to be made of black obsidian. The buildings loom over a parking lot that holds eighteen thousand vehicles. James Parker sat in the bowels of one of the buildings in a small cubicle in a quarter acre of identical cubicles. He was staring at a computer monitor, trying to make a decision.

On the screen in front of Parker was a short e-mail originating from the iPhone of a man named Kenneth Winston that was sent to a woman named Jane Moore. The text of the e-mail said, "Jane, just wanted to wish you a Happy Birthday." The e-mail had an attachment, and the file name of the attachment was *BDayCard.jpg*.

Kenneth Winston worked for Zytek Systems, a company that manufactured sonar equipment for the U.S. Navy. "Jane Moore" was one of the cover names used by a woman named Lin Mai, who worked for a Chinese trade association in Washington, D.C. The NSA had been monitoring calls to and from employees of the trade association for years, knowing it was a front for industrial and military espionage. The attachment to the e-mail—BDayCard.jpg—was encrypted in a code the Chinese thought was unbreakable but that the NSA had broken two years ago.

The attachment was only forty-five kilobytes and contained less than four hundred characters of what appeared to be computer source code. Parker had no idea, however, what the significance of the source code might be; most likely only experts in sonar technology would be able to understand it—but Parker didn't need to understand it. All he cared about was that the e-mail was proof that the Chinese had a spy at Zytek.

Parker had no idea what had caused Winston and Lin Mai to do something so dangerous; that is, communicate by e-mail. The whole time the NSA had been monitoring the trade association, it had been almost pristine insofar as not exposing Chinese operatives. So the e-mail meant one of two things. One, that Winston, who appeared to be Lin Mai's agent, had gotten careless, thinking that because the e-mail and the attachment were so small and seemingly innocuous that it wouldn't be noticed in the trillions of e-mails sent each day in the United States. The second possibility was that they knew it might be noticed, but the information contained in the e-mail attachment was needed so urgently that they decided to take the risk. Whatever the case, it didn't matter to Parker. He didn't care about the intelligence value of the e-mail.

What James Parker cared about was that the e-mail was the key to his salvation.

Parker printed out a copy of the e-mail and the attachment using a printer in a different section of the office. He then spent the next half hour doing everything he could to make the original e-mail and the instructions to the printer disappear. He knew that they wouldn't ever really disappear—they would still exist as fragments of computer code buried inside the NSA's servers—but he hoped he had made it impossible for another technician to find them and, more important, trace the documents to the machines in Parker's wee cubicle.

DAY 1—8 A.M.

Parker told his section head that he had a dental appointment that he'd forgotten about. The supervisor, who had never liked Parker—hardly any of Parker's co-workers liked him—looked as if he suspected Parker was lying, but all he said was "You need to get back here as soon as your appointment's over. I have three people on leave this week, so I'm shorthanded."

"Sure," Parker said.

Parker left the base and headed toward Washington. He passed the pay phones closest to Fort Meade, thinking those might be monitored. He stopped at a 7-Eleven in Greenbelt and made the call.

"No names," he said when she answered the phone. The way her voice sounded, he'd woken her up. "I have something you're going to love. It concerns the brothers."

"What is it?"

He laughed. "Are you crazy? Over the phone? We need to meet, right away, because I have to get back to work. Pick a place in D.C. I'm headed there now."

She named a restaurant in southeast D.C. and he told her he'd be there by nine a.m.

DAY 1—9 A.M.

Parker was already seated, drinking coffee, when Sally Ann Danzinger walked into the restaurant. She beamed a smile at him and came toward him in long-legged strides. She was wearing Levi jeans and a man's short-sleeved plaid shirt unbuttoned over a white T-shirt. She was an impressive-looking woman because she was six feet tall and had the broad shoulders of a former swimmer. She was now in her sixties, her hair was long and completely gray, and she had a network of wrinkles around her eyes and mouth appropriate to her age—wrinkles she could've gotten rid of any time she wanted. Danzinger, however, would never avail herself of a plastic surgeon, any more than she would dye her hair to hide the gray. Parker simply couldn't understand why a woman with her money would want to look and dress the way she did—but then, Danzinger was a nut.

She immediately said, "What did you find?" Before Parker could answer, she said, "I'm so excited I'm practically peeing my pants."

"Uh, yeah," Parker said, not knowing what else to say. He handed her the copy of the e-mail attachment.

"What is this?" she said. The document was obviously gibberish to her, as it would be to 99 percent of the people on the planet.

"It's computer source code related to submarine sonar technology."

"How do you know that?" Sally Ann asked.

"Because I know what computer source code looks like and I know it's related to submarine sonar because of where the e-mail came from." He paused dramatically. "The e-mail was sent by a guy who works at Zytek Systems to a . . . to an operative of a foreign government, a government not friendly to the United States. In other words, there's a spy at Zytek who's giving military secrets to our enemies."

"Oh my God!" Sally Ann said. Then she frowned and said, "Are you saying the Layman brothers are involved in this?"

"The CEO of Zytek is Bob Layman's middle son," Parker said, telling Sally Ann something she already knew. Parker was confused by her confusion.

"I know that," Sally Ann said, "but did Ted Layman send the e-mail?"

"No. It was sent by a guy who works for him. But can't you see the headlines? A spy in a Layman company? This is huge. I mean, you know how the Laymans are always going on about what superpatriots they are."

Sally Ann shook her head. "This doesn't do me any good, James. As much as I loathe the Laymans, I would never accuse them of being traitors. I mean, they're xenophobic, and one of the many things I despise about them is their so-called patriotism, but they wouldn't condone or ever be part of something like this. And if the e-mail you intercepted didn't come directly from Ted Layman . . . Well, like I said, this doesn't do me any good. I need proof that the Laymans are committing crimes and this doesn't implicate them at all."

Parker couldn't believe her. Was she obtuse? Before he could object, she said, "You need to turn this over to whoever deals with this sort of thing. The FBI, I suppose."

"Are you insane?" Parker shrieked. Lowering his voice, he said, "You think I'm going to go to my boss and say, 'Hey, I've been eavesdropping on the Layman brothers for Sally Ann Danzinger and I just happened to run across this e-mail that shows there's a spy at Zytek'?"

"Well, you need to figure out a way to do the right thing. I mean, I don't want you to get in trouble, James, but somebody in law enforcement or counterintelligence needs to know about this."

Before Parker could speak, she asked, "Who was the e-mail sent to? The Russians? The Chinese? North Korea?"

Parker didn't answer the question. Instead he said, "Look, I need money. I've gotten myself into some serious financial trouble, and I need eighty-five grand. I thought you'd be willing to pay for something as big as this."

Then the bitch turned righteous on him. "I'm not going to pay you for this. And this isn't the sort of information I wanted you to get for me." She reached out and patted one of his hands. "James, I've always appreciated your willingness to help in my fight against the Laymans, and I'll never tell anyone that you've been helping me, but you need to do the right thing. Now, are you going to tell me who sent the e-mail and who the recipient was?"

"No."

"Then I have to leave," she said and pushed back her chair.

"Wait a minute! Goddamnit, just wait! I've been risking my job to help you. Hell, I could go to prison for what I've been doing."

"I'm sorry," Sally Ann said. She stood, the copy of the e-mail attachment still clutched in her clawlike hand, and turned to leave.

Parker shouted, "Hey! Give me back that paper. You can't take that with you."

"Well, I am. Because if you don't do what's necessary, then I'll be forced to."

Parker started to get up. He was going to rip the document right out of her hand. Then he noticed the dozen other customers in the restaurant, including three big guys wearing hard hats, and one of them was eyeing him. The hard hats would definitely try to stop him and might even call the cops.

Before he could do or say anything else, Sally Ann was out the door. *Son of a bitch!*

DAY 1—9:10 A.M.

As Sally Ann drove back home, she tried to decide what to do. She could wait to see if Parker would contact the Bureau or tell his superiors—although the only way she would know if he did was if the media reported that a spy had been arrested at Zytek—but it was obvious to her that he wasn't going to do anything. He was too afraid that he'd get in trouble.

She'd met James Parker at a rally at the Capitol. It was one of those 99-percenter protests. The Layman brothers and Sally Ann were both part of the elite 1 percent—but Sally Ann sided with the masses while the Laymans did everything they could to crush the dreams of the poor and the middle class. Parker didn't know who she was when she met him. He was just standing next to her, holding his WE ARE THE 99 placard, and they started talking. When she found out that he worked at the NSA, she invited him to dinner and used all of her considerable powers of persuasion to get him to assist her.

Parker wasn't a likeable man. He was a boorish, arrogant egomaniac, and he was bitter because people he considered fools had been promoted instead of him. He assisted Sally Ann because it thrilled him to put one over on the idiot who supervised him, but he'd also seemed genuinely interested in helping her bring down the Laymans. All he agreed to do for her was keep his eyes and ears open for anything the NSA scooped up, and if he came across anything related to the Laymans, he'd pass it on to her.

In the nine months she'd known him, he'd twice provided voice recordings of Bill Layman, the older of the two Layman brothers, talking to the senior senator from Kansas. The recordings proved that the Laymans were trying to persuade the senator to pass legislation the Laymans wanted, but nothing said was overtly illegal. The recordings simply demonstrated that the Laymans had a cozy relationship with a politician they supported financially.

But Parker had never asked for money before. She had no idea what sort of financial trouble he was in and she couldn't help but wonder if it had happened recently. He seemed so desperate that she wondered if he might try to sell the information he'd intercepted, although she didn't know who would buy it. A more likely possibility was that he'd destroy the illegally intercepted e-mail, and if he did, the spy at Zytek would never be identified. Whatever the case, she needed to do something quickly.

Sally Ann's house didn't have a garage, so she parked in the driveway. The house was a two-story, four-bedroom home built after World War II in a racially mixed neighborhood in southeast D.C. When she bought the place, it was a dilapidated wreck surrounded by similar wrecks, but she used local contractors to restore the house and did everything she could to bring the neighborhood back to life.

Latisha Taylor, the young woman who lived with her and acted as her secretary and general assistant, was already up and working. Sally Ann said good morning to her, then went to the bedroom on the second floor that she used as an office. She looked again at the piece of paper she'd taken from Parker. It was just a bunch of numbers and symbols and absolutely meaningless to her.

Who should she talk to about this? There were a dozen progressive politicians who would be in a position to help, but she didn't want this politicized. She could always go to her contacts in the media, but that didn't seem right either. She could, of course, take the information directly to the FBI, but she wasn't on the best of terms with the Bureau, who considered her a radical activist.

She suddenly realized who she should call.

DAY 1—9:15 A.M.

Parker sat brooding in the restaurant for five minutes after Danzinger left, then headed back toward Fort Meade. He didn't know what to do. He was confident that Sally Ann wouldn't tell anyone that he'd been collecting information on the Layman brothers. She would protect his identity the way a reporter would protect a source. She might, however, give the attachment to the FBI, and if the FBI was somehow able to figure out that it had come from someone at the NSA, then they might be able to identify him.

But then he thought, no, they wouldn't. He'd buried the e-mail and his handling of it so deep in the NSA's servers that it would never be traced to him. It was like the original e-mail was a bottle he'd smashed, and then he'd thrown the pieces of broken glass onto a pile of broken glass that was as high as a mountain. It wasn't a needle in a haystack; it was a needle cut into a thousand pieces, and *then* tossed into the haystack.

So he should be safe, but he still needed money and he needed it desperately—and suddenly he had an idea. It would be dangerous, but he didn't have any other choice. He took the next exit he came to and drove around until he found a pay phone.

DAY 1—9:30 A.M. (2:30 P.M. IN LONDON)

Olivia Prescott was in a taxi on her way to Thames House for another meeting with the good people from MI5. She'd been in London for two days meeting with the NSA's counterparts in the U.K. and would be returning home the next morning. The meetings were primarily so that the NSA could share the latest eavesdropping and encryption tools they were using with their British brethren—which, of course, weren't really the *latest* tools in their tool bag. But what they did share impressed the British, and they were appropriately grateful. The other purpose of the meetings was to subtly reassure the British that the NSA wasn't spying on their politicians—not that long ago they'd been caught spying on the German chancellor—but, of course, they were.

Prescott didn't recognize the number on the caller ID when her phone rang. She thought for a moment about letting the call go to voice mail, but having nothing better to do while the cab was stuck in traffic, she answered.

"Yes," she said.

"Olivia, it's Sally Ann."

For a moment Prescott was too shocked to speak. She hadn't spoken to Sally Ann Danzinger in three years. They had been at a Princeton reunion, and they got into a terrible row, and Sally Ann called her a fascist.

"What can I do for you, Sally Ann?" Her tone made it clear that she hadn't forgiven her.

"Olivia, this is important and it's not about politics. I was given a copy of an e-mail this morning by a . . . a *person* who works at the NSA. The e-mail, according to this person, is a fragment of computer source code, whatever that is, related to sonar technology manufactured by Zytek Systems."

"What?" Prescott said. She couldn't believe what she was hearing.

"This person said the e-mail had been sent from someone at Zytek to a hostile foreign government."

"Why on earth would an NSA employee give this to you?" Prescott asked.

"I'm not going to tell you that, nor will I give you the person's name. And I don't know who sent the e-mail or who it was going to. The copy I have is just the attachment—just a bunch of numbers and symbols— and doesn't have the e-mail addresses on it."

"Sally Ann, please don't say anything for a moment. I need to think."

If she was telling the truth—and there was no reason for Prescott to believe she wasn't—there was a mole in the NSA passing information on to Sally Ann, most likely information about the Layman brothers. Prescott could have someone at the NSA pick up the e-mail attachment from Sally Ann right away and begin an investigation, but if there was a mole in her house, she didn't know who she could trust—at least not until she understood more. But she also wanted the document out of Sally Ann's hands. You could never tell what Sally Ann might do.

"Okay, Sally Ann, here's what I need you to do. I'm not in D.C. right now, so I want you to put that e-mail attachment in a sealed envelope. Under no circumstances are you to make a copy of it. Then I want you to take it to a man named Thomas Callahan. Callahan has a company on K Street called the Callahan Group. He's a civilian now, but he's ex-CIA, an old friend, and I trust him. His office isn't far from your house, so please do this quickly."

That was a lie; Callahan was not a friend and Prescott didn't trust him any farther than she could spit his fat body.

"Give Callahan the envelope," Prescott said, "and tell him to put it in his safe. I'll get it from him when I return from London tomorrow. But don't tell Callahan what's in the envelope. Just go to his office and tell him I asked you to deliver it to him. Do you understand?"

"Yes. I know we've had our differences, Olivia, but I trust your judgment in these matters."

"Good. I'll see you when I get back."

Prescott disconnected the call. She wasn't going to phone Callahan. It was bad enough that she'd mentioned his name on a cell call, but there was no way she wanted there to be a record of her contacting him. With the type of phone she had—there were only a couple thousand like it on the planet—it was highly unlikely that anyone could monitor her conversations, but you never know.

There was one thing Olivia Prescott knew for sure, though: She'd find Sally Ann's mole and she'd crush him like the small rodent he was.

DAY 1—9:30 A.M.

Lin Mai was sitting at her desk in the Chinese Trade Association on New York Avenue in Washington, D.C. The mission of the trade association was to encourage the American government and American businesses to buy and borrow from the Chinese. The trade association employed almost two hundred people, and two-thirds of those people were American citizens: lawyers and ex-politicians and others of that ilk who could lobby the U.S. Congress and develop position papers to persuade those who had to be persuaded.

Lin Mai was an active participant in the trade association's legitimate endeavors. She attended meetings and conventions; she socialized with powerful American officials; she hosted parties at her home in Georgetown. She had a more important job, however. She was a spy. Or, to be precise, she was a Chinese intelligence officer who controlled a number of American spies.

She was sitting at her desk, reading a draft of a bill that would soon be introduced in the House of Representatives. It would limit the sale of certain computer technologies to China and it was just one more of the Americans' futile attempts to stay ahead of her country. The bill was so new that few members of Congress had seen it, and Lin Mai knew that most members wouldn't even read it before they voted on it; they would vote based on summaries prepared by low-ranking aides— and she might be able to influence one of them. As she was struggling to grasp a complex paragraph, one of the four phones in her purse rang.

All four phones were marked with a plastic stick-on label, which identified in Chinese characters the name Lin Mai was supposed to use when she answered. She was shocked to see the phone that was ringing was the one she used to communicate with Winston. Why would he be calling her? She and Winston never *talked* on the phone; on very rare occasions she would send him encrypted text messages. She figured someone must have dialed the number by mistake but decided to take the call.

"Yes?" she said.

"Happy birthday, Jane. Or should I say, Happy birthday, Lin Mai?"

Lin Mai almost dropped the phone, like she'd just realized she was holding a poisonous snake in her hand. The man calling was not Winston but he knew her name and her cover name. Even Winston didn't know her real name. And the caller knew about the e-mail Winston had sent her yesterday. She wondered if this phone call would simply end her career or if it would end her life.

"What do you want?" she said. She could hear the tremor in her voice.

"This morning I was forced to give a copy of the attachment—you know, the birthday card—to someone. But if you act very, very quickly you can protect yourself and the man who sent it to you. If you don't give me what I want, however, then the birthday-card sender will be arrested and you'll be deported. Who knows what will happen to you after that. Your masters are not known for their forgiving natures."

"What do you want?" she asked again.

"A hundred thousand."

"Dollars?"

"Of course, *dollars*."

"Okay," she immediately said. She wasn't going to haggle with him; protecting herself and Winston was more important than money. "But it will take me some time to get that much."

"Bullshit. You can get your hands on that amount of cash in no time at all. That's one reason I'm asking for so little. I could have asked for a million, but I'm in a hurry. But take all the time you want. Just keep in mind that if you don't act fast, the person I gave the attachment to will give it to somebody else. And then this whole mess will be out of your control."

"How do I reach you?" Lin Mai asked. "I need to talk to my superior."

"I'm calling from a pay phone. I'll wait half an hour, and then I'm leaving." He gave her the phone number and hung up.

DAY 1—9:40 A.M.

Lin Mai squeezed her eyes shut, trying to keep the tears from leaking out. It was not her fault that she was in this situation. It was the fault of people back in China who told her she needed to get the information immediately, that it was extremely urgent, but she was not told why.

She normally obtained documents or flash drives from Winston from a drop box they used, and she would then send them to China via diplomatic pouch. That was the safest way.

This time, however, she was given a lengthy technical document that had been overnighted from China. The document was too scientifically complex for her to understand, so she couldn't summarize it and it was too long to read to Winston over the phone, not that she would have ever used a phone. So she flew up to Boston, met with Winston so he could read the document, and then told him that he was to give her what the people in China wanted via e-mail as soon as he had the information. She and Winston both knew that sending an e-mail was dangerous, but it was urgent. Winston had not been happy when she gave him the order but he complied; he had no choice if he wanted to get paid.

Kenneth Winston was a physicist at Zytek Systems. The company was located in Cambridge, Massachusetts, and Winston had been providing information on American submarine sonar technology to the Chinese since 2010. He was fifty-seven years old, and he was one of those destroyed by the American financial crisis. He had been planning to retire at the age of sixty-two, sell his home for a large profit, downsize to something smaller, and live off his investments. Thanks to Wall Street, however, Winston's dreams of retiring to a condo in Florida were blown to smithereens. His 401(k) was reduced to almost nothing, his one-point-four-million-dollar home became worth approximately eight hundred thousand dollars, and his wife lost her job.

Winston made a good salary—he was a talented man involved in cutting-edge work at Zytek—but he depended on both his and his wife's salaries to support their lifestyle and pay their mortgage. He had also accumulated over seventy thousand dollars in credit card debt. Lin Mai was always surprised that even brilliant people could dig their own financial graves.

Following the American financial meltdown—which became a global financial meltdown—four hundred Chinese analysts were put into a warehouse filled with computers and they worked eighteen hours a day for six months looking for people like Kenneth Winston: people in sensitive positions who were now financially vulnerable. It was simple to access credit card and mortgage and bankruptcy records. Winston was one of eighteen people eventually recruited, and Lin Mai was the one who recruited him.

Lin Mai sat for only another minute pondering her potential fate and blaming the fools in China who had done this to her, then she called Fang Zhou. She told Fang they needed to meet immediately. She said that she had less than half an hour to resolve a critical situation, and it would take her twenty minutes to drive to the Chinese embassy. She asked Fang to meet her halfway between the embassy and the trade association. Fang Zhou agreed.

Fang Zhou terrified her.

Ten minutes later she was sitting in Fang's car in the parking lot of a restaurant that was closed, and she quickly told Fang what the man had said to her. Fang didn't waste time reprimanding her; he knew there was no time for that.

"Okay. Call him back and tell him you'll give him what he wants." He looked at his watch and said, "Tell him you'll meet him in forty-five minutes at a park in Anacostia. Tell him you chose that location because you don't want anyone to see the two of you together. Try to sound timid and frightened when you talk to him."

"What's the name of the park?" Lin Mai asked. She wouldn't have any problem sounding frightened.

While Lin Mai was speaking to the blackmailer, Fang drove them back to the Chinese embassy. From a safe in his office, he took an untraceable .38 revolver and a handful of bullets. He also grabbed a briefcase; Lin Mai would need to carry something large enough to hold a hundred thousand dollars. They then drove to the park in an older model sedan that didn't have diplomatic plates.

Fang Zhou had no idea what had gone wrong between Lin Mai and

Winston. He had no idea what information Winston had sent. His job was not overseeing their spies. Fang Zhou was Damage Control. His job was fixing things when they went wrong—and this time, something had gone very wrong. He actually felt sorry for Lin Mai. He'd known her for several years and she was an intelligent, appealing woman, but a bit full of herself. He was certain this experience would make her much more humble.

As they were driving toward the park, he said, "Tell me about Winston. How valuable is he?"

"Extremely valuable. As you must know, we are building the next class of ultraquiet diesel submarines. The more we know about American sonar capability, the safer our submarines will be."

She was right. One day China and the United States might fight a real war as opposed to an economic war, and if that happened, every American submarine had to be located before they could fire their nuclear missiles, and Chinese subs needed to be so quiet that the Americans would not be able to target them. Submarines were the most powerful weapons in each country's arsenal and very few things were as important as counteracting America's capability for hunting Chinese subs.

Two blocks before they reached the park, Fang pulled over so Lin Mai could drive. He got into the backseat of the sedan and crouched down on the floor out of sight. This was not easy because he was so tall. He was also annoyed because he hadn't had time to change and was wrinkling his expensive suit.

DAY 1—10:45 A.M.

Parker didn't like the place Lin Mai had selected for their meeting. It made him nervous. It looked like a place where a person could get mugged.

The park was on the banks of the Anacostia River in a poor section of Washington. At one time it had contained a couple of swings, a teeter-totter, and a small wading pool, and there had been a patch of grass for those who wished to picnic. The grass was now gone, replaced by weeds that were two feet high. Paper cups, wine and beer bottles, and Styrofoam fast food boxes littered the ground. The wading pool had an inch of water in it that was covered with a film of green scum. A car, minus its tires, had been set on fire in the small parking lot, and only the blackened, charred body remained.

As he drove toward the parking lot, Parker could see a Chinese woman sitting in a car by herself. He looked around to see if anyone was lurking in the untended bushes surrounding the park but they were too dense, and he couldn't be sure that no one was there. It appeared they were alone, but just to be safe, he backed his car into a parking space so that it was facing the exit.

FIVE MINUTES AFTER Lin Mai and Fang parked, an unwashed Honda Accord drove into the parking lot. Lin Mai could see the driver, a man, looking around, checking to see if she'd come alone. Then he backed his car into a parking space a few yards from where she was parked. Barely moving her lips, she told Fang what she saw.

Fang whispered from the backseat, "Get out before he decides to take off. Take the briefcase with you and go sit in his car. Move! I want him to remain in his car and I don't want him driving away."

Fang waited until he heard the door of the Honda slam shut before he slithered out the back door and peeked over the trunk. Lin Mai was in the passenger's seat of the Honda and the man's head was turned toward her. Fang ran up to the Honda, yanked open the driver's door, and placed the muzzle of the .38 against the man's head. "Don't move," he said.

In Chinese, he told Lin Mai to walk up to the park access road and to call him if she saw anybody approaching, then he took Lin Mai's place in the passenger seat of the Honda.

The man was in his thirties. He had a short, scraggly beard that was darker than his thinning blond hair. He wasn't fat but he had the soft body of a man who spent all day sitting behind a desk. He wore a blue short-sleeved shirt with a button-down collar, beige pants, and white running shoes; his shirt and pants were clean but in need of ironing. Fang suspected that he didn't have a wife.

"Hey, look," the man said. "You don't want to kill me. I can be useful to you. Really."

Fang almost laughed. Two minutes ago the man had been a blackmailer; now he was applying for a job.

"Maybe," Fang said. He wanted him to remain hopeful. "What's your name?"

"Parker. James Parker. Jim."

"Show me your driver's license, Jim," Fang said.

Parker pulled out his wallet and showed his license to Fang. His name was indeed James Parker.

"Put your wallet back in your pocket, Jim," Fang said. "Now tell me who you work for." Fang was pretty sure he already knew who employed Parker, but he asked anyway.

And Parker confirmed what Fang suspected. "The NSA," Parker said.

"So tell me about this e-mail. You told Lin Mai you gave a copy of the attachment to someone. I want to know everything you did and what you told this person."

Parker didn't hesitate; he was too frightened. He told Fang about his relationship with Sally Ann Danzinger—whom Fang had never heard of—and about Danzinger's political war against the Layman brothers. Fang had heard of the Layman brothers, and privately admired them. According to Parker, he'd been helping Danzinger for the last nine months, attempting to gather incriminating information against the Laymans. Fang didn't ask why he was helping Danzinger, but when he asked

Parker why he had decided to betray Danzinger, Parker hesitated, so Fang pinched a nerve in the man's neck, causing Parker considerable pain.

After Parker was able to speak again, he explained that Danzinger had refused to pay him for the information.

"What will Danzinger do with the information you gave her?" Fang asked.

"I think she'll eventually give it to somebody who will try to arrest Winston, but I don't know who. Maybe the FBI. Maybe a politician. I don't know, but she'll give it to someone."

"And you only gave Danzinger a copy of the e-mail attachment? You didn't give her the e-mail that showed the contact information?"

"No, just a copy of the attachment. I didn't tell her Winston's name and I didn't say who he sent it to. I just told her that the e-mail was going to a foreign government. I swear. I did tell her the attachment came from Zytek. I had to tell her that much so she'd know it was important."

"How do you know Danzinger won't tell somebody that you gave her the attachment?"

"She won't. You don't know Sally Ann, but I do, and I know she'd never give me up. She'd go to jail first. In fact, she's the type that would *want* to go to jail. She'd love the publicity of being a martyr."

"How do you know Danzinger hasn't already given the copy to someone?"

"I don't. I met with her about"—he glanced at his watch—"an hour and a half ago. So maybe by now she has, but I doubt it. She'll have to figure out who to give it to and then set up a meeting to hand it over. She won't scan and e-mail it like, well, you know. So if you act fast, maybe you can stop her. All I was trying to do was let you know that your spy at Zytek is vulnerable. I figured that information would be worth a lot to you."

Then Parker, who was not totally stupid, began to bargain. "Look," he said, "I can be very valuable to you. I have access to—"

"Shut up," Fang said, "I need to think."

He needed to decide if it was still possible to save Winston. Parker knew about Lin Mai, he knew about Winston, and he knew what the e-mail contained. But all Danzinger knew was that the e-mail had come from Zytek. Yes, Winston could be saved, but only if Fang acted quickly.

"If Danzinger gave the e-mail attachment to the FBI, could they trace it back to you at the NSA?"

"No, no way. After I made a copy of the e-mail I buried that information so deep and in so many places that nobody will ever be able to trace it to me. The FBI wouldn't even know where to begin to look for it. And even if somebody at the NSA saw the attachment, they still wouldn't be able to trace it to me."

Fang wondered about that. This arrogant fool had probably done everything he could to make sure that no one could figure out he'd intercepted the e-mail. But was Parker really smart enough to hide his identity? And although Parker was confident that Danzinger would not give his name to the FBI, what if the FBI forced it out of her? Then they might be able to force Parker to confess.

"Where is the copy of the e-mail you made? You said you gave the attachment to Danzinger, but what did you do with the e-mail?"

"It's right here," Parker said, and removed a folded piece of paper from his shirt pocket and handed it to Fang.

Fang would burn the document later—after he had dealt with Parker.

"Look," Parker said. Sweat was beaded on his forehead. "You don't have to pay me today. Consider this a favor. But like I said, I can really be useful to you, and in the future—"

Fang placed the muzzle of the .38 directly against Parker's right temple and pulled the trigger.

Being careful not to get Parker's blood on himself, Fang lowered the driver's-side window, wrapped Parker's right hand around the weapon, and fired a second shot out the window so Parker would have gunshot residue on his hand. He then opened the chamber of the revolver, removed the four bullets that had not been fired and the two empty shell casings. He took a handkerchief, wiped his fingerprints off the gun, off all the unfired bullets, and off one of the shell casings. He reloaded the revolver—using the handkerchief again to avoid leaving fingerprints—so it contained five unfired bullets and a single shell casing, and it would appear that only one shot had been fired. Finally, he placed the gun in Parker's dead hand, inserted Parker's finger in the trigger guard, and pressed Parker's finger down on the trigger.

Fang didn't know Parker's personal circumstances, but it was logical to assume that the man was desperate for money. Why else would he risk his job and his freedom by contacting them? Whatever the case, staging a suicide was the best Fang could do on such short notice.

Fang needed more information. He got back into his car and picked up Lin Mai, who was still waiting on the access road, holding the empty briefcase in her hand.

"Would the FBI be able to trace the e-mail attachment to Winston if they saw it?" Fang asked her.

"What?" she said.

He looked over at her. She was weeping, thinking about what might happen to her, and not about his question. He backhanded her hard enough to make her head bounce off the passenger-side window. "Pay attention!" he said and repeated the question.

"I don't know," she said. "Zytek employs fifteen hundred people and works with numerous outside contractors. But I would think that the number of people who would have access to the source code would be limited. Fifty people, a hundred? I have no way to know. I'd have to ask Winston."

In China, if they suspected that a group as small as fifty people contained a spy, it would take less than a day to find him. In the United States, however, with its bizarre concerns for the legal rights of criminals, it might be possible for Winston to avoid capture and continue to be a valuable asset. But to determine this, Fang needed to know what Danzinger had done with the attachment.

DAY 1—11 A.M.

Sally Ann had planned to take the e-mail attachment to this Callahan person right after she spoke to Olivia Prescott, but then Latisha reminded her that she had a teleconference at ten a.m. The conference call was about an advertising campaign for Planned Parenthood, one that she was personally funding, and involved an ad agency in New York, a well-known Hollywood actress, and a number of Planned Parenthood people. She thought about rescheduling it, but that would be difficult. Since Olivia wouldn't pick up the envelope until tomorrow, she didn't think that a one-hour delay would matter.

Following the teleconference, she had Latisha call her a cab—she didn't want the hassle of trying to find a parking spot on K Street—and told her that she'd be back soon. When Latisha asked where she was going and if there was anything she could do to help—Latisha was really the sweetest girl—she said that it was just a small problem she needed to deal with personally.

She found the Callahan Group's office, but when she turned the doorknob to enter, it was locked. She'd noticed a surveillance camera over the door—which seemed odd to her—and wondered if anyone could see her standing in the hall. She rapped on the door and heard the lock click.

Sitting behind a desk in a small foyer was a large, intimidating man. His shoulders were so broad she wondered if he had to turn sideways to pass through doors.

"What can I do for you, ma'am?" he asked.

"I need to see Thomas Callahan," she said.

"May I ask your name, ma'am, and why you want to see him?"

"I'm not going to tell you my name. Just tell Mr. Callahan that I have something very important to give him and that a friend of his asked me to come here."

"Ma'am, unless you give me your name and show me some ID, you won't be allowed to see Mr. Callahan."

Sally Ann hesitated. She finally decided that it didn't matter if he had her name, but she wasn't going to tell him anything more. She showed him her driver's license and then he spent a minute tapping on his laptop. Finally, he picked up his phone and spoke to someone so softly she couldn't hear what he said. She assumed he was speaking to Callahan or Callahan's secretary. He concluded the phone call, saying, "Okay, boss, I'll let her in."

"I need to wand you for weapons," he said to her.

"What?" Sally Ann said.

He stood up and she saw an enormous revolver in a holster on his belt—the gun looked big enough to kill an elephant. "Ma'am, I need to wand you," he said.

Who were these people? She'd glanced at the Callahan Group's website to find Callahan's address, and from what she'd seen, it was some sort of lobbying firm. But why on earth was the receptionist armed? And why would he check to see if *she* was armed? But considering that Callahan was Olivia Prescott's friend, who knew what sort of activities they might be engaged in?

"Oh, all right," Sally Ann said. "This seems rather silly, but go ahead."

He passed two devices over her body. One looked like those gadgets they use at airports when people set off the metal detectors. She didn't know what the other one did. He led her through a second locked door and down a long corridor, stopping at an office at the end of the corridor. She noticed another surveillance camera over this door. The receptionist knocked, a lock clicked, and the receptionist held the door open for her.

Sitting behind a large mahogany desk was an overweight man with unruly gray hair and a pale face. He was wearing a wrinkled blue shirt and his maroon tie was loosened. His eyes were the same color as his shirt. He smiled at her—he had a charming smile—and said, "Hi. I'm Thomas Callahan. What can I do for you, Mrs. Danzinger?"

"I'm here because Olivia Prescott told me to come. I have—"

"And how's Olivia doing? I haven't seen her in quite some time."

"I don't know how she's doing, to tell you the truth," Sally Ann said. "The last time I saw her was at a college reunion a couple of years ago. At any rate, I have an envelope in my possession and Olivia told me to bring it to you. She said you were to put it in your safe and keep it until she could pick it up."

Sally Ann glanced over at the large safe mounted in the wall on the right-hand side of Callahan's desk. The door was partially open but she couldn't see what was inside. She handed the envelope to Callahan.

"What's in the envelope?" he asked, still smiling slightly.

"Olivia told me not to tell you, just that she'd pick it up tomorrow when she got back from London."

"Olivia's in London?"

"That's what she said."

"I see," Callahan said. He was now tapping the envelope on his desk, studying her. He was rather sneaky looking, Sally Ann thought. She wondered if he would open the envelope after she left, and she wished now that she'd used wax to seal it—but she didn't have a wax seal.

Callahan got up from his chair with a grunt, put the envelope in his safe, then shut the safe and spun the dial. "Okay. Mission accomplished."

She rose and said, "Thank you. The only other thing I'll say is that it's extremely important that Olivia receives that envelope."

"Okeydokey," Callahan said. "This is all very mysterious, but then Olivia has always been a bit of a mystery herself."

As Sally Ann was waiting for a cab, she realized she was hungry.

She hadn't had breakfast and it was almost noon, so she decided to have a bite to eat before she headed back home. As she walked down K Street, she thought about Callahan and was absolutely certain that he was going to open the envelope she'd given him.

DAY 1—11:30 A.M.

Fang decided that he needed to question Danzinger, but he had to be sure the interrogation couldn't be traced back to the Chinese. He dropped the weeping Lin Mai off near the trade association—glad to be shed of her—and proceeded to an office building on Vermont Avenue.

The building was four stories high and was occupied by a number of small businesses: independent insurance agents, one-man public relations firms, website designers, a travel agency, and a company that employed thirty people who made thousands of cold calls each day trying to sell various products to people who didn't want to talk to them. Fang had an office adjacent to the cold-call company. Inside his office was a phone, which was listed as belonging to the cold-call company so no one would be able to trace his calls back to the embassy.

Fang's first call was to his researcher, whom he told to quickly find Danzinger's address. While he was waiting for the researcher to call back, he went online to learn more about Danzinger.

Five minutes later, the researcher called with the address, which was in a racially mixed, working-class area of D.C. It appeared that Mrs. Danzinger was making some sort of social statement.

Fang's next call was to Jamal Howard.

Jamal was a gangster. He was only twenty-four years old, but he was intelligent and very accomplished for his age. He ran a string of prostitutes; he sold drugs, weapons, and false identity documents; he stole cars; he robbed people. He was quite the entrepreneur. The .38 that Fang had used to kill James Parker had come from Jamal, and Fang had purchased drugs from him several times when he was entertaining guests from out of town. More to the point, he'd used Jamal twice in the past when he needed a smart, vicious thug. Once, he had Jamal beat a man so badly that he was unable to attend a meeting that Fang didn't want him at. The second time, he had Jamal kill a man who had accidently seen something he shouldn't have. Jamal Howard was one of the most ruthless young men Fang had ever met, and Fang was convinced that if Jamal had gotten a decent education, he could have ended up on Wall Street, where the truly amazing American criminals resided.

Fang told Jamal to go to Danzinger's house immediately, restrain her, and call him back. Then he told Jamal how much he was willing to pay.

"You shittin' me?" Jamal said.

Fang was fully versed in American slang, but "You're shittin' me" was a phrase that had never made sense to him. Nonetheless, he knew the correct response: "I shit you not," he said. "Go online and find out what she looks like."

"Okay, but what if she's not home?" Howard asked.

"Then wait for her."

"What if the house is alarmed?"

"Then you must find a way to deal with that. Just get her and call me back." Fang knew that no matter how fast Jamal moved, it would take at least half an hour to capture Danzinger, and that was assuming she was home. But he couldn't do anything to make things move faster. And if Danzinger had already given the information to someone else, there wasn't anything he could do about that, either. But either way, he had to know what Danzinger had done with the document so he could decide what to do about Winston.

DAY 1—12:30 P.M.

"She's not home," Jamal Howard said.

"Are you in her house?" Fang asked.

"Yeah."

"So she didn't have an alarm."

"She's got one, but a young bitch let me in."

"Who is she?"

"Danzinger's secretary. She lives with her."

"Do you have people with you?"

"Yeah. Two of my boys."

"And I'm assuming none of the neighbors saw you."

"Nah. The house has a bunch of bushes and shit around it and there wasn't nobody on the street when I knocked. I let my boys in the back door."

"What's the status of the secretary?"

"Status?"

"Her physical condition."

"She's alive. I had to hit her a little to settle her down, but I didn't hurt her bad or nothing."

"Good. Now ask her where Danzinger is."

Fang heard muffled words and Jamal came back on the line. "She says she doesn't know. She said Danzinger got a cab about eleven and left the house."

"Ask her again."

A moment later, Fang heard the secretary scream, then scream again. Jamal came back on the phone and said, "She still says she don't know."

"Do you believe her?"

"Yeah."

"Okay. Tie her up and gag her. Wait for Danzinger, and when she arrives, tie her up, too, and call me."

"Uh, this young bitch," Jamal said. "While we're waitin', can we . . ."

"No. I haven't decided how I'm going to play this. Just tie her up and wait for Danzinger."

While Fang waited, he learned more about Danzinger on the Internet. He discovered that she was absurdly wealthy, and although much of her money had been inherited, she and her late husband were also very astute business people; they'd provided the start-up capital for a number of companies that were household names today. She was worth over a billion dollars. When she was about fifty—she was sixty-three now—she shifted her focus from business to politics and charity work.

Her battle against the Layman brothers was well documented, as were the numerous lawsuits she'd filed against them. Danzinger, Fang concluded, was liberal to the point of silliness. Had Fang been an American, he probably would have voted Republican, although he didn't agree with Republicans on abortion or taxation. Abortion was a necessary tool in controlling population growth and invaluable in keeping the gene pool strong. Insofar as taxation, he felt that the ruling class shouldn't be taxed too heavily, but the masses should be taxed as much as necessary to support the needs of the state. Well, maybe the Republicans felt the same way.

All the articles described Danzinger as aggressive, unwilling to back down, and uncompromising in her beliefs. An adjective used frequently was *fearless*. In her youth, she'd skied and sailed boats and even drove a race car for a brief period. *We'll soon see how fearless she truly is*, Fang thought.

DAY 1—1 P.M.

Jamal Howard called Fang. "I got her. She's tied up next to the secretary."

"Put your phone on speaker so she can hear me.

"Mrs. Danzinger," Fang said, "this morning you met with a man named James Parker and he gave you a copy of an e-mail attachment. I want to know what you did with the attachment and if you discussed it with anyone."

"Who are you?" Danzinger asked. She didn't sound sufficiently frightened to Fang. In fact, she sounded defiant.

"Jamal, ask the secretary what her name is."

A muffled sound, then, "She's Latisha Taylor."

"Jamal, shoot Latisha in the face."

"Wait!" Danzinger screamed. "I'll tell you what you want to know."

She told Fang what he already knew: that Parker had given her a document that proved there was a spy embedded in Zytek Systems, but he had refused to tell her anything else. Then Danzinger said she called a woman named Olivia Prescott who worked at the NSA and told her about the e-mail and her meeting with Parker. "So you're too late, whoever you are," Danzinger said, sounding smug.

Fang cursed in Chinese.

"Did you give Prescott Parker's name?"

"No."

"What did Prescott tell you to do next?" Fang asked.

"She said that she was in London and would pick up the attachment when she returns tomorrow."

"Where's the document now?"

"I don't have it," Danzinger said. That smug tone was back.

"You didn't answer my question. Where is it?"

Danzinger didn't respond. "Jamal, cut off one of Latisha's fingers. Mrs. Danzinger isn't being forthcoming with me."

"No, wait!" Danzinger screamed.

"Go on, Jamal. Do it. The little one on her left hand."

A few moments passed in silence, then it sounded like two women screaming through gags.

"Okay," Jamal said. "But the bitch is bleeding like a bitch."

"If you don't want Latisha to suffer anymore, Mrs. Danzinger, answer my question. What did you do with the attachment?"

"You bastard," Danzinger said. "You son of a bitch. You didn't have to—"

"I don't have time for this," Fang said. "Jamal, cut off another finger."

"No!" Danzinger screamed. "I put it in a sealed envelope and took it to a man named Thomas Callahan."

She proceeded to tell Fang that Callahan had an office on K Street and he was an old friend of Prescott's. She said she saw Callahan put the envelope in his safe.

"Did you tell Callahan what was in the envelope?"

"No. Olivia told me not to."

Fang was beginning to feel a glimmer of hope. Saving Winston might still be possible.

"Now tell me more about Callahan, his office, and the type of building it's in."

To Fang's dismay, Danzinger wasn't able to provide much in the way of detail; she hadn't been all that observant. She only remembered that the safe was large and mounted in the wall, but she couldn't recall the brand. She said there weren't any security personnel in the building. Fang thought he heard a false note in her voice, but he decided not to pursue it.

Satisfied that she had told him everything, Fang asked Jamal to take him off speaker. "I can't let Mrs. Danzinger and her companion live," Fang said.

"Yeah, I could kinda see that coming, especially when you kept sayin' my fuckin' name."

"I need you to make this look like a home invasion."

Jamal laughed. "It *was* a home invasion."

"Kill them both and take anything that you can carry. And Jamal, this is very important: I want you to throw away everything you steal. I can't afford to have you caught with stolen property."

When Jamal didn't immediately respond, Fang said, "I'll double the amount I agreed to pay you."

"All right," Jamal said. He said this in the odd way that gangsters do, making *all right* sound like *awight.*

"And make sure you don't leave any evidence behind. You know, fingerprints, DNA—"

"This ain't my first rodeo. You just make sure I get the money today. And that's no shit."

DAY 1—2 P.M.

Fang left the office on Vermont and walked a block to a Starbucks down the street. He smiled at the pretty barista, and she smiled back. He ordered a coffee and a sandwich on a croissant, and took a seat near a window.

Danzinger had said that the Prescott woman was in England and would pick up the document tomorrow. And once Prescott saw the attachment, she might be able to figure out which NSA employees were likely to have intercepted the e-mail based on their work assignments and trace it to Parker and then to Winston. But if Fang could get the attachment before Prescott saw it, there was still a chance to maintain Winston's cover.

There was another potential problem, however. This man Callahan might have looked in the envelope.

He sipped his coffee and came to a conclusion: He had to make an attempt to retrieve the envelope before Prescott got it and he needed to kill Callahan—and he had the perfect man for the job.

Dylan Otis was the consummate professional. Fang had used him twice before when the Chinese required items to be removed from secure facilities.

Fang had learned of Otis from one of his contacts in the FBI. "This guy isn't some junkie who has to steal so he can buy dope," his contact told him. "He isn't a gambler, and he isn't the kind of guy who walks away with only fourteen hundred bucks from the teller's drawer. Otis does one or two jobs a year, and he usually nets anywhere from a quarter to half a million."

"If you know all this," Fang asked, "why haven't you arrested him?"

"Because *knowing* a guy's guilty isn't the same thing as *proving* he's guilty. Otis doesn't leave evidence behind, he launders the money carefully, and he and his guys always have alibis. We're going to have to catch him literally coming out of a bank if we're ever gonna nail him."

"Tell me more," Fang said.

"Otis and his guys are—I guess you'd say blue collar. They're all good with tools. Otis restores old cars. He'll buy a beat-up '56 Chevy for ten grand, fix it up, then sell it for sixty to some collector. And he pays his taxes. The guys he works with are the same kind of people, guys who are good with tools and alarm systems, pros who keep low profiles."

DAY 1—2:30 P.M.

Fang returned to his office on Vermont and called Dylan Otis. A woman answered, and he could hear a couple of kids yelling in the background. Fang knew that Otis was married but didn't know much more about his personal life.

When Otis got on the phone, Fang said, "This is John. Meet me at the Iwo Jima Memorial as soon as you can. This is a big deal and I'll pay accordingly."

Otis didn't know Fang's real name and had no idea that he worked for the Chinese government. All Otis cared about was how much he'd be paid.

Half an hour later, standing near the famous sculpture of the six Marines raising the American flag, Fang told Otis what he needed done: Break into the safe in Callahan's office, remove whatever was inside it, and kill Callahan. And he needed the job done today, as soon as possible. He gave him a photo of Callahan he'd found online.

Otis refused, saying it was too risky. Fang handed him a gym bag and Otis almost dropped it, not expecting the bag would weigh so much.

"That's a million in gold bars. I didn't have time to get that much cash, but I had the gold on hand. You'll get another million when the job is complete."

Otis hesitated, then said, "Okay. But it might be easier to just take the safe from the office and open it later."

"Then do that," Fang said.

"And it's going to take me a few hours to round up my crew and get the equipment I'll need."

"Just move quickly, Mr. Otis. Time is of the essence," Fang said.

DAY 1—7 P.M.

Otis and his crew entered the building on K Street.

DAY 1—8:45 P.M.

Otis called Fang to tell him he had the safe and that Callahan had been killed. Also that two of his own men had been killed as well. Fang ordered Otis to take the safe to a garage in Arlington.

DAY 1—10 P.M.

The nightly news reported that four people had been killed in a building on K Street. Apparently, it was an attempted robbery, but the police weren't giving out any additional information, except that there were two survivors—and Fang Zhou thought: *Shit*.

9

Kay was still sitting in Prescott's apartment, still trying to digest everything that Prescott had told her. It also occurred to her that Prescott had told her a lot of things she didn't need to tell her—and it was not the nature of the NSA to divulge information to people outside the agency. In fact, it was the nature of the NSA to hide almost everything they did from the public. So why had Prescott shared so much?

"What do you plan to do next?" Kay asked.

Prescott rose from the couch where she'd been sitting. "It's been a long, rather stressful day. I need a drink. Would you like one?"

"No," Kay said.

"Then I'll be back in a moment," she said and left Kay sitting in the living room. Kay heard a toilet flush and a few minutes later heard Prescott in the kitchen. She came back to the living room holding a tumbler containing either Scotch or bourbon. She drank it neat. She resumed her seat on the couch and then just sat there looking at Kay with her pale blue eyes. She reminded Kay of a cobra staring down at its prey—and Kay was the prey.

"I asked what you plan to do next," Kay said.

"The first thing I plan to do is locate the e-mail that I believe Parker intercepted. We don't destroy information at Fort Meade, but it can be hidden if a person is smart enough to know what to do. Since we only hire smart people, I'm sure the e-mail has been hidden in some very clever way, but my people will find it."

"Then what?" Kay asked.

"Then I'll find out which government received it and who their spy is at Zytek. What else would I do?"

"But what are you going to do about the people who killed Danzinger and Callahan's people?"

"I'll do what I can, but that's not my job. That's up to the police—or you, if you choose to pursue it."

"What?" Kay said. "Not your job! Callahan worked for you! It's your fault he was shot."

Prescott shook her head as if Kay were being childish. "You keep saying that Callahan worked for me. And I'm telling you that Callahan was just an old friend I trusted. That was the extent of our relationship."

"That's bullshit—" Kay said. She stopped and stared at Prescott and Prescott just stared back, looking . . . what? Amused?

Kay knew *exactly* what Prescott was doing, and now she also understood why Prescott had told her so much: Prescott was planning to use her. Prescott wasn't going to go anywhere near the investigation into the attack because that might expose her true relationship to Callahan. Kay also realized that Prescott must know about her background with the DEA and what she did for Callahan. How else would Prescott know that she had the ability to track down the people who shot Callahan?

But was Kay going to allow Prescott to use her? And the answer to that question was: Yeah, goddamnit, she was. She was going to get to the bottom of this.

"Okay," Kay said. "I need to know everything the cops know. Right now all I have is the name of the man I shot and that he has a record for armed robbery. He wasn't a spy or an operative for some foreign government, and the cops aren't going to tell me more. Do you have any influence over D.C. Metro?"

Prescott shrugged. "When the NSA calls a law enforcement institution in this country, they know we wouldn't be calling unless it was something related to national security. Most people also know that we can't tell them why we're calling, and they cooperate because they know if they don't, considerable pressure will be brought to bear. We have sufficient weight to crush careers. So I believe I can get someone at Metro to meet with you."

"Then do it," Kay said. "And I want the meeting tonight. The trail's getting cold."

Prescott smiled slightly. She was probably thinking: *Good dog.* She walked over to a table where she'd placed her purse, removed a phone, and punched in a number from memory.

"Detective, this is Olivia Prescott. Very well, thank you. A woman named Hamilton is going to call you soon and ask for a meeting with you tonight. You are to give her your utmost cooperation. Is that clear?"

Prescott hung up and gave Kay the phone number of a man named Eagleton.

"There's one thing you need to understand, Ms. Hamilton. Everything I told you about the e-mail and Zytek is classified. If I find out that you've talked to anyone about what you learned this evening, I'll have you arrested and prosecuted. Divulging classified information is a federal offense."

"Then why did you tell me in the first place?" Kay asked.

"Because I thought you had a right to know."

Kay barked out a laugh. "I don't know how many lies you've told me, but that's definitely one of the bigger ones. You didn't tell me because you thought I had a right to know, you told me so I could help you catch these guys."

"Be that as it may, I'm serious. If you talk to anyone about the e-mail, you'll end up in prison. And that's not a lie."

"Yeah, whatever," Kay said, rising from the uncomfortable chair. "Give me a phone number where I can reach you in case I need to talk to you."

"No," Prescott said. "I don't want you calling me. But I'm sure I'll be able to reach you if I need to."

10

The Chinese government maintained a database on Chinese nationals who'd immigrated to the United States, and as soon as Fang learned that Callahan had been taken to George Washington University Hospital, he had his researcher check it. Fortune was on his side. Four Chinese émigrés worked at the hospital, and one was a nurse.

As Kay was leaving Prescott's apartment, Fang Zhou was watching the nurse. She had just finished her shift and was waiting for a bus. She was a short, slightly built, moonfaced woman in her early thirties.

Fang joined her at the bus stop, and in her native tongue, said, "Little sister, we need to talk."

"Who are you?" she asked, looking up at him. He was six-foot-three and he loomed over her. She had no particular reason to be afraid—he hadn't spoken to her in a threatening manner—but he could see that she was. Which was good.

"I know you're on your way home," Fang said, "and that you must be tired from your long day at work. But I need a few minutes of your time. Let's go to that restaurant over there and have a cup of tea."

"But what do you want?" the nurse said.

K STREET | 101

"Tell me," Fang said, "how is your uncle in Chaohu? Have you spoken to him recently? Is he doing well? And your uncle in Huaibei. How is his family doing? And your brother in Trenton. I was pleased to hear that he was recently promoted."

"What do you want?" she asked again, her lower lip quivering. He noticed she didn't ask again who he was because she knew he must represent the Chinese government. She knew that he held the lives of her uncles in China and their entire families in the palm of his hand. She knew her brother's life, even though he lived in Trenton, New Jersey, was also in danger.

"Come, little sister," he said. "We'll be more comfortable in the restaurant. And if you do what I ask, you'll be rewarded. So don't be afraid. I'm not going to harm you."

She walked beside him, head down, as they crossed the street to the restaurant. For his own amusement, Fang almost told her to walk five paces behind him, and he knew that if he had, she would have obeyed.

Inside, he asked her if she wanted coffee or tea. She said tea so softly he could barely hear her, and then tears began to well up in her eyes. He wagged a finger at her. "No, no, don't do that. I'm telling you, everything is going to be fine."

He told the waitress to bring them two hot teas—Lipton or whatever they had would be acceptable. While they waited, he ignored the nurse and checked his phone for messages. The waitress brought the teas. "Drink," Fang said. "The tea will relax you." But he knew it wouldn't.

He waited until she obediently took a sip, then said, "There's a man in your hospital named Thomas Callahan. I want you to go back to the hospital before you go home and find out his condition. I'm sure you can figure out a way to do that. You're a smart woman. Then I want you to tell me what you've learned. Call me before you leave the hospital." He wrote his phone number on a napkin and handed it to her. "That's my number. Okay, little sister? Will you do me this small favor?"

He pulled out his wallet and handed her several twenty-dollar bills; he didn't know how many for sure, but there were at least six of them. "That's for cab fare because I've made you miss your bus. Now go. I'll be waiting here until I hear back from you."

Without looking at him, she left the table. Fang knew she'd catch the bus home instead of taking a cab.

FANG HAD TWO PROBLEMS. His people had not yet been able to break into Callahan's safe to verify that it contained the envelope, and Callahan was still alive.

He had been dismayed to hear on the news last night—contrary to what Dylan Otis had told him—that two people had survived the attack. Fang, a committed atheist, prayed that one of the survivors had not been Callahan. After he heard the news report, he contacted a high-ranking detective in the D.C. Metro Police force and asked if he could find out the names of the survivors and anything else the police knew about the attack.

Fang had many contacts throughout Washington, contacts he'd built up in the eight years he had lived in the city. And this contact's services came cheaply: Fang compensated him by allowing him to use his season tickets for the Redskins. Fang never used them; he thought American football was an idiotic game.

The detective told him that Callahan was one of the survivors and that two of Callahan's people had been killed—Fang didn't bother to note their names—and that two of the robbers, both men with prior convictions for armed robbery, had been killed as well. But that's all the police knew at this point.

"Who killed the two robbers?" Fang asked.

"A female security guard killed one," the detective said. "She was the other survivor. It looks like Callahan killed the other guy before he was shot."

"A woman killed one of them?" Fang said.

"Yeah. Her name is Kay Hamilton."

Fang was shocked to learn that a woman had killed some of Otis's men, but the security guard seemed unimportant. Fang assumed she had been doing her rounds and simply blundered onto Otis's operation. He thanked the detective, and because the football season was still a couple months away, he said he would send him a case of single-malt Scotch that was priced at over a hundred dollars a bottle. The detective was appropriately grateful; Fang was going to miss him when he retired.

That Callahan had survived was disappointing, but that didn't necessarily mean all was lost. If the information Fang had forced out of Danzinger was correct, Callahan had no idea what had been inside his own safe.

FIFTEEN MINUTES AFTER leaving the restaurant, the little nurse called. She told him that Callahan had survived a difficult, lengthy surgery but it was possible that he still might die. She said that right now he was unresponsive. "Has he had any visitors?" Fang asked. The nurse said she didn't know. "Find out," Fang said. "I know you can. You're very clever."

Half an hour passed before she called back. She said a woman police officer, a detective named Platt, came to see him but he was unconscious. His daughter also visited him. "His daughter?" Fang said.

"Yes," the nurse said. "Right after he got out of surgery, but he was probably still unconscious from the anesthesia."

"Thank you, little sister, you did well. Now all you have to do is monitor Callahan's condition. If he dies, call me. If he regains consciousness, you must call me immediately. And if you do these things for me, your aged mother will no longer have to go all the way to the basement in your apartment building to wash clothes. She'll soon have a very nice washer and dryer that will fit right inside your apartment. Don't worry. I have your address."

Now what? It probably didn't matter if Callahan lived or died, but he'd certainly feel more comfortable if the man was dead. The fact that Callahan had a daughter could be useful if he needed to force him to cooperate.

He called his researcher and told her to find out about Callahan's family, where they lived and so forth, and to do so quickly. Next, he called his secretary and told her to arrange for the nurse's parents to receive a washer and dryer—one of the stackable units because their apartment was small.

After he spoke to his secretary, he took a cab to the Mandarin Oriental Hotel. It was one of his favorite places to eat in D.C. because of the chef, not the name. He took a seat at the bar and ordered a Grey Goose martini. He noticed a woman in her thirties sitting at the other end of the bar. She was slender and blond. Very pretty. She reminded him of a Russian ballerina he knew but hadn't seen in years. He raised his martini glass in a toast to her loveliness. She responded with a smile.

Most women liked Fang. He was—and he wasn't being immodest—a handsome man. He dressed well, he spent money freely, and he could be quite charming. The blonde was charmed. To his annoyance, his researcher called back just as they started to share an appetizer: the chef's quail satay.

The researcher reported that Callahan had no family. He had four ex-wives but no children. So who was the woman who had gone to see him and claimed to be his daughter? Fang wondered. He'd call the little nurse later and tell her to find out the woman's name. But not right now.

He asked the blonde if she would like another glass of wine.

11

Kay walked into the McDonald's on 17th Street NW. The place was almost empty. There were three teenagers staring at their cell phones, ignoring each other, and one old woman who was probably homeless who was wearing three layers of clothing on a hot, humid night. The last customer was a heavyset man in his fifties wearing a cheap blue suit, a white shirt, and no tie. He was eating Chicken McNuggets.

Kay figured the McNuggets eater had to be Eagleton—Prescott's connection in the Metro P.D. Kay had called Eagleton right after she left Prescott's apartment and told him she wanted everything they had on the attack on Callahan's office and the murder of Sally Ann Danzinger. Eagleton had told her to meet him at the McDonald's, but the earliest he could get there was ten p.m.

Kay walked up to his table. "Are you Eagleton?"

"Yep. You must be the lady from the NSA. You got ID?"

"No," Kay said. And she didn't see any reason to disabuse Eagleton of the notion she was NSA.

"Well, all right then," Eagleton said. "Have a seat." Kay sat.

"You want a McNugget?" Eagleton said.

"Tell me what you know," Kay said.

"Okay. Regarding the Danzinger homicide, we don't have shit," Eagleton said. "None of the neighbors saw anyone going into or coming out of Danzinger's house. It doesn't help that this went down during the middle of the day when people were working and that it was so fucking hot that nobody was outside. The forensic guys found a million prints inside the house and we're still sorting through them. We'll get a couple of slugs from the autopsies, and if we find a gun, maybe we'll be able to match it to the slugs. The only other thing we found is a partial footprint from a Timberland boot when one of the killers walked through some blood.

"The house had been ransacked but we don't know what they took so we can't put out a list to pawnshops. We didn't find the victims' cell phones, and when we tried to locate them, we couldn't find their signals, meaning the killers probably disabled them." Eagleton shoved another McNugget in his mouth and said, "So, like I said, we got shit."

"What about K Street?" Kay asked.

Eagleton shook his head. "We've got almost a hundred shell casings and not one of them has a print on it. We have a bunch of tools, the kind you can buy at any Sears, and none of them have prints, either. We should have been able to get some information off surveillance cameras, but we couldn't."

"Why not?"

"The cameras don't record. They show a real-time picture of what they're seeing."

Detective Mary Platt had already told Kay this and that meant that the D.C. cops still hadn't figured out how to get into the guts of Callahan's security system.

"What about the dead guys? I don't mean Callahan's employees, but the intruders who were killed."

Eagleton nodded. "Their names were Jack Quinn and Ray Brown, both convicted in their misspent youths for armed robbery. Neither one had been arrested recently, and they both had legitimate jobs.

Quinn was an electrician who worked on boat shit. You know, alternators, generators, radars, sonar systems. Brown was a welder and a mechanic. He worked part time at a garage in Fairfax."

"What about known associates?" Kay said. "Somebody these guys worked with in the past?"

"We haven't identified anybody like that yet—they never committed a crime in the District—but we're still checking with federal agencies and other police departments. Maybe we'll get a lead from one of them."

"Well, shit," Kay said. "There has to be something that will connect these guys to the others involved. Tell me more about them."

"There's not much to tell. Quinn was married once but his ex-wife now lives out west." Eagleton laughed. "He lived with a pit bull who is now among the faithful departed."

"What?" Kay said.

"We sent a couple detectives to search Quinn's double-wide. Deputies from Prince William County assisted us. When they went into Quinn's trailer, this fuckin' pit bull that weighed about a hundred pounds attacked one of the deputies and almost tore his arm off. They had to kill it." Eagleton shook his head. "Damn pit bulls have become the house pet of choice for lowlifes. It seems almost any place we raid these days, there's a fuckin' pit bull there."

"But what did you find in Quinn's trailer?"

"Nothing. Nothing to tie him to the job on K Street and nothing to give us a lead to whoever else was involved."

"Did you look at his phone records?"

"Yeah. He didn't have a landline, but he had a cell phone. The cell was in his trailer, along with his ID. All the calls made from the cell phone were to places related to his day job. He probably has a burner phone somewhere, or maybe a pager, but we didn't find it."

"What about Brown?"

"Brown lived with his sister. Never been married. Neither has the sister. They were both raised in a bunch of foster homes and we think they were probably abused. You know, sexually. Brown did time for a bungled bank job a dozen years ago, but nothing since then. The sister's been arrested a couple of times for assault. Both times, she was in a bar, drunk, and she went nuts when some guy made a pass at her. She split one guy's head open with a beer bottle and she beat up another guy with her fists. The sister's a trip.

"Anyway, when we sent people to tell her that her brother had been killed and to search the house, she went ballistic. Crying and screaming, throwing things, and when they started the search, she attacked one of the detectives and they had to cuff her. They would have thrown her in jail for interfering with the search but they felt bad because she'd just lost her brother. But they didn't find anything in the house that we could tie to the robbery or to anyone else who might have been involved."

"And the sister didn't give you anything? Guys her brother hung with, people he's worked with in the past?"

"No. Like I told you, she was so upset we couldn't interview her. Maybe we'll try again later."

"Anything else?"

"Yeah, the U-Haul they used to take the safe away. We found it in a parking lot three blocks from the building on K Street. We checked with the place that rented it and found out the guy who rented it died eighteen years ago. The U-Haul place has cameras outside but the cameras only caught the guy's back and the top of a baseball cap. When we asked the clerk what the guy looked like, he said, 'Shit, I don't know. He was just a big white guy wearing coveralls.'"

Leaving the McDonald's, Kay thought, *Now what?*

Well, there was nothing more she could do tonight. She'd get a good night's sleep and continue the hunt first thing tomorrow. Kay smiled slightly. Even though she knew she was being manipulated by Prescott, she loved hunting for two-legged prey.

12

O livia Prescott had been in her office at Fort Meade since dawn. She spent some time reviewing e-mails, various logs, and reports, and catching up on what had happened while she was in London. There was one interesting phone call that had been intercepted: a call between a Saudi prince who had aspirations to be the next bin Laden and a retired Russian colonel—a colonel who once held the keys to a site where the Russians stored a number of nuclear weapons. She would definitely follow up on that one.

She picked up the phone on her desk and told Ackerman to come to her office. While waiting for him to arrive, she watered a ficus plant that she was convinced was suicidal. She'd done everything she could think of to keep the plant alive: installed a special bulb to trick it into thinking it was getting sunlight; loaded the soil around its roots with enough nutrients to bring back the dead. Even the water she used was special, the equivalent of water from Lourdes. But nothing helped. The plant looked *limp;* its broad leaves had a jaundicelike yellow tinge. Prescott knew she wasn't popular at the agency and she couldn't help but wonder if someone was sneaking into her office at night and slowly poisoning her plant.

Ackerman rapped on the frame of her office door. "You wanted to see me, boss lady?" Then he sat, uninvited, in the chair in front of Prescott's desk.

Boss lady. She felt like ripping his head off.

Ackerman was a repulsive individual. He was six-foot-four and morbidly obese, at least a hundred and fifty pounds overweight. Standing, he looked like a mountain of white Jell-O; sitting, his stomach occupied his lap. He had limp black hair so long it touched his shoulders and it glistened with some sort of gel—or maybe it was just naturally greasy. At the age of thirty, he still suffered from acne and he would wear the same clothes three or four days in a row. Worse than his appearance, however, was his personality: He was an annoying, condescending, abrasive smart-ass. The only reason Prescott tolerated him was because he was a genius, and as he had no wife, girlfriend, boyfriend, or pet, he would work twenty-four hours a day—provided he got overtime pay.

"James Parker," Prescott said.

"The yahoo who offed himself?" Ackerman said.

"Yeah, that yahoo. He intercepted an e-mail with an attachment from somebody who works for Zytek Systems. I know he printed out the attachment because he gave a copy to someone. I want you to find that e-mail and figure out who sent it and who received it."

Ackerman stood up. "Okay. Parker was an idiot. It shouldn't be that hard."

She picked up her phone as soon as Ackerman left her office. "This is Prescott. Tell Fortus I want him."

Fortus was ex–Naval Intelligence and was now a civilian in charge of internal security at the NSA. He had an important job: making sure all the NSA's many secrets remained secrets. He had replaced the man who occupied the position when Edward Snowden decided to share all he knew about the NSA with the media.

nutes later, looking like he'd just run

, Fortus gave her the respect her posi-

-looking individual in his fifties, hair as

litary. He no longer wore a uniform, but

a plain blue tie, and blue pants, he looked

so well polished he could use them as

tus as soon as she heard James Parker was

why Parker would kill himself or be killed.

he might have sold his services to Sally Ann

"Online gambling," Fortus said. "Texas Hold'em. He owed seventy-eight thousand."

"Goddamnit! Why in the hell didn't we know about this?"

"His security review wasn't scheduled for four months and we had no indicators."

NSA employees with Top Secret security clearances are subjected to periodic security reviews. These reviews look at a number of factors that could indicate whether an employee was spying for someone or likely to be turned into a spy. Phone records were examined. Home computers were checked remotely for evidence of adultery or criminal activity such as child pornography. The NSA's concern was that if a foreign government determined an NSA employee was having an affair or committing a crime, then the individual would be susceptible to blackmail.

The main thing Fortus's people looked at was an employee's finances. Was he or she carrying a large amount of debt? Had he suddenly purchased something that was outside his income range? If a person was in over his head, then a foreign operative might offer him money in return for information. If a person was suddenly living above his means, it could mean that he'd already been turned.

It appeared that in the case of James Parker, he'd gambled himself into a money pit. At least now Prescott knew why he had betrayed the National Security Agency.

Prescott had a briefing to attend, but before she left her office, she made two phone calls. One was to a man named Grayson; the other to a man named Lincoln. She said the same thing to both men, "We need to meet," and specified the time. Neither man asked where they were meeting or why. They already knew.

13

Fang Zhou walked into the garage, an auto body shop owned by a Chinese immigrant. The garage smelled of acrid smoke. Two Chinese men wearing soiled gray coveralls stood at attention behind the safe from Callahan's office. They'd finally opened it and it was sitting on the floor in front of them, making Fang think of two filthy cats displaying a dead mouse for their master.

As soon as Otis had informed him that the safe had been taken from Callahan's office, Fang had ordered him to deliver it to the garage, then sent two men from the embassy over to open it. He sent a third man to collect the gym bag containing Callahan's laptop and the papers taken from his office, and bring it back to the embassy.

Fortunately, the Chinese embassy in Washington employed a number of skilled workers who performed whatever maintenance was required. The embassy didn't want to use Americans to fix air conditioners or plumbing or dishwashers; it would be too easy for American intelligence officers to pose as workers and install bugging equipment. However, the Chinese maintenance people were not safecrackers. It took them over thirty hours to open the safe. Fang knew it would have been more efficient to have had an experienced robber like Otis open it, but he didn't want Otis to know more than he already did. At any rate, the embassy maintenance men called Fang an hour ago and said they had finally succeeded.

Fang had already looked through the papers from Callahan's office. They all appeared to be related to the stated mission of the Callahan Group and Fang found nothing that made it appear that the Callahan Group was anything more than what its website claimed. The laptop was different. Fang tried to look at its contents but it was password protected, so he sent it to the embassy's computer experts and asked them to unlock it. A technician came to him an hour later, looking like a dog expecting to be beaten. He said that when they tried to get around the computer's security system, it self-destructed. Callahan's laptop was now nothing more than a plastic brick. Why would Callahan have that sort of a security on his computer, Fang wondered.

Fang walked carefully through the garage, taking care not to rub up against any of the greasy items. He squatted on his heels and peered into the safe, which looked like a can that had had its lid removed with jackhammers. The only things in it were a single white business envelope and a few stacks of American currency. He'd expected more but he was certain that the workers hadn't taken anything.

He removed the envelope first, saw that it was sealed, and placed it in the inside pocket of his suit. He then flipped through the bills, and estimated that there was about fifty thousand dollars, in hundreds, fifties, and twenties. Fifty thousand seemed like a lot for a lobbyist to have on hand, but maybe not. American politicians didn't come cheaply.

He barked an order for one of the incompetent safecrackers to find him something to carry the money in, and the man brought him a brown paper Safeway bag with handles. He took about two thousand dollars and, without making any attempt to make sure each man got the same amount, gave the money to the two men. He took another small stack of Callahan's cash, maybe five hundred dollars, and gave it to the owner of the auto body shop.

"Good work," he said to the men and left the garage. It was always wise to praise and reward people for a job well done. He also decided that he should be rewarded for the job *he* had done: He would keep the rest of the money from the safe. No one but he and the two mechanics knew about it, and the mechanics were smart enough to know that if they told anyone, they would be on the next slow boat to China.

BACK INSIDE HIS TOWN HOUSE, Fang found a message waiting for him on the answering machine. It was from his wife. It appeared that his oldest son was acting out and his wife wanted Fang to speak to him. Maybe he would call them tomorrow. Fang only saw his wife when he had to return to China, and the last time he'd seen her was four months ago. He didn't miss her at all when they were apart, but when he did see her, he was always happy to be with her. He wondered how he would feel if they lived together all the time. Whatever the case, he knew he'd never divorce her, at least not while her father lived; her father was too politically powerful.

He took a seat in his living room and removed the envelope from his suit pocket. He studied it carefully and could see no evidence that it had been opened, but if someone had given him an envelope and told him not to look in it, he didn't think he would be able to resist. He would be too curious.

Fang opened the envelope and examined the document it contained: a single sheet of white paper with an incomprehensible string of letters, numbers, and strange symbols. At least it was incomprehensible to him; it would mean something, he assumed, to whoever had asked for the information. He walked to the nearest bathroom, tearing the document into pieces as he went, and flushed it down the toilet. There was no need to keep it because people in China already had the original.

He poured a glass of orange juice and walked out to the patio behind his town house, a lovely little brick patio surrounded by plants and flowers. Gardeners from the embassy maintained it because the house belonged to the People's Republic. He took a seat under an umbrella that provided some relief from the July sun and lit a cigarette.

So. Was there anything else he needed to do to protect Winston?

Regarding the e-mail that Winston had sent, he believed he'd done everything that could be done. He'd prevented Prescott from seeing the attachment, and Parker had assured him that Prescott would never be able to find the original e-mail in the NSA's computers. He would have to accept that, because there wasn't anything he could do about it if Parker was wrong.

He did need to get Lin Mai out of the country. It was possible that only the late James Parker, because he'd intercepted the e-mail, knew that she was a Chinese intelligence officer—but Fang couldn't take that chance. Lin Mai had to go. He had no idea what would happen to the other spies she'd been running, but that wasn't his problem. Someone in China would assign them a new controller.

But what about Winston? If he was arrested, the Chinese would lose a valuable asset, but Winston didn't pose a danger to Chinese intelligence. The only person Winston knew in the intelligence apparatus was Lin Mai—and Lin Mai would soon be out of the picture. In any case, Winston's fate would ultimately be decided by people back in China, but Fang would recommend that they leave him in place, assign him another handler, and hope for the best.

The only loose end that he could see was Callahan. It would really be best if Callahan died, just in case he'd opened the envelope.

He called the nurse. "Little sister," he said, "how is our patient?"

"He is in terrible shape," she said, sounding concerned for Callahan.

"After the surgery, he developed pneumonia and then an infection. He's on a respirator and being given antibiotics."

This was *very* good news. "Is he conscious?"

"No. He may never regain consciousness."

"Have more people been to see him?"

"Not that I know of, and like I said, he can't talk. But now there is a very large man who sits outside his room. He appears to be guarding him."

"I see," Fang said. "Is this man a policeman?"

"I don't know. He doesn't wear a uniform."

"Is he armed?"

"I didn't see a weapon on him, but he wears a jacket."

"Very well. Keep careful watch on Mr. Callahan's condition and call me immediately if he appears to be recovering. Oh, how do your parents like their new washer and dryer?"

"They are very happy with them," the nurse said, but she didn't *sound* happy. She sounded like she was weeping again. Some people were impossible to please.

Fang thought for a moment about hiring Jamal Howard to kill Callahan, then decided he would wait since it sounded like Callahan might die from infection or pneumonia. The other thing that occurred to him was that even if Callahan had seen the attachment, it wouldn't mean anything to him, and unless he had a photographic memory, he probably wouldn't be able to remember what he saw. For now he'd leave Callahan alone and let nature take its course.

Satisfied there was nothing more he needed to do, Fang called the Chinese ambassador's secretary and said he needed to meet with her boss. It was time to tell the ambassador where things stood. As he was driving to the embassy, he remembered the woman who had visited Callahan in the hospital, the one claiming to be his daughter. He suspected the woman might be the security guard, Kay Hamilton, who'd killed Otis's man. But since the nurse had said that Callahan had been unconscious when the woman visited him, he didn't see how she posed a threat. He wouldn't worry about her.

DAO YUNYI, ambassador of the People's Republic of China, listened in silence as Fang Zhou gave his report. Dao prided himself on his self-control; he was a master at concealing his feelings. He was sixty-seven years old and had served as the ambassador to the United Kingdom before being assigned to the most prized post in the Chinese diplomatic corps. He had been educated at Oxford and spoke English well—though not as well as Fang.

Dao did not like Fang. He thought the man was arrogant and disrespectful. He also didn't like that Fang had affairs with American women, affairs he claimed were necessary to develop connections. Unfortunately, even though Fang was listed as a member of the embassy's staff, Fang didn't work for Dao; he worked for the intelligence apparatus in China. Fang was only telling him what he'd done because he was obligated to keep him informed.

Dao didn't necessarily disagree with the actions Fang had taken to save the valuable asset at Zytek Systems, but it infuriated him that Fang had not bothered to include him in any of the decisions he'd made. He also thought Fang had been dangerously reckless using American thugs to steal the safe, but he had to concede that it had been necessary for Fang to work quickly.

Fang completed his report and bowed his head respectfully—although Dao could see the mockery in the gesture. The only good news, as far as Dao Yunyi was concerned, was that if Fang's plan fell apart, only Fang would be blamed. Dao would make sure of this.

14

Otis was in his shop, sanding the right front fender on a 1965 Ford Thunderbird. The body of the vehicle wasn't in bad shape, but he figured he'd probably spend about three hundred hours sanding before he put on the first coat of primer. The engine would have to be rebuilt, maybe the tranny, too. And the previous owner had put a lot of aftermarket shit on the car that he'd have to replace with original equipment that he'd have to scour the country to find. He figured it would take him seven or eight months to fully restore the Thunderbird, and estimated he would put at least ten grand into it, but when he was done, he'd be able to sell it for sixty or seventy.

He restored cars mainly because he enjoyed it and because he could work for himself. He'd never liked having a boss. He also did it so he could show a legitimate income to the IRS or the FBI. Right now, though, he was working on the car to avoid doing something he knew he had to do: talk to Ray Brown's sister, Shirley.

Otis knew Shirley would be out of her mind with grief—she probably went berserk when the cops had given her the news about Ray—and she'd blame him for her brother's death. He'd told himself that he hadn't gone to see her because the cops would start looking into him if they saw him, but the real reason he hadn't gone was because he wasn't ready to face Shirley's wrath.

Otis had never known siblings closer than Ray and Shirley. He knew their mom had abandoned them when they were little and they never did discover who their father was. They'd been raised in one shitty foster home after another, sometimes together, sometimes apart. And they'd both been seriously fucked up: molested, raped, and battered. By the time they were old enough to be on their own, they were so messed up that neither of them ever had a normal relationship. But they told each other everything—and that was a problem: Otis had no doubt that Ray had told crazy Shirley that he was working with him the day he died.

The only good thing he could tell Shirley was that, since Quinn had been killed, she'd get five hundred grand instead of the four hundred Ray had originally expected. But Shirley wouldn't care about the money; the only thing she'd care about was that Ray was dead.

Otis heard the side door to the shop bang against the wall and he thought that one of his kids had flung it open. But it wasn't one of his kids.

"You son of a bitch!" Shirley Brown screamed. "You motherfucking son of a—"

Then she was coming at him, and along the way she scooped up a fourteen-inch crescent wrench off the workbench. She swung it at his head and would have caved in his skull, but he ducked under her arm and wrapped his arms around her. She tried to break his grip and knee him in the balls. Fortunately, she missed and hit his thigh, then she quit fighting him and started sobbing.

Otis's wife, Ginnie, was now coming through the door. Shirley must have barged right past her, screaming and scaring the hell out of the kids. While he was clutching Shirley, he looked at his wife and made a head gesture telling her to go back in the house. Ginnie stood there for a minute, then the fear and anger faded from her face and she just looked sad—sad for Shirley. Ginnie had a good heart.

Otis just kept saying, "I'm sorry, I'm sorry, I'm sorry."

Shirley Brown looked like a biker chick. She had a thin, angular face that had once been pretty but had turned hard and lupine as she'd aged. Her hair was dark and cut short—or *chopped* short. She liked to wear sleeveless leather vests—like the one she had on now—tight jeans, and boots. Like her brother, she had lots of tats on her arms, her neck, her lower back, and probably more in places that couldn't be seen. The funny thing was that Shirley was really domestic. She liked to cook and garden, and she spent most of her free time fixing up her house; she and Ray had remodeled their kitchen themselves, completely gutted it and replaced everything, and Shirley had done at least half the work. She also took care of a couple of her neighbors' kids sometimes; Otis bet it took quite a while for the soccer moms to trust Shirley with them.

As he hugged her, Otis could smell the cigarette smoke in her hair and the booze on her breath. The booze was a really bad sign. Shirley had been going to AA for the last two years. The court had made her go after the last time she was arrested, but she stuck with it after that. But she was seriously off the wagon now, and who knows what she might say unintentionally?

Finally, the sobs slowed down, and he walked her over to a bench and sat next to her, his arm around her shoulder.

"What happened, Otis?" she said. "Tell me why he died."

He told her, and he didn't try to make excuses. He said they all took the job because the guy was paying them so damn much they couldn't pass it up. He told her that he hadn't had time to plan the way he normally did. "But I told all the guys that it was going to be risky and asked if any of them wanted to back out. Nobody did."

"Who killed him?" Shirley said. "The cops won't tell me."

"It was a fat guy in his sixties in a fucking office. I never thought for a minute that he'd have a gun. When Ray broke down his door, he was standing off to one side and he shot Ray as soon as he entered. I just never expected—"

"I want his name, Otis. I'm gonna kill him."

"I think I may have already killed him for you, Shirley. Quinn shot a bunch of bullets through the wall after he shot Ray, and at least one of the bullets hit him. Then I shot him again. I put one right in his chest. I heard on the news that they took him to the hospital, but I doubt he'll make it. He was bleeding like a stuck pig."

"Well, you find out if he made it and get me his name."

Otis knew the guy's name, but no way was he going to tell Shirley because she'd go to the hospital and kill Callahan if he wasn't dead already. So Otis lied. "I will, Shirl, I promise. And if he survives, I'll take care of him myself and that's a promise, too. As soon as I get the rest of our money, I'll give you Ray's share."

"I don't give a shit about the money!"

"I know you don't care about it now, but one of these days you'll be glad you have it." Shirley didn't have a job and was too much of a mental case to hold one down if she found one; he had no idea how she'd support herself now that Ray was dead.

"Have they released his body to you yet?"

"No. They . . ."

And then she started sobbing again. Sobbing so hard she started to hiccup.

15

The morning after meeting Detective Eagleton at McDonald's, the first thing Kay did was go to the hospital to check on Callahan. She hoped he'd be able to talk; she wanted to see if he could confirm the things Olivia Prescott had told her. She didn't necessarily trust Callahan, but she trusted him more than she trusted Prescott. She got off the elevator on the ICU floor and walked past the nurses' station without stopping. She wasn't about to ask for permission.

She saw Henry sitting on a chair outside the door to Callahan's room. He stood up when he saw her. He was wearing a lightweight jacket and Kay was willing to bet that the .44 Magnum he preferred was holstered under it.

"How's he doing?" she asked.

Henry shook his head and for a minute he couldn't speak.

"He's in bad shape, Kay. He's got pneumonia and some kind of nasty infection, the kind that's hard to treat. They're pumping him full of antibiotics, but from what the nurses are saying, it's an uphill battle."

"Can he talk?"

"No, he's on a respirator and he's unconscious. And you shouldn't go into his room. He might catch something from you that could infect him even worse."

"I just want to look in on him," Kay said, and she cracked the door to Callahan's room. He looked fragile lying there in bed—and she'd never thought of him as fragile. Tubes snaked down from IV bags dripping drugs into his bloodstream. Because of the respirator, she couldn't see much of his face, just his high forehead and his gray hair. She closed the door.

"Who's helping you guard him? You gotta sleep sometime."

"A buddy of mine. He's a vet and a licensed PI. He's good and I trust him."

As they were speaking, a short Asian nurse came down the hall. She nodded at Henry and Kay, put on a mask, and entered Callahan's room.

"They won't let me go in there when they're working on him."

"Just do the best you can, Henry."

"What are you doing?"

"I got the names of the men that Callahan and I killed, and I'm following up on them to see if I can get to whoever planned this."

"Do you need help?"

"Not at this point. Call me when Callahan's able to talk. I really need to know what he knows."

KAY DIDN'T RETURN TO HER CAR. Instead, she went to the cafeteria. The food may have been inedible, but the coffee was adequate. She would go and see Ray Brown's sister next. If Brown and his sister were as close as Detective Eagleton had said, Shirley Brown might know who her brother had been working for. The cops hadn't been able to get anything from her, but maybe Kay could because she had an advantage over the cops: She didn't have to play by the rules. But she didn't think that asking nicely for the names of her brother's accomplices was going to cut it. She wanted some leverage, some way to apply pressure.

Kay called Eagleton; she woke him up. She suddenly remembered that he worked nights. Too bad.

"This is the lady you met at McDonald's," she said.

"Yeah, Jesus. What time is it? What do you want?"

"I need Ray Brown's Social Security number, DOB, and his current address."

"Can't your own people get that for you?" he said, still under the impression Kay worked for the NSA.

"Yeah, but since there are probably ten thousand Ray Browns living on the Eastern seaboard, I figured you can get it faster."

"Yeah, all right. I'll have to call the office. Give me ten minutes."

Twenty minutes later, he called her back and gave her the information. He concluded with, "Try to remember that I work swing shift the next time you want to talk to me."

KAY USED HER PHONE to look up the general number for the NSA. Prescott had refused to give her a private phone number, so what else could she do?

She told the NSA operator that she needed to speak to Olivia Prescott. The operator asked, "And may I say who you are, ma'am, and what this is in regard to?"

"Sure," Kay said. "My name is Kay Hamilton. I work for Thomas Callahan and I just wanted to tell Ms. Prescott that Mr. Callahan's still alive."

A long minute later, Prescott screamed into the phone, "What in the hell do you think you're doing?"

"Hey, I asked you to give me a number and you wouldn't. I need you to do something for me."

"I am not going to discuss anything on a telephone."

"Olivia, the only people monitoring this call work for you. Tell them to stop."

"Now you listen to me—" Then Kay heard Prescott take in a deep breath to calm herself. "Where are you?"

"At the hospital. I was checking on Callahan."

"Oh," Prescott said. Then, sounding almost human, she asked, "How is he?"

"Not good. He got pneumonia and some kind of bad infection after the surgery. He's unconscious, on a respirator, and they're pumping antibiotics into him."

"I see. Anyway—"

"*Anyway?*" Kay said. "That's all you have to say?"

Prescott ignored the jibe. "Where exactly in the hospital are you?"

"The cafeteria."

"Stay there. A man will meet you in an hour to give you a phone that's more secure than the one you're using. After you have the phone, call me. My number will be in the contacts list."

"All right," Kay said.

PRESCOTT HUNG UP and made another call. "Brookes, I want one of your people to take one of the new cell phones to a woman at George Washington University Hospital. She'll be waiting in the cafeteria. She's tall, blond, and very good looking. Her name is Hamilton."

"Okay," Brookes said.

"That's not all," Prescott said. "I want you to program the phone so we can listen to whatever she's saying, whether the phone is on or not. Got it?"

"Yeah, sure."

"I also want you to personally monitor the phone until I tell you otherwise. I want to know where Hamilton is every moment of the day and I want a recording of everything she says or texts from that phone. With one exception. When she's speaking to me, stop monitoring and recording. Do you understand?"

"Yes, ma'am."

. . .

ALMOST EXACTLY ONE HOUR after Kay spoke to Prescott, a guy wearing black-framed glasses, jeans, a white short-sleeved shirt, and a narrow green tie entered the cafeteria. The end of his tie was about halfway between his waist and his collar. When she saw his head swiveling about as if he was looking for someone—there were only three other people in the place and two were older than God and the third was in a wheelchair—Kay raised a hand and he walked toward her table.

"Are you Hamilton?" he asked.

"Yeah," she said.

He handed her a plastic bag and walked away. Inside was a phone, a regular charger, and a car charger. She took out the phone. It looked like an iPhone. Even had the little bitten apple on the back. Kay didn't realize it, but the phone was just slightly bigger in every direction than a standard iPhone.

"HERE'S WHAT I WANT," Kay told Prescott, using her new phone. "The guy Callahan killed was an ex-con named Ray Brown. He had a sister named Shirley, who lived with him. I want all of her bank accounts frozen and her credit and debit cards canceled. If she has a safe deposit box, make sure that she's denied access to it. And she and her brother might have joint accounts, so make sure all of Ray's accounts are frozen as well. You understand?"

"Yes," Prescott said. "But do you understand that this isn't the sort of thing the agency does?"

"But you can do it," Kay said. "You can fuck up anything that relies on a computer, and I want you to fuck up Shirley Brown's finances."

"Why?" Prescott asked.

"Because I want to make her give me the names of the men her brother was working with. I also need you to monitor Shirley's phones, and I *know* that's something you can do."

Prescott hesitated. Kay figured Prescott didn't have a problem morally or ethically doing what Kay wanted; she was just trying to decide if it was in her own best interest. Finally she said, "Okay."

"How long will it take you?" Kay asked.

"I don't know. The banking stuff, three or four hours, maybe less."

"I have Ray Brown's basic information. SS number, DOB."

"Give it to me," Prescott said, and Kay rattled off the numbers.

"Call me when it's done," Kay said. "I want to go see Shirley as soon as possible."

"I don't work for you, Ms. Hamilton."

"That's right, and I don't work for you. But if you want me to track down who shot Callahan—and I know you do—then you'll do as I ask." Kay hung up before Prescott could respond.

KAY NOW HAD three or four hours to kill, and she didn't want to spend the time at the hospital. She wanted to do something either productive or pleasurable. Nothing productive occurred to her, but something pleasurable did.

She called Eli Dolan. "Where are you?" she asked.

"K Street. I finally got the cops out of here. When I got here yesterday, one of their technicians was trying to log on to a computer and two other guys were searching desks. I informed the detective in charge—"

"Mary Platt?"

"Yeah. What a charmer. Anyway, I told her we were willing to be cooperative but we weren't going to allow them access to our computers without a warrant. Then I had a nasty lawyer deliver the same message. At any rate, they've cleared out of the office and I'm trying to put the place back together. I've got carpenters coming to replace doors and carpets, and to patch up all the bullet holes. I couldn't believe how many bullets were fired, Kay. It's a miracle you weren't killed. I also sent Henry over to protect Callahan."

"Yeah, I know," Kay said. "I saw him. I went to the hospital first thing this morning to check on Callahan. I was hoping he'd be conscious, but he wasn't."

"Henry told me that Callahan's in really bad shape. The infections you can get in hospitals these days are worse than gunshot wounds."

"Aw, he's too ornery to die. Even the devil wouldn't want him." Kay was trying to sound lighthearted, but she was genuinely worried about Callahan.

"How are you handling the cops?" Kay asked.

"I gave Platt the names of half a dozen people who work the cover side, just to give her people to talk to. They're all telling her the same thing: that they had no idea what was in Callahan's safe or why anyone would want to steal it. But Platt knows I'm stonewalling her, and she's pissed. Now, tell me what you've been doing."

"Why don't we meet at your place," Kay said, "and I'll fill you in. And we can also . . . you know. It's been a while since I've seen you."

Eli laughed. "How soon can you get there?"

"Half an hour."

Kay wondered if people still used the term *nooner* anymore.

BROOKES, BACK AT FORT MEADE, wondered who Eli Dolan was. The machines had given him Dolan's name as soon as Hamilton called him. Prescott hadn't told him anything about why he was monitoring Hamilton or who she was—which was typical of her.

The iPhone Prescott had given Hamilton was a whole level above any other iPhone on the planet. Its battery would last for days instead of hours—the Apple people would kill to get their hands on it—and Brookes would be able to hear anyone in the same room with her. He would be able to read her e-mails and text messages, and see anything she looked up on the Internet. And naturally the phone was equipped with GPS. Right now Brookes could see that Hamilton had left the hospital and was moving toward Georgetown. As she drove, she was humming a song he couldn't identify. She sounded happy.

On another computer, he called up everything the government had on Dolan. It was just basic information, the sort that could be obtained by accessing tax returns, property records, and military and criminal databases. He didn't spend much time looking at Dolan's information; he figured if Prescott wanted to know more, she'd tell him. But he couldn't help but note that Dolan was extraordinarily rich and was currently employed as a consultant for the Callahan Group—whatever the hell that was. He had previously worked for Goldman Sachs, then over in Treasury and the OMB. Dolan looked like some kind of financial heavyweight.

Brookes routed the recording of Hamilton's brief conversation with Dolan to Prescott's computer, then went back to working on his novel. He figured he'd get fired if it was ever published because, although it was fiction, it was based on things he'd observed the last fifteen years working for the NSA. He would need a literary agent who could get him an *enormous* advance—like seven or eight figures enormous—enough to compensate for the pension he'd lose and enough to retain all the lawyers he was going to need.

ELI DOLAN'S TOWN HOUSE was filled with high-end furniture and expensive artwork, and Kay could imagine photos of it in some glossy magazine. Kay had even met the decorator once when she was having dinner with Eli at a restaurant in the District. The woman had a sexy Southern accent, what Kay thought of as blow-job lips, tresses the color of a raven's wings, and a body that turned every head in the room. When Eli had introduced her as his decorator, Kay got the impression that the woman had once spent time in Eli's bedroom doing more than picking out the wallpaper.

Eli asked Kay if she wanted lunch and she said yes, and he started digging things out of the refrigerator to make sandwiches. As he was digging, he asked her what she'd been up to.

She wasn't sure how much to tell him. She knew she should tell him about Prescott and what Prescott had told her about the e-mail attachment, but was reluctant to do so. Prescott had threatened to have her arrested if she divulged the information, but she wasn't worried about herself. She was worried about Eli and what he might do. She didn't want to put him in the NSA's crosshairs. So rather than tell him the whole story, she told him the part that really mattered.

"I got the names of the two robbers who were killed," she said.

"You told me you got the name of the guy you killed from Platt," Eli said. "How did you get the other one?"

"From a DEA guy I worked with in Miami. He put me in touch with a D.C. Metro narc, and the narc got the other name for me."

Keep track of all the lies you tell.

"Anyway," Kay said, "the guy Callahan killed was another ex-con named Ray Brown, and he lived with his sister. I'm going to lean on her for more information. The cops couldn't get anything out of her, but maybe I'll be able to."

"Because you're a woman?" Eli said.

"No. Because I'm going to do something mean to her if she doesn't tell me what I want to know."

Eli laughed.

Kay watched as Eli prepared the sandwiches, completely absorbed with the task, his long graceful fingers placing meat and cheese on slices of freshly baked bread. He had his cold cuts delivered from the best deli in D.C. He was wearing jeans and a blue dress shirt with the tails untucked. He was normally clean-shaven, but today he had a couple days' worth of stubble. Shaven or unshaven, he turned her on.

She almost said, "We need to talk." She needed to tell him that she was planning to quit the Callahan Group. But she had always hated discussions that started that way. She remembered a couple of past relationships that she had terminated after beginning with, "We need to talk."

Well, the relationship with her first husband hadn't ended that way. She married her first husband, who'd also been a DEA agent, when she was twenty-three and then divorced him when she found out he was cheating on her only eight months after they said their vows. The marriage had ended with: "Get the hell out of my sight before I shoot you."

At any rate, she wasn't in the mood for talking. She got up from the chair at the kitchen table where she'd been sitting and walked over to him.

"Why don't we eat later," she said and started to unbutton his shirt.

BROOKES HEARD A THUMP, like the iPhone had hit the ground. The next thing he heard was two people making love—and Brookes was really getting turned on. He had a woody that was threatening to break his zipper—which also made him feel like a voyeuristic creep. But he had to find some way to put this scene into his novel, which could use a bit more sex. He played back the recording and typed up the dialogue, Hamilton saying things like, "Oh, yes. Don't stop. Don't stop."

PRESCOTT WAS THINKING about the Russian colonel who was, almost certainly, trying to sell nuclear materials to the Saudi prince. The NSA had done all the things it was supposed to do. The CIA, the FBI, Homeland Security, and the president's national security advisor had all been informed. Com satellites were hovering in space hoping to pick up more chatter between the greedy colonel and the royal nut in Arabia.

But Prescott knew it wasn't enough. They might be able to stop the Russian from selling materials for a suitcase nuke this time, but he'd try again. And if he couldn't sell what he had to the Saudi prince, he'd find another buyer. As for the prince, if he couldn't get what he needed from *this* Russian colonel, he would find another Russian colonel.

If Prescott were the president, she would order a SEAL team to eliminate the colonel and schedule a drone strike on the tent in the desert where the prince was sleeping with a couple of his wives, but she knew the current resident in the White House would never do this. And this was exactly the reason why the Callahan Group had been formed. If Callahan wasn't dying, she would have told him to send somebody—maybe even Kay Hamilton—to take these maniacs off the board.

Brookes interrupted her reverie with another recording of Hamilton speaking to Eli Dolan. She heard Hamilton tell Dolan that she'd obtained the name of the man Callahan had killed and was planning to go see Brown's sister, which Prescott already knew. She stopped the recording when Hamilton and Dolan started having sex. Prescott couldn't remember the last time she'd had sex and didn't want to be reminded of the fact.

Fortunately, Hamilton hadn't told Dolan about Danzinger and the e-mail attachment, and maybe she didn't because she was trying to protect him. The truth was, Dolan didn't worry her as much as Hamilton did. He'd worked for Callahan for years and had proven himself to be completely loyal. And, unlike Hamilton, he either believed that Callahan worked for the president or he didn't care who Callahan worked for. Even before Callahan had been shot, Prescott had thought that Dolan might be the person to replace Callahan if something should happen to him. She knew they could work with Dolan. But Hamilton . . . she was a whole different story. Nobody could work with that woman.

As she was stewing, there was a rap on her door. It was an elfinlike technician named Natalie Jones. Natalie was about five feet tall, wore jeans with ripped knees, tinted her hair purple, and wore a ring in her nose—but Prescott didn't care. Natalie was a shark when it came to her job.

"Those bank accounts you wanted frozen? They're ice."

"Good," Prescott said. It had only taken Natalie two hours.

After Natalie left, Prescott called Hamilton. She figured by now Dolan and Hamilton *must* be finished. How long could they possibly go on? The phone rang several times before Hamilton answered, and Prescott thought she sounded . . . well, *languid* was the only word she could think of. Prescott said, "Those accounts you wanted frozen have been frozen. The sister now only has access to the money in her purse."

"Thanks," Hamilton said and hung up.

16

K ay pulled up in front of Ray and Shirley Brown's house in Spring-field and was surprised. It was a brick rambler with a manicured lawn and brightly colored perennials in the flower beds. There was a boxwood hedge surrounding the front yard, but it might as well have been a white picket fence. Eagleton had told her that Quinn—the man she killed—lived in a double-wide with a pit bull and Kay had been expecting Brown's place to be similar. Instead it looked like a place where Mr. and Mrs. Beaver Cleaver would dwell.

Kay rang the doorbell, and when no one answered, she started pounding on the front door with her fist. The door flung open a moment later.

"What the hell do you want?" Shirley Brown said.

Kay's reaction was: *Whoa!* Shirley was one tough-looking lady. Kay had an immediate image of Shirley riding on the back of a Harley with a fat bearded guy driving. When she got off the bike the inscription on the back of the guy's leather jacket would say: IF YOU CAN READ THIS, THE BITCH FELL OFF.

Once Kay got past the woman's hard face, the tats on her muscular arms, and the raggedly chopped hair, she noticed the red-rimmed eyes.

Shirley Brown was grieving for her brother. She was also drunk; her breath smelled as if she'd been gargling with Jack Daniel's.

"I need to talk to you," Kay said.

"If you're another cop, you can fuck off. I don't have anything else to tell you and you already ripped my house apart."

"I'm not a cop."

"Then you can definitely fuck off."

Shirley started to close the door, but before she could, Kay said, "Shirley, I'm a whole lot worse than a cop."

"What the hell does that mean?"

"It means I want some information from you and if you don't tell me, I'll—"

"I'm not going to tell you shit."

"That's what I thought you'd say. After you slam the door in my face, I want you to call your credit card company. They're going to tell you that your card has been canceled. Then I want you to try and make an ATM withdrawal, and you're going to find out that your bank accounts have been frozen. If you have a safe deposit box, you won't be granted access. In a couple of days, the electric company is going to shut off your power because their records are going to show that you haven't paid your bill for six months. Ditto your phone bill. If your brother had a will, it's going to be frozen solid in probate. You won't be able to get at his assets for a year. And if this place has a mortgage, your bank is going to discover that you're behind on your payments and they're going to foreclose. You've heard of identity theft, Shirley? Well, I'm not going to steal your identity. I'm going to steal your fucking life."

"You can't do all that shit! It's not legal."

"I *am* doing all that shit, Shirley. Call your bank. Call your credit card company. I'm leaving now, but I'll be back in an hour. That should give you enough time to find out that I'm not bullshitting you." Kay took a breath. "You need to understand something, Shirley. Your brother and his pals didn't rob just any ol' office in D.C. They robbed a guy connected to national security."

"What are you talking about?"

"Look, I'm sorry about what happened to your brother, but whoever he was working with stepped into something way over their heads. I'm sure they had no idea when they stole that safe."

"What safe?"

"You don't know about the safe? Your brother's friends stole a safe that contained something a lot more important than money. Now I need to know who your brother was working for. We're not going to arrest anyone. We just want back what is ours. In fact, we're willing to buy it back. I guess you could say that I'm the negotiator, and I need a name to negotiate with."

That was a lie; Kay had no intention of negotiating with anyone.

Shirley stood there for a moment, a frown on her face, trying to digest what she'd just been told. Finally, she came up with a response: "Fuck you," and slammed the door.

BROOKES SENT PRESCOTT the recording of Hamilton speaking to Shirley Brown. When Prescott heard it, she closed her eyes. Did Hamilton *have* to tell Brown the Callahan Group was connected to national security? Jesus Christ! What was wrong with that woman?

KAY WENT BACK to her car to wait and see what Shirley would do. But Kay didn't even have to wait ten minutes before a car pulled out of the garage. Kay was surprised to see that the Hells Angels poster girl was driving a Prius. Shirley came out of the driveway fast, the driver's-side tires running over part of her well-tended lawn and crushing one of the boxwood plants. Shirley was way too drunk to be driving, and Kay hoped she didn't get pulled over by a cop; the last thing Kay wanted was the cops hauling Shirley away in handcuffs.

Shirley didn't go more than half a mile before she pulled into a shopping mall on Braddock Road. She drove up to a PNC bank, jumped out of her car, leaving the door open, and ran to the ATM. She fed her card into the machine—and Kay smiled when Shirley began hitting it with her fists.

Kay thought that Shirley would drive back to her place, but instead she drove for half an hour and ended up in Fairfax, stopping in front of a fair-sized house on a corner lot. In addition to the attached two-car garage, most of the large backyard was occupied by a sheet-metal building that had roll-up garage doors.

Shirley walked up to the front door and pounded on it like she was trying to batter it down.

OTIS WAS SITTING with his family in the living room having what Ginnie thought of as an "intervention," something she'd picked up from a reality show. Ginnie had found a pack of cigarettes in their twelve-year-old daughter's backpack and was giving her hell while Otis and the boys just sat there, not sure what they were supposed to do. Every once in a while, Otis would say, "Yeah, that's right," to support his wife, but he was really thinking that Ginnie would be in a much better position to lecture their daughter on the evils of tobacco if she herself didn't smoke. His two sons were just sitting there, trying not to grin, watching their older sister catch hell. Usually they were the targets of Ginnie's wrath.

Ginnie was in mid–finger wag when someone began pounding on the front door.

"Jesus, who's that?" Ginnie said.

"I'll get it," Otis said. He was afraid that the next words he would hear would be: *Open up. It's the police.* He looked through the peephole and sighed. "It's Shirley. Let me see what she wants."

Otis opened the door, stepped outside, and closed the door behind him before Shirley could enter the house. "What's going on, Shirl?" he said.

"I got a big problem," Shirley said.

"Why? What happened?"

Shirley told him a woman had showed up at her house and wanted to know who Ray had worked with on his last job.

"Was she a cop?"

"No. She said she was worse than a cop, whatever the fuck that means. She said you took a safe from the office of a guy hooked into national security. National security, Otis! Then she told me that if I didn't give you up, she was going to freeze all our bank accounts and cancel our credit cards."

Otis noticed she said *our*, like Ray was still alive.

"I thought she was bullshitting me, so I called Visa, and sure as shit, my card had been canceled. Then I went to the bank and tried to get cash out of the ATM, but the statement said my checking account balance was zero. What am I going to do, Otis? What are *you* going to do?"

"What did you tell her?"

"I didn't tell her shit. But what are you going to do? I don't have a job. All I've got is the house and the money we've put in the bank. And she threatened to have the bank foreclose on the house. What the hell am I supposed to do?"

"Calm down," Otis said, "and quit screaming. The whole damn neighborhood can hear you and you're probably scaring my kids."

"Fuck you, calm down. I—"

"What's this woman's name?"

"She didn't give me a name."

"Then what did she look like?"

"Shit, I don't know. Tall, blond ponytail, pretty."

Blond ponytail? Otis wondered if it was the same woman who'd killed Quinn.

"Okay," Otis said. "I'm going to see the guy we did the job for tonight to collect the rest of what he owes us. When I see him, I'll get some answers about this national security shit. And since Ray's cut was five hundred grand, you'll be okay for money until we can sort out all this bank account stuff."

"But what about my house? What if the bank forecloses like she said?"

"We'll sort it out, Shirley. Trust me. Now go home. I'll call you later."

"Okay, Otis," she finally said. Then she started blubbering. "God, I miss him. I'll be sitting there in the house and I'll catch this motion out of the corner of my eye, like Ray's still there. I can *feel* him in the house. I don't know what I'm going to do without him."

Otis stayed on the porch, watching Shirley until she got in her car and drove away. Just looking at her, you'd never guess how fragile she was. If something ever happened to Otis, Ginnie would grieve and she'd miss him, but she'd be okay in the end. She could survive without him. But Shirley . . . he didn't know.

He wondered if Shirley had been told the truth—had they messed with national security? You rob a bank, they assign half a dozen agents to track you down; you fuck with national security, the entire government comes after you.

He remembered the aftermath of the Boston Marathon attack and the way they went after those two little Chechen shits: thousands of cops working twenty-four hours a day, going door to door, talking to every person the bombers ever knew, looking at every surveillance camera and seemingly every cell phone photo in Boston. He'd never seen a manhunt like that, and he sure as shit didn't ever want to be the focus of one.

Otis walked back to the living room and took a seat. If the intervention was having any effect on his daughter, it was hard to tell; she just had this stubborn, *You can't make me do anything* look on her face that reminded Otis of Ginnie when she wasn't going to back down.

"Is everything okay?" Ginnie asked him.

"Yeah, everything's fine," he said.

"What did Shirley want?" Ginnie asked.

"I'll tell you later," he said, then he pointed his finger at his daughter's sullen face and said, "And you. You're gonna knock off the smoking shit. You got it?"

FROM HER CAR, Kay watched Shirley scream at the guy who came out of the house. He had short dark hair, was tall, broad-shouldered, and handsome in a rough way. He was wearing boots, jeans, and a white T-shirt that showed off hard biceps and a flat stomach.

She could tell by the body language that he was trying to calm Shirley down and wasn't having much luck. But he must have said something to reassure her, and ten minutes later, Shirley walked unsteadily back to her Prius and drove away. Kay didn't see any reason to follow her. She needed to know who the guy was. When he went back inside the house, she used her NSA smartphone to do a property search. The house belonged to a guy named Dylan Otis, wife named Virginia.

BROOKES COULD SEE that Hamilton was stationary in Fairfax, Virginia, and it sounded like she was listening to the radio in her car. He watched on another monitor as Hamilton used her phone to do a property search, and discovered that a house near her location belonged to one Dylan Otis. With a few keystrokes, Brookes learned that Otis had served time for a bungled armored-car robbery when he was seventeen, had no convictions since then, and according to his tax returns, he remodeled cars. He called Prescott immediately.

KAY TAPPED HER fingers on the steering wheel, thinking, then checked her watch. It was after four. Eagleton should be on duty. She called him.

"I need to know what you've got on a guy named Dylan Otis. He lives in Fairfax."

"I have a job you know," Eagleton said. "Right now I'm at a double homicide. Two dead bangers. They were selling dope off their designated corner when a couple guys in a car drive by, shoot off about a hundred rounds, blowing out half the windows on the block. Luckily, only the corner boys were killed."

"I don't give a shit," Kay said. "What I'm working on trumps dead dope dealers. Call somebody and have them look up Dylan Otis."

"Yeah, all right. I'll get back to you as soon as I can."

Kay wondered how long she should watch Otis's house. He could stay inside for the rest of the day. She decided to wait until she heard back from Eagleton. Otis could be one of the people who worked with Ray Brown or he could just be a guy who Shirley ran to when she had a problem, a guy with broad shoulders to cry on. But Kay doubted that. And even if Otis was one of the people who stole the safe, Kay didn't have a plan for what she should do about him.

FORTY-FIVE MINUTES LATER, Eagleton called her back.

"Otis did time for an armored-car heist when he was seventeen. And get this. One of the guys who pulled the job with him was his old man. Anyway, his father was killed during the robbery and Otis and two other guys were caught. Otis did five years. He probably would have done more time if he'd been older.

"We don't have anything on him other than the one conviction. He's never been arrested here in the District and he's never been convicted of another crime. But I was curious about him, so I called an FBI guy I know who works banks. He said the Bureau has had Otis on its radar for years. They're pretty sure he runs a crew that's pulled a bunch of big-money capers, but they've never been able to nail him."

"Okay, thanks," Kay said.

"How did you come up with Otis's name?" Eagleton asked.

"Just stumbled across it," Kay said.

"Yeah, right. Are you going to tell Mary Platt about him?" Eagleton asked.

"No," Kay said. Then she added, "At least, not yet. And you're not going to tell her anything either, Eagleton. You do not want to get in the middle of what's going on here. This is *way* above your pay grade. You understand?"

"Yeah, I understand," Eagleton said.

Kay disconnected from Eagleton. Now what? She was pretty sure that she'd found the guy in charge of the break-in, but—just like the FBI—she didn't have any hard evidence. She was also pretty sure that Otis was working for somebody. Otis robbed banks and Callahan's office wasn't a bank, which meant that somebody had most likely hired him—but she had no idea who that could be. All she knew was that it had to be somebody who cared about the attachment—like the foreign government that the e-mail had been sent to. Otis wasn't the guy at the top—and she wanted the guy at the top.

BROOKES CALLED PRESCOTT to tell her about the conversation between Eagleton and Hamilton, and when Prescott didn't answer, he forwarded the recording to a machine in her office. Brookes wondered where she had gone.

17

Prescott was the first to arrive at the Key Bridge Marriott in Arlington. The room had a magnificent view of Lincoln's Memorial, which she ignored. The first thing she did was close the drapes on the extremely remote chance that somebody was pointing a directional microphone at the window, attempting to eavesdrop on the meeting.

Grayson arrived next. Like Prescott, he was in his sixties. He worked at the Pentagon, was privy to intelligence gathered by the DIA, saw the daily briefing reports given to the Joint Chiefs and, most important, controlled large amounts of money given to the DOD. Grayson was tall and lanky, his hair was white and softer than goose down, and he wore wire-rimmed glasses and favored tweed suits. You might mistake him for a college professor—which would be a big mistake. In his youth, Grayson had been a Delta Force soldier who had slit more than a few throats.

The first words out of Grayson's mouth were, "How's Callahan doing?"

"He's still among the living, but just barely. I'm not sure he's going to make it."

"Do you have any idea yet who was behind the attack on his office?"

"Let's wait for Lincoln to get here," Prescott said, "so I don't have to tell the story twice."

Grayson walked over to the minibar, ignored the alcohol, and pulled out a can of ginger ale. "Would you like anything, Olivia?"

"No." Actually, she felt like having a Scotch but knew she'd be returning to Fort Meade and most likely spending the night there, so she had to keep a clear head.

As they waited for Lincoln, they chatted about some idiotic thing the president had said at a news conference that morning. Neither of them could remember a president they didn't think was a complete fool.

Lincoln arrived ten minutes later—ten minutes after the stated start time. It was almost unheard of for Lincoln to be tardy.

"I apologize for being late," he said. "Some idiot ran into another idiot right outside the main gate at Langley." It was also almost unheard of for Lincoln to apologize.

Lincoln was a big man, six-foot-four, and weighed about two hundred and fifty pounds. He had short, gray hair and a big-nosed, craggy face, like it had been chipped out of stone by a myopic sculptor. Not a handsome man, but an impressive and intimidating one.

"Would you like a drink, Lincoln?" Grayson asked.

"No, nothing for me. Well, Olivia, would you care to enlighten us?"

For some reason, Lincoln—to Prescott's great annoyance—always assumed that he was the one in charge, but the fact was that they were all equals.

As soon as Prescott heard about the attack, she had immediately called Grayson and Lincoln. There was nothing unusual about her talking to these men, considering their relative positions in the intelligence community. She said the same thing to each of them: "I'll take the lead on the K Street event. I have background you don't have." Neither man had asked any questions, but now they wanted to know what had happened.

Prescott quickly told them everything that had transpired since

Danzinger called her in London, about the e-mail attachment, and Parker, and what Hamilton was doing.

"Have you identified the spy at Zytek yet?" Grayson asked.

"No, but I'll find him," Prescott said. "I have my best man working on that. Then I'll have the FBI arrest him and find out how much damage he's done. The spy at Zytek isn't my biggest concern. The bigger problem is Hamilton." Prescott shook her head. "If that stubborn bastard Callahan had gotten rid of her after the fiasco in Afghanistan . . ."

"Why on earth did you tell Hamilton anything?" Lincoln said. He'd been brooding the whole time Prescott had been talking.

"I *told* you why," Prescott said. "Weren't you listening? She threatened to give my name to the cops and the media."

"She was bluffing," Lincoln said.

"I don't think Hamilton bluffs," Prescott said. "The other reason I told her what I did is because we need to know who was behind the attack, and Hamilton is good enough to find whoever it was."

Lincoln started to object, but Grayson said, "Lincoln, I don't think we need to worry about Hamilton. All she really knows is that Prescott knew Callahan from his days at the CIA. She has no proof whatsoever that Prescott is working with the Callahan Group."

Ignoring Grayson, Lincoln said to Prescott, "Are you sure that she doesn't know about Grayson or me?"

"Am I sure? No. But as far as I know, Callahan only gave her my name. If Callahan ever regains consciousness, I'll ask him what else he told her."

"I'll say it again," Grayson said. "I don't think we need to worry about Hamilton. She can't talk about the covert missions she did for Callahan because she'd be implicating herself. I also think that young woman is bright enough to know that exposing the Callahan Group could have a disastrous effect on the intelligence agencies, and I don't think she'd want that to happen."

"The problem," Prescott said, "is that we don't know what she might do in the future. If she's ever arrested or needs money, maybe she'll talk. I do not *ever* want to face the day when she testifies to a congressional committee about the Group and names me as part of the leadership."

No one said anything for a moment as they envisioned Hamilton telling a roomful of senators about Callahan's missions, but a Senate investigation would be the least of their problems. They'd be fired, of course, and could even end up in jail.

But it wouldn't end with them. They had taken funds from their respective agencies—funds earmarked for legitimate operations and programs—and used them to carry out unsanctioned missions. This meant that the organizations they worked for obviously lacked sufficient internal controls, and their bosses would be forced to resign and the president would be crucified by the opposing party. The worst consequence, however, would be that the entire intelligence community would be put under a magnifying glass and Congress would hobble it even more by demanding increased oversight.

Softly, almost as if she were thinking aloud, Prescott said, "We're vulnerable because of Hamilton. Maybe it would be best if . . . well, if Hamilton was gone."

"Do you mean kill her?" Grayson said bluntly.

Prescott didn't answer.

"I won't be part of that," Grayson said. "We formed the Callahan Group to deal with enemies of the United States. Kay Hamilton is not an enemy. Find some other way to get this back in the box, Olivia."

Prescott didn't respond—and neither did Lincoln—but Prescott was thinking that it was easy for Grayson to be sanctimonious. Hamilton didn't have his name.

AFTER LINCOLN AND GRAYSON LEFT, Prescott changed her mind about having a drink, removed a small bottle of Glenlivet from the minibar, and poured the liquor into a glass. She opened the blinds so she could see the Lincoln Memorial and stood there, sipping the Scotch.

They formed the Callahan Group about eighteen months after 9/11. Around that time, the 9/11 Commission was trying to understand how the intelligence agencies had failed so badly, and the agencies, in turn, were doing their best to understand what had gone wrong—while trying to avoid being blamed for incompetence.

One night, after a long, frustrating joint intelligence group meeting to brief the president on Iraq, Callahan, Grayson, Lincoln, and Prescott retired to the bar of the Hay-Adams Hotel, which was opposite the White House. After twenty years at the CIA, Callahan was now working for Bush's national security advisor. Prescott, Grayson, and Lincoln held senior positions at the NSA, the Pentagon, and the CIA respectively. They'd all known one another for years, and although they never socialized together, they respected one another and worked surprisingly well together. Their views about how the United States should respond to threats were virtually identical.

The four of them were all frustrated that it took weeks to make decisions because the president felt he needed to analyze *everything*: the potential downsides, the reaction of the American public, the reactions of countries who were supposedly our allies, and the reactions of countries who were definitely not our allies. Nothing happened quickly, and they had all seen, far too many times, opportunities for dealing with the country's enemies slip away.

It was Callahan—drinking heavily as usual—who essentially came up with the idea of the Callahan Group. He said, "Maybe we should be the ones who ought to decide what should be done."

Now, if this had been any other group of people sitting in a hotel bar, someone would have laughed at Callahan's outrageous statement. But this wasn't just any group. These were four people who had spent their entire careers dealing with threats to national security, four people who had engaged in numerous dangerous, top secret operations. So no one laughed.

Instead, Grayson said, "Exactly what do you mean, Callahan?"

"I mean, if we see a problem, we deal with it ourselves, quickly and quietly."

"But how?" Prescott asked.

And from that simple beginning, the Callahan Group came to be.

Callahan set up what appeared to be a legitimate company that would have logical reasons for sending its employees to various parts of the world. He recruited operatives who could be trusted and could execute covert operations. Prescott, Grayson, and Lincoln would analyze the information collected by their agencies, decide if action should be taken, and secretly assist Callahan in any way they could. Most important, they would provide the funding Callahan needed. Each of their agencies—particularly the Pentagon and NSA—had so damn much money at their disposal it was almost impossible for the bean counters to keep track of it all. Then came the wars in Iraq and Afghanistan and money flowed like a water main had burst.

They soon found that their worldviews were so similar that they had no trouble isolating threats and deciding on an appropriate course of action. And the beauty of the Callahan Group was that if Callahan was ever caught, only Callahan would be blamed. The United States government couldn't be held responsible for the actions of a private corporation, nor could the agencies that Lincoln, Prescott, and Grayson worked for.

Many times over the years they had discussed what might happen if they were ever found out and exposed to the world. They all agreed that if that day ever came, they would stand proud and take whatever punishment was dished out to them. They believed that they had done the right thing, had acted in the country's best interest, and they wouldn't apologize. But now the possibility of being exposed was *real*—thanks to

Hamilton—and the one who would be forced to swallow the castor oil would be Olivia Prescott.

Prescott had always envisioned retiring in about ten years. Callahan, Lincoln, and Grayson would retire at the same time and the Callahan Group would be dissolved. Then Prescott, like General MacArthur's old soldier, would simply fade away. But she was not going to end a brilliant career in a federal penitentiary, being pilloried by the media and useless politicians. That was *not* going to happen. And not because of Kay Hamilton.

18

Prescott returned to her office at Fort Meade, still preoccupied by her meeting with Grayson and Lincoln. She glanced over at the leather couch in her office, thinking she'd probably be sleeping on it tonight. She couldn't afford to leave with Hamilton running around, doing God knows what. Then she smiled slightly when she realized that that wasn't really true: God may not have known what Hamilton was doing, but the NSA certainly did.

She called Brookes. "Where is she now?"

"She's in Fairfax. She's stationary, near the home of a man named Dylan Otis. I sent you two recordings of her talking to a cop named Eagleton, and apparently Otis is some kind of thief, like a bank robber."

"And Hamilton is watching his house?" Prescott said.

"Yeah, it looks that way. She's been there since about four."

"Okay," Prescott said. "Stay awake and stay on her."

She didn't know why she'd said that. Brookes was too afraid of her not to stay awake.

.   .   .

PRESCOTT LISTENED TO the recordings of Eagleton talking to Hamilton and came to the same conclusion Hamilton had: that Otis was most likely the ringleader of the group that attacked Callahan. As she was still mulling this over, the large, gross form of Ackerman filled her office door.

"Got him," Ackerman said.

He dropped down into the chair in front of Prescott's desk, again without being invited to sit, and Prescott was surprised the chair didn't collapse under his weight. She noticed his pupils were dilated, and she wondered if he was using amphetamines to stay alert.

Ackerman said, "The e-mail went from a bozo named Kenneth Winston at Zytek to a gal named Jane Moore, who is actually a gal named Lin Mai, who works for our friends in the Chinese Trade Association on New York Avenue. Lin Mai, by the way, got on a plane to Beijing today. She checked four suitcases, so I think she may be gone for good. You see, what I did was write a subroutine that—"

"I'm sure you did something brilliant, Ackerman, but tell me how you did it later. Right now, just give me the e-mail, then go home and get some sleep."

After Ackerman left—disappointed that he hadn't been able to tell her exactly how he'd found Winston and Lin Mai and the e-mail that Parker had intercepted—she thought about the current state of play. She had confirmed that James Parker had been working for Danzinger; she had found the spy at Zytek and had proof that he worked for the Chinese; and, thanks to Hamilton, she knew Dylan Otis led the people who stole the safe. She didn't know if Lin Mai had ordered Otis to steal the safe or if some other Chinese operative was behind the break-in, but she didn't see that that really mattered. All that mattered was that Kenneth Winston was a Chinese spy and she'd caught him.

Prescott decided that she'd let Hamilton pursue things a bit longer and she'd continue to have Brookes monitor her. It would be good to know if another Chinese operative had been involved in the attack and to learn who else was working with Otis. It also occurred to her that if she ordered Hamilton to stop, she probably wouldn't.

But right now her problem wasn't Hamilton. She needed to focus on arresting and interrogating Winston. He had to be dealt with immediately.

PRESCOTT CALLED HER BOSS, the director of the NSA, a four-star army general, and filled him in on Winston, saying only that they'd intercepted an e-mail from Winston to a suspected Chinese intelligence officer and the e-mail contained information related to American submarine sonar systems. She didn't mention Danzinger, Callahan, or Parker. From this point forward, Parker would be remembered as a sad, depressed analyst who'd committed suicide. The general didn't ask if the e-mail had been legally intercepted. He was smart enough to know that he didn't want to know the answer to that question.

When the general asked Prescott what she planned to do, she said, "I'll coordinate with the FBI and Naval Intelligence, of course."

The general concluded with, "Good work. Keep me informed."

"Yes, sir," she said.

Prescott looked at her watch—it was almost eight p.m.—and then realized she didn't care what time it was. She called the appropriate people at the FBI and the Pentagon and suggested they all meet at the Pentagon in one hour.

Before she left the building, she stopped by Brookes's office for an update.

"Where's Hamilton now?"

"She's still sitting near Otis's house."

"Huh," Prescott said. What the hell was Hamilton planning?

. . .

PRESCOTT WAS THE LAST to arrive at the meeting, which was being held on the C ring of the Pentagon in a conference room with a table large enough to seat thirty people. There were two FBI agents, a three-star navy admiral, a two-star admiral, two captains, and two commanders. Prescott was the only woman present. She assumed the navy folks were either Naval Intelligence or technical types who understood sonar systems. She knew only one of the men—the three-star admiral—and she only knew him by reputation.

The man's name was Kincaid. While he wasn't physically impressive—he was about five-foot-nine, slim, thinning gray hair, pale blue eyes—what was impressive about Kincaid was his mind. He was a genius, possibly the smartest man to wear a navy uniform since Hyman Rickover, the man who had developed the first nuclear submarine. Kincaid had actually worked for Rickover when he was an ensign, and even Rickover had been impressed by Kincaid's intellect.

Prescott had always been worried that Kincaid might one day be appointed director of the NSA; she was worried because he was bright enough that he might be able to figure out she was funneling money to the Callahan Group. At the moment, Kincaid managed the Naval Sea Systems Command, the organization responsible for ship construction and modernization. The navy was about to start building a new class of nuclear aircraft carriers that would need fewer men to operate and would carry more planes and weapons. They would also be cheaper to construct and maintain than earlier models—and Kincaid was the person most responsible for the ground-breaking design. The Naval Sea Systems Command was also the organization that managed contractors who developed new technologies for submarines, such as sonar systems.

Prescott told the group what she knew about Winston and passed out three copies of the e-mail and its attachment. Kincaid just glanced at the attachment, then passed it to one of the commanders.

"How much damage has this guy done?" the senior FBI man asked.

Kincaid looked at the FBI agent like he was a fool, but didn't say anything. Prescott said, "We have no idea. Like I said, we intercepted just the one e-mail."

Kincaid turned to one of the captains and asked, "Do you know Winston?"

"Yes, sir," the captain said. "He's been at Zytek a long time and he's one of the main guys working on the sonar upgrade. He knows everything about the new system and could have given the Chinese everything."

"Well, we need to arrest him before he can do any more damage," the FBI man said.

Kincaid shook his head but didn't address the FBI man. "Did you intercept the e-mail from Winston to the Chinese legally?" he asked Prescott.

"It's a gray area," Prescott said.

Kincaid smiled slightly. "Yeah, that's what I thought."

"I can get a team in place by tomorrow to start tearing this guy's life apart," the FBI agent said. "And I know we can get a FISA warrant to start monitoring his communications. I suggest we watch him for a couple of weeks while we do the background work, then arrest him. Then we'll break him. Believe me, he'll tell us everything."

The senior FBI agent was a beefy, red-faced man who looked like he might have been a lineman on his college football team. He was a take-charge, full-speed-ahead type—even when he didn't know where he was headed.

Kincaid shook his head again. The FBI man was too busy talking to notice the gesture, but Prescott did.

"Do you disagree, Admiral?" Prescott asked.

Kincaid said, "Yes. I want everyone out of the room except the senior FBI agent and Ms. Prescott."

The room cleared—the two-star admiral miffed that he'd been booted out with men he outranked.

"This situation provides us a great opportunity," Kincaid said. "We shouldn't arrest Winston. We should leave him in place and let him keep feeding information to the Chinese."

"What?" the FBI man said.

Kincaid ignored him, speaking directly to Prescott. "I need to do an in-depth technical analysis for confirmation, but we may be able to use Winston to provide the Chinese information that will allow us to detect their submarines. We can turn their sonar systems into broadcasting stations and they won't even know it. Or we might be able to disable their systems remotely any time we choose. So, the NSA will get the proper FISA warrant to monitor all of Winston's communications, the FBI will begin watching him, and I'll complete the technical review. Then, at some point, we'll very quietly drag Winston into a room and tell him that he's become a double agent."

Prescott smiled. As far as she was concerned, everything regarding Danzinger and Winston had been brought to a successful conclusion. The only thing left was to get Hamilton under control.

19

Kay had been watching Dylan Otis's house for four and a half hours, and it was starting to grow dark outside. She'd been hoping that Otis would leave so she could question him—and she wouldn't be gentle. If Otis lived alone, she would have simply knocked on his door and pointed Eloise Voss's Beretta at his face and talked to him inside his house. But Otis was married and Kay had seen two boys who looked like they were about eight and ten.

At that moment, the door on the two-car garage attached to Otis's house rolled up and a black Toyota Tundra pickup with a crew cab backed out. Otis was driving. Kay smiled; this was the opportunity that she'd been waiting for.

She needed to be careful. Following the drunk, distraught Shirley Brown had been easy, but Dylan Otis was a different sort of animal. The good news was that it was almost dark and getting darker and Kay's car would just be a pair of headlights in Otis's rearview mirror. Twenty minutes later, Otis pulled into the empty parking lot of a high school in Falls Church. What the hell was he doing there?

Kay drove past the parking lot entrance, then made a U-turn and drove up the street and parked. There was a ball field on one side of the parking lot and the high school was on the other side. She put on a baseball cap and a jacket she kept in her car, tucked her hair up under the cap, and walked past the parking lot. It was still empty except for Otis's pickup.

This was the perfect place to grab Otis, but she figured he had to be waiting for someone. What other reason would he have for just sitting there? She crossed the street, walked back in the direction she'd come from, and continued until she found a gate to enter the ball field. It was elevated above the parking lot and she couldn't see Otis's pickup from where she was standing. She ran quickly across the field, then dropped to the ground onto her belly, crawled the final thirty yards to the edge of the field, and looked down at the parking lot. Otis was still alone, sitting in his pickup.

Five minutes later, a sedan arrived and a man got out. Otis left his vehicle and joined the man. There was only a single light near a walkway that led to the school, but it was too far away to illuminate the new man's face. All she could see was that he was slim and about an inch taller than Otis. *Damn it.* She needed to see his face.

FANG PARKED HIS CAR in the high school parking lot and got out carrying a gym bag that contained the remainder of Otis's fee.

As he had done on previous jobs, Otis had insisted on getting half of the money upfront. The only way Fang had been able to pay the first part of Otis's fee was in gold bars that the embassy had available; there hadn't been time to round up a million dollars in cash before the attack on Callahan's office. Tonight, however, Otis would receive the other million Fang had promised him, and it would be in good old-fashioned American greenbacks.

Fang walked up to Otis, who was standing next to his pickup truck.

Fang would never understand why anyone would want to drive a vehicle like that. It was so . . . pedestrian. "I'm disappointed you failed to kill Callahan, Mr. Otis."

"I can't believe the guy didn't die. He had two bullets in him." Then Otis frowned. "Are you saying you're not paying me because of that? You gave me no time to plan the job and two of my people were killed. You oughta be fuckin' grateful I was able to get the safe at all."

"Calm down, Mr. Otis. And I am grateful. You did an excellent job. I'm just disappointed that you didn't do everything I asked."

"So what are you saying? You want me to go after Callahan in the hospital?"

"No. There were complications following Callahan's surgery and he may yet die. And if he does need to be killed, I have someone else who can do the job."

Fang handed Otis the gym bag, and he unzipped it and looked inside, which Fang found somewhat insulting. Thankfully, Otis didn't waste time counting the money.

"We have a problem," Otis said.

"And what is that?" Fang asked. He noticed that Otis didn't mention there being a problem until he had the bag in his hand. Fang wondered if he could take Otis if he had to. Otis was a powerful man and he was certainly armed, but Fang, although not armed, had been trained to kill in numerous ways.

"A woman came to see Ray Brown's sister today," Otis said. "She told her that she'd frozen all her assets and wouldn't unfreeze 'em until Shirley gave her the names of the men Ray had been working with. She also said the bank was going to foreclose on her house. Shirley told her to go to hell and then came to see me."

"I see," Fang said. "So you're saying that Ms. Brown knows you did the job with her brother."

"Yeah. I always worked with Ray, and Ray told Shirley everything."

This was not good. "Are you concerned that Ms. Brown will give this woman your name?"

"No. Shirley would never do that."

"Are you sure? Maybe you should eliminate her. I mean, for your own safety."

"I'm not going to do that. Shirley's good people. Like I said, I know she'd never give me up. But I have to do something to help her out of the mess she's in. I can't let her lose her house."

"Who was the woman who threatened Ms. Brown?"

"I don't know," Otis said, "but the way Shirley described her, I think she might be the same woman who shot my other guy, Quinn."

"I see," Fang said. Hamilton. Fang could kick himself for not taking the security guard—who he was now sure was not a mere security guard—more seriously.

"But that's not the worst of it," Otis said. "This woman, whoever she is, told Shirley that Callahan's connected to national security. Is that true? Is Callahan connected in some way to the government?"

"No," Fang said. "She's lying."

"Then how was she able to freeze Shirley's accounts? Who but the government could do that?"

Fang smiled and shook his head as if Otis were being naïve. "It's funny," he said, "but people are always worried about the government spying on them and about the government's power. It's not the government that people should fear, Mr. Otis. It's people like me and the people this woman works for."

"What are you talking about?" Otis said.

"Like myself, Mr. Callahan works for a large, international company, and it would have been easy for his company to get into a bank's computer systems. In fact, I wouldn't be surprised if the company that Mr. Callahan works for owns the bank where Shirley Brown keeps her money. At any rate, the government is not involved, and I'm very sorry that Ms. Brown has been caught in the middle of all this."

"Yeah, but I have to do something to help her."

"Her problem is easy to solve," Fang said. "It just takes money. How much do you think her house is worth?"

"What? Shit, I don't know. Three, four hundred thousand."

"Fine. We'll pay off Ms. Brown's mortgage. I'll also have a lawyer speak to her bank. The lawyer will tell the bank that he will tell the media that their computer systems are vulnerable, that Ms. Brown's accounts have been hacked, and that she intends to sue for damages, distress, and whatever else the lawyer can think of. And when the bank looks into Ms. Brown's accounts, they will find out that they have indeed been hacked and they will unfreeze her assets. That may take some time, but in the meantime, you will give Ms. Brown her brother's share of the money."

"You'll do that? You'll pay off Shirley's mortgage?"

"The people I work for will," Fang said. Otis had no idea that Fang was employed by the Chinese government. "The stakes are very high, which was why you were paid so much in the first place. Another four hundred thousand is of no consequence." And for the Chinese government, it really wasn't.

"But what do we do about this woman who's looking for me?"

"I'm not sure," Fang said, and he was being honest. "But right now I'm inclined to do nothing."

"Nothing?"

"Yes. All that this woman appears to know is that Ms. Brown is Mr. Brown's sister. And if Ms. Brown refuses to tell her anything, then she'll have no other leads to follow."

"What if we kill her?" Otis said.

"That's always an option, but I'm not sure it would do much good. Like Mr. Callahan, she's an employee of an organization that has many employees, and if she's killed, someone will replace her. I think the best strategy at this point, as I said, is to do nothing and avoid exposing ourselves."

What he'd just told Otis wasn't exactly true. Fang always had the option of calling his young friend, Jamal Howard, and having him eliminate both Shirley and Otis if that should become necessary.

KAY STILL COULDN'T CLEARLY SEE the guy Otis was talking to and now his back was to her. She couldn't make out his license plate either, and she couldn't hear what they were saying to each other.

She wondered what was in the gym bag that the guy had given Otis. She had to get back to her car so she could follow him.

She started to scoot backward—away from the edge of the ball field where she lay—when the man talking to Otis got into his car and drove out of the lot. Goddamnit! She belly-crawled as fast as she could, and when she was far enough away from Otis, she got to her feet and sprinted to her car.

She jumped into the car and drove toward the parking lot exit. She hoped she'd be able to see the guy's taillights—but she couldn't. There was an intersection half a block from the parking lot, and she knew that the guy hadn't headed straight because she would have seen him. He'd taken either a left or a right, but she couldn't see taillights in either direction. *Shit!*

She made a U-turn and drove back to the parking lot. If she was fast enough, Otis would still be parked and she would make him tell her who the guy was. But she was too late. Otis was already pulling out onto the road.

She decided to follow Otis again. Maybe she'd get lucky and he'd stop someplace along the way, someplace where she could get him alone and question him.

OTIS LOOKED AT HIS WATCH. It was almost ten, but he called McCabe. "I'm on my way," he said. "I've got the second installment."

He called Simpson next but he didn't answer. Irritated because he'd told Simpson to stay by his phone, Otis left a message: *I'm headed to Billy's right now. Get there as fast as you can. I've got the second installment.*

He hesitated before he made the third call, but finally decided it was the right thing to do. He called Shirley Brown.

"Has that woman contacted you again?" Otis asked.

"No, that bitch. And my accounts are still frozen."

She sounded like she was drunk, but Otis needed to get Shirley her brother's share of the money. He could do that tomorrow, but he'd decided he wanted to get her out of her house and someplace where that woman couldn't squeeze her anymore.

"Are you sober enough to drive?" he asked.

"Yeah," she said. "Why?"

"You know how to get to Billy's place on the river?"

"Yeah, Ray and I went there a couple of times for barbecues."

"Good. I'm headed there now and I want you to meet me."

"Why?"

"Shirley, just meet me there. Okay? I've got some good news for you, but I'm not going to say any more on the phone."

"Okay," Shirley said, and Otis ended the call.

PRESCOTT DROVE BACK to Fort Meade after her meeting at the Pentagon, and the first thing she did was call Brookes to find out what Hamilton was doing.

"At about nine, she left Otis's place in Fairfax and drove to a high school in Falls Church."

"A high school?"

"Yeah. She was parked there for about twenty minutes, and now she's on the move again. I don't know where she's headed."

.   .   .

KAY WONDERED WHERE OTIS WAS GOING. She thought he would've headed back to his home, but he didn't. He headed south. Forty-five minutes later, outside the town of Lorton, he turned onto a narrow, unpaved road. Kay didn't follow him—he would spot her tailing him if she did—so she drove past the turnoff and parked. She pulled up Google maps and saw that the only thing at the end of the road was the Occoquan River. She was pretty sure that Otis was meeting someone; he certainly wasn't going fishing at eleven at night.

Kay parked and started to take a flashlight from the glove box, but then she looked outside and saw the pale half-moon. It would provide enough light to see by, and a flashlight beam bouncing around in the woods wouldn't be good. Holding the Beretta, she left the car and started down the road Otis had taken, moving cautiously, staying to one side of the road. There were trees and bushes on both sides, and if anyone else came down the road, she could hide in them.

Less than a hundred yards later, she could see lights ahead of her and a one-story, ranch-style house. It looked like one of those prefabricated, manufactured homes. Otis's pickup was parked near it and another pickup was in the carport. Off to one side of the house was an ATV and a boat on a trailer. She remembered that Quinn had a pit bull and that it had almost gnawed the arm off one of the deputies that had searched Quinn's house. She sure as hell hoped that whoever owned the house by the river didn't have a damn dog.

BROOKES CALLED PRESCOTT, who was still in her office. He could imagine her sitting there in the dark, like an ancient spider at the center of its web, waiting for some helpless prey to blunder into the sticky mesh.

"After she left the high school in Falls Church," Brookes said, "she drove to Lorton and stopped near the Occoquan River. Right now it looks like she's walking toward the river. There's a house close to where she parked, and it belongs to a guy named William McCabe. He's like Dylan Otis, another guy with a record for bank robberies."

Prescott hung up without saying anything, but Brookes, in his mind's eye, could see the spider's legs twitching.

Prescott scared the shit out of him. He knew that she had come to the agency in the late '80s with a doctorate in math and started out working on technical stuff, but she soon proved that she had the Machiavellian political skills to rise in a large, complex, backstabbing bureaucracy. She was there during the Cold War and the War on Terrorism, and every other war that the United States had fought in the last thirty years, and she found a way to make herself indispensable. Within the NSA, there was hardly anyone more powerful.

Rumors about her abounded. Some said she was gay, but one of the old hands said she'd had a male lover, a CIA officer who died in Afghanistan when the Afghans were fighting the Russians. Brookes had also heard that her older brother had died in the Marine barracks bombing in Lebanon in '83. If those stories were true, maybe they explained her fanaticism and why she did nothing but work. The only hobby she was known to have was photography, and the depressing photos in her office of leafless trees and collapsing barns and fallow fields had been taken by her. The one thing Brookes knew for sure was that crossing Olivia Prescott was tantamount to career suicide.

PRESCOTT FIGURED THAT MCCABE was one of the men who'd helped Otis steal Callahan's safe and Hamilton was now sneaking down toward his house. But what was Hamilton going to do?

The only logical conclusion was that Hamilton planned to question Otis to find out who'd hired him. But then what? It would be acceptable if she killed Otis and his pal, but the last thing Prescott wanted was Otis and McCabe being arrested for stealing Callahan's safe. She didn't want them talking to the police about who'd hired them. She didn't want anything to happen that might possibly interfere with Kincaid's plan to use Winston as a double agent.

She needed to stop Hamilton. She needed to tell her to back off until she had decided how she wanted to deal with Otis and his crew.

She picked up her phone and called Hamilton. The phone rang four times and went to voice mail, but Prescott didn't leave a message. She didn't want there to be a recording of her speaking to Hamilton.

Goddamnit! Now all she could do was sit back and see what Hamilton did next—and pray to God that she didn't turn Otis and McCabe over to anyone in law enforcement.

She also decided she didn't want Brookes monitoring Hamilton any longer. He didn't need to know more than he already did. She called Brookes and said, "Come to my office and set up your equipment so I can monitor Hamilton myself." Minutes later, Prescott was sitting at her desk, watching the red dot that was Hamilton's iPhone moving on a monitor toward the Occoquan River.

She told Brookes, "Go find a place to sleep, but stick around in case I need you."

"Yes, ma'am," he said.

20

Kay was still in the woods but now within fifty feet of the house by the river. She could hear the river but couldn't see it, and figured the front of the house faced it. Otis had parked his pickup by the back door, and she could see concrete blocks that served as steps leading up to a small porch and a window in the back door.

With her gun in her hand, she started forward—and the phone in her back pocket vibrated, startling her. Thank God she'd turned off the ringer. She looked at the caller ID screen but the number was blocked. She could think of only one person who could be calling her on the NSA iPhone: Olivia Prescott. But why was Prescott calling and why was she calling now? Most likely she wanted an update on what Kay was doing. Whatever the case, this was no time to have a conversation with Prescott or anyone else. She'd talk to Prescott after she'd dealt with Otis.

She continued forward until she reached the back of the house, then ascended the concrete block steps, staying low, keeping her head below the level of the back-door window, and crept forward until she could press her ear against the door. She didn't hear anything.

She turned the knob; it wasn't locked. After the homeowner had let

Otis in, he apparently hadn't seen any reason to lock the door. She decided to take a chance and raised her head for a quick look through the window. She could see the kitchen—a small table, appliances, a single unwashed plate on the kitchen counter—but she couldn't see Otis or whoever he was meeting.

Now what? Should she go in and try to take down Otis? If it was just Otis and one other guy, she was confident she could do it. They wouldn't be expecting her, and if she moved quickly, she'd be the only one holding a gun. But she wasn't sure how many people were in the house. If there were more than two, the situation could get unmanageable in a hurry.

Screw it. She was going in. Once she was inside and had the drop on Otis, she'd make him tell her who had hired him. She'd make him give her the name of the man he met in Falls Church. She wasn't sure *how* she'd make him talk, but one way or the other, Otis was going to give her what she wanted.

She turned the doorknob and entered the house. She could hear a man talking, but didn't know if it was Otis or someone else. She crept through the kitchen until she could see Otis and a younger man who was about thirty. They were sitting in the living room, the man on an old brown leather couch, Otis in a rocking chair near a potbellied, wood-burning stove. On a coffee table in front of the couch were stacks of bills and small gold bars. It was a *shitload* of money.

Kay stepped into the living room. Both men were startled and began to stand up, but she shouted, "Don't move! I'll shoot both of you. I swear to God I will. Just stay where you are."

Otis was wearing jeans and a plain blue T-shirt. The other man wore a sleeveless wifebeater and cargo shorts. Neither of them appeared to have a weapon.

"Put your hands on your knees," she said. Both men did. They were surprisingly calm—they'd probably had guns pointed at them before.

"If you take your hands off your knees," Kay said, "I'm going to shoot you. Who else is here?"

"Nobody," the younger guy said. Then he added, "You're the one who killed Quinn, aren't you." Again she noticed how relaxed he seemed, and then smelled the odor of marijuana. He was high, but not so high that he wasn't able to function.

"That's right," Kay said. "I killed Quinn and I'll kill you two if you force me to. What's your name?"

"Billy," the man said.

Speaking to Otis, she said, "I want to know who hired you to take the safe from Callahan's office. And I want to know who you met with tonight in Falls Church."

"You followed me to the school?" Otis said.

"Yeah. I followed Shirley to your place, then followed you to Falls Church. So who hired you?"

Kay could tell that Otis felt like a fool for having allowed her to tail him, but he didn't answer her question.

"Otis, I'm not screwing around here," Kay said. "I don't care about you—you're just hired help—and I don't care about all that gold and cash on the coffee table. Give me a name or I'm going to shoot Billy. Then I might as well shoot you, too."

THANKS TO THE PHONE Hamilton was carrying, Prescott could hear everything. The sound quality was excellent. But who was the man in Falls Church whom Otis had met? Was he another Chinese operative? It sounded like she'd find out pretty soon, because she had no doubt that Hamilton would get the information she was after. But the next thing Prescott heard was a woman's voice saying, "Hey, Billy, where the fuck are you guys?"

OH, GOD, KAY THOUGHT. It was Shirley Brown, and she sounded drunk. Her damn Prius was so quiet that Kay hadn't heard it approaching

Billy's house. Shirley stepped into the living room and when she saw Kay, her eyes widened in shock.

Kay pointed the Beretta at her and was about to tell her to sit down on the couch next to Billy, but then Shirley did the very last thing she expected.

"You bitch!" she screamed—and she charged at Kay.

It had never occurred to Kay that the damn woman would do something so stupid. She had less than a second to react; less than a second to decide if she should shoot Shirley. But she hesitated and then Shirley smashed into her, knocking her backward into a wide-screen television that was on a low table. She heard the television crash to the floor, and then she lost her balance when the back of her knees hit the table. Now she was on the floor with Shirley on top of her, and Shirley took a swing at her face. Kay was able to move her head enough so that the blow hit her on the side of the head instead of in the face, but it still hurt.

As soon as Shirley slammed into her, Otis and Billy came at her like a couple of linebackers blitzing a quarterback. Kay tried to aim the gun at Otis but didn't have a chance with Shirley pummeling her. Otis clamped one big hand over her right wrist and ripped the Beretta out of her hand. Shirley, still cursing, hit Kay again—this time on her left cheekbone— but before she could swing again, Billy pulled Shirley off her. When Kay looked up from the floor, Otis was pointing her own gun at her.

"Okay," Otis said. "Now *you* go sit on the couch."

PRESCOTT DIDN'T KNOW exactly what was going on but it sounded like Hamilton was in trouble. A minute later, Prescott was positive she was.

"WHAT'S YOUR NAME?" Otis said.

Kay thought about lying, but she had her wallet in the left-hand back pocket of her jeans with her driver's license, and they would find it if they searched her. In the other back pocket of her jeans was the cell phone Prescott had provided. "My name's Hamilton," Kay said.

"Who do you work for?"

"Callahan. The guy you shot."

"What are we going to do with her, Otis?" Billy said. He was holding on to Shirley's upper right arm, restraining her from attacking Hamilton again.

"I don't know," Otis said to Billy.

"Well, I think we oughta dump the bitch into the river," Billy said.

"Not until she unfreezes my bank accounts," Shirley screamed, and then she made a move toward Kay, but Billy yanked her back.

"Goddamnit, Shirley, settle down," Otis said. Then he added, "And you gotta knock off the boozing. Now go sit down over there in the rocking chair."

WHEN BILLY SAID, "We oughta dump the bitch into the river," Prescott thought: *Hamilton, you should have answered when I called.*

OTIS COULDN'T DECIDE what to do.

If John had told him the truth, Hamilton was a cog in a big machine and his troubles wouldn't end by simply killing her. But at the very least, he needed to know how much she knew and who else she'd told.

"I'm not going to lose my house because of her," Shirley said. Then she screamed at Kay, "I'll get a knife and cut your fucking nose off if you don't unfreeze my money. You won't be so pretty then. In fact, I'm gonna get a knife right now."

Shirley got up out of the rocking chair and Otis hit her in the chest with his open palm, pushing her back down.

"Shirley, knock it the fuck off. I gotta think."

The night was supposed to have been about splitting up the cash, but the situation was quickly unraveling. It got worse when Hamilton said, "You guys have stepped into a national security shit pile. There were classified documents in Callahan's safe."

"Oh, bullshit," Otis said, but he wondered if she was telling the truth.

Someone was lying, either her or John, but which one? John had said this was a private sector thing, one big company going after another. Otis had always assumed John was American—Chinese-American, but American. But now he wasn't so sure and had the horrible feeling that the person telling the truth was Hamilton.

"Otis, what about my bank accounts?" Shirley screamed. "What about my house?"

Otis had to get Shirley out of there. He couldn't think with all her screaming. He also didn't want her to see him kill Hamilton if it came to that. He didn't want Shirley to be an accomplice to murder, but more important, he didn't want her to be a witness to a murder.

"Billy," Otis said, "I'm going to take Shirley to a motel in Lorton, and then you and I will deal with this."

"I'm not going anywhere," Shirley said.

"Yeah, you are, Shirley. You gotta lay low someplace. Nobody's looking for you, but the way you're drinking, you're a problem for me and Billy and an even bigger problem to yourself. And you don't need to worry about your house or your bank accounts. That's being taken care of."

"How?"

"I'll explain on the way to the motel. I'm driving you because you're too fucking drunk and the last thing we need right now is you getting pulled over. Billy, you got any booze in the house?"

"Yeah. Sure."

"Get a bottle for Shirley." Otis figured that Shirley would drink until she passed out, and that was the best condition she could be in right now. He would take her cell phone when he dropped her off.

Otis handed Billy Hamilton's Beretta. "Keep that gun pointed at her while I'm gone. She tries anything, just fuckin' shoot her. And I mean it. Just shoot her."

"How do you know a SWAT team isn't going to come through the door any minute now?" Billy asked.

"That's not going to happen. If she had backup, they would have been with her when she came into the house. She's on her own. We'll find out why and what she knows when I get back."

But Otis was already starting to think that maybe the smartest thing to do at this point was run. This whole thing was getting way out of hand.

PRESCOTT WAS THINKING that if she wanted to, she could send in a team to rescue Hamilton. She could have an armed NSA security force in a helicopter in five minutes and they could probably be in Lorton in less than half an hour.

But there was no way she was going to do that.

How could she possibly justify sending NSA agents into Virginia for a civilian who had no official connection to the agency? And what would she do with Otis and Billy if they were captured? Everything she could do to save Hamilton could result in exposing herself and her connection to the Callahan Group and she couldn't allow that.

She also no longer needed Hamilton. As far as she was concerned, it didn't really matter that the men who shot Callahan would never be brought to justice. She wasn't in the justice business. Nor was she in the revenge business.

It was really a shame about Hamilton, but she'd gotten herself into this situation and had no one to blame but herself. She also couldn't help but think that if Hamilton was killed, she wouldn't have to worry about her ever talking about Prescott's connection to the Callahan Group. Yes, it was regrettable, but it would be best for everyone if Hamilton was gone.

21

Billy was a good-looking guy: short blond hair, two or three days of stubble, solid pecs, big biceps, tats on both arms. He seemed completely relaxed—probably thanks to the pot he'd been smoking—but he was also alert. He made Kay think of a happy guard dog, but one that would still bite your head off if you made the wrong move.

Kay pointed at the money sitting on the coffee table, the stacks of gold bars and cash. "The smartest thing you could do right now is take that money and leave before Otis gets back. There must be over a million there. Throw it in a suitcase and split. Buy yourself a nicer place on a nicer river far away from here."

Billy laughed.

"The people I work for don't care about the money, so if you take it, we're not going to come after you. All I want is the name of the guy who hired you."

"We killed a couple of people," Billy said.

"But are you the one who killed them?"

"No. I didn't kill anybody. I tried to kill you after you shot Quinn, but you ducked into that room before I could."

"The point is, Billy, if you're telling the truth, you didn't kill any-one. And even if you're lying, I don't care. This thing you stepped into is bigger than murder. It's bigger than the money. So take the money and run, but before you do, give me a name."

Billy smiled. "That's not going to happen, honey."

She could see she wasn't going to convince him, and she'd better come up with something soon. Otis could be back any minute.

She needed to get closer to Billy, close enough to hurt him. She also needed some kind of weapon.

"I need to go to the bathroom," she said.

"Nah, you can hold it."

"Come on, Billy. Are you afraid of me? You're the one with the gun. All I want to do is take a pee. Do you want me to pee on your couch?"

Billy hesitated for a second. "Yeah, okay. But if you try anything, I will shoot you."

"Trust me when I tell you that the last thing you want to do is shoot me. The people I work for will track you down and throw you into a hole for the rest of your life. There won't even be a trial."

IN HER DARK OFFICE, Prescott muttered, "Oh, Billy, you fool."

KAY ROSE TO HER FEET. "Where's the bathroom?"

Billy pointed to a hallway that she assumed led back to the bed-rooms. He stayed about five feet behind her as she walked, which wasn't good. He needed to be closer for her to do anything. She reached the bathroom and started to step inside when he said, "Hold it."

She stopped and he came up behind her and placed the Beretta directly against her spine. "I want to make sure you don't have another gun. I'd feel kinda stupid if you shot me."

He ran his left hand over her body. When he felt the phone in her back pocket, he removed it and put it in one of his pockets. He finished frisking her, paying particular attention to her lower legs, making sure she wasn't wearing an ankle holster.

"Okay," he said.

Kay stepped into the bathroom and walked over to the toilet. She started to undo the top button on her jeans, then stopped. "Close the door," she said.

"I don't think so."

"I never figured you for a pervert, Billy. Are you going to stand there and watch me? Or maybe you're one of those golden shower guys, and what you'd really like is if I peed on you."

Billy's face reddened, not from anger but from embarrassment. He started to pull the door shut, but before he closed it, he said, "The window doesn't open and if you break it and try to get out, I'll hear you and I'll shoot you in the back. I use an electric shaver not a razor, so there's no point looking in the medicine cabinet."

He closed the door.

Kay pulled down her jeans and peed, figuring Billy would be listening at the door. She used toilet paper, stood up, buttoned her jeans, then pulled the toilet paper dispenser out of its recess in the wall. She put the roll of toilet paper on the window ledge next to the toilet, flushed the toilet, walked over to the sink, and ran the water so Billy would think she was washing her hands. While the water was running, she disassembled the toilet paper dispenser.

It was a standard dispenser consisting of two pieces of hollow aluminum tubing and a spring. She dropped one half of the dispenser and the spring into the wastebasket next to the toilet and palmed the other half. She turned off the water and opened the door. She didn't think Billy would notice the roll of toilet paper sitting on the window ledge because she'd be blocking his view as she came out of the bathroom.

Billy was down the hall, to her right, when she stepped into the hallway. He again stayed four or five feet behind her as she walked back toward the living room. She had to get closer to him. As soon as they stepped into the living room, she stopped abruptly and pointed with her left hand at the television set lying on the floor.

"Sorry about your TV, Billy," she said. "It looks like the screen's cracked."

But she didn't move—and then he did just what she wanted him to do: He prodded her in the back with the barrel of the Beretta and said, "Go sit back down on—"

As soon as the barrel touched her, she swung around fast, right arm extended, and hit him on the right side of the head, on the corner of his right eye.

When the tube hit him, Billy screamed in pain and staggered to his left from the blow. By now Kay had completed her spin and was facing him, and she struck again with the tube, hitting him again in the face. She aimed for his left eye, hoping to blind him completely, but missed and hit his forehead.

Billy staggered backward and raised the Beretta, but Kay hit him one more time in the face with her fist. She hit him hard on the nose and heard a satisfying crunch. Billy was now almost blind and his nose was bleeding, but he was still holding the gun, so Kay did the only thing she could do: She ran.

She ran through the living room to reach the corner that turned into the kitchen. She prayed that Billy wouldn't shoot her in the back. He shot, but his shot went high and to the right, just missing her head. Kay reached the corner, barreled through the kitchen, and banged through the back door.

But she didn't run when she got outside. She figured that Billy would be right behind her, and if he could see her at all, he'd shoot. So she stood to the side of the back door, her back against the wall, and when Billy came running through the door, she stuck out her foot and tripped him. He fell face-first down the concrete block steps and hit his head hard on the last step.

Kay jumped off the porch and kicked him in the head as hard as she could. But she didn't knock him unconscious as she'd been hoping to— Billy had a hard fucking head. Although Billy was dazed by the kick, he was still holding the gun. So she kicked him a second time, then stomped hard on his hand and reached down and ripped the gun from his hand.

She backed up so she was five or six feet from him. She'd just beaten the shit out of him, but he *still* wasn't finished. He started to get to his feet—maybe he was so dazed that he didn't realize she was holding the gun—and Kay yelled, "Stop! Stay on the ground."

But Billy didn't stop. The damn guy got to his feet, staggered a bit, then lunged toward her—and she shot him in the chest. No hesitation at all this time.

PRESCOTT DIDN'T KNOW what was going on. She'd heard Hamilton tell Billy to close the bathroom door and the idiot did. The next thing she heard was Hamilton say something about Billy's television screen being cracked, and then she heard someone cry out in pain. It was hard to be sure, but it sounded like it came from Billy, not Hamilton. After that, she heard what sounded like a fight, someone being punched, and then a gunshot. Then there were more punching sounds, and finally Hamilton said, "Stop! Stay on the ground"—and then another gunshot.

KAY WAS BREATHING HARD as she stood looking down at Billy's body. She stood until her breathing slowed and she could think clearly. She bent down, pressed the barrel of the Beretta against Billy's head, and checked for a pulse. Nothing. For a brief moment she felt sorry for him. Then she thought about Callahan and his people, and stopped feeling sorry.

She would wait for Otis to come back and make him talk. She grabbed Billy by the feet and dragged his body around the side of the house so Otis wouldn't see it when he drove up. She started to go back to the house, then remembered that Billy had her cell phone. She found it in one of the leg pockets of his cargo shorts.

She walked back into the house and did her best to remove her fingerprints while she waited for Otis. She washed the blood off the half of the toilet paper dispenser she'd used on Billy, wiped down the other parts of the dispenser, then reassembled it and put it back where it belonged. The only other things she'd touched in the house were the flush handle on the toilet, the bathroom doorknob, and the back-door doorknob. She wiped them all down.

She glanced at her watch. Otis ought to be back soon.

22

Kay studied Billy's house the way a general would analyze a potential battlefield, trying to figure out the best way to use the terrain to her advantage. Off to the side of the kitchen was a laundry room. She stepped into it and partially shut the door. Ten minutes later, she heard Otis open the back door.

Otis walked into the house and Kay could see him through the crack in the laundry room door as he passed through the kitchen. She heard him call out from the living room, "Billy! Where are you?"

Kay stepped out of the laundry room and walked into the living room. Otis's back was to her; he was looking down at the pile of gold and cash on the coffee table. Then he turned—and she shot him in the left knee. He dropped to the floor, landing on his side, and started to reach behind his back as Kay said, "If you pull out a gun, the next bullet is going to be in your head." Otis stopped.

Kay walked over to him, keeping the gun pointed at his face. "Roll over onto your stomach," she said.

Otis rolled over and she pulled out the .45 he had in the waistband of his jeans and tossed it on the couch.

"Okay," she said, "now roll back over so you can look at me." Otis rolled onto his back.

"Where's Billy?" he asked through clenched teeth.

Otis's eyes were closed and his face was contorted because of the pain. Kay could recall banging her kneecap a couple of times—and it always hurt like a son of a bitch. She wondered how much worse the pain would be from a bullet.

"Open your eyes," she said, "and look at me."

Otis complied.

"Billy's dead."

"How did you—"

"Listen to me, Otis. Tell me who hired you. If you don't, I'll put a bullet in your other knee. Nobody's going to hear gunshots out here."

"You're going to kill me anyway," Otis said.

"Not necessarily," Kay said. "I tried to tell Billy that, but he didn't believe me. I don't care about you; I just want the guy who hired you. Give me what I want, and I'll leave. I can always find you again if I need to."

Otis didn't respond.

"Otis, you're running out of time."

"I don't know his real name. He goes by 'John' but—"

"Okay, have it your way," Kay said, and aimed the gun at his right knee.

"Wait a minute! I'm telling you the truth. I don't know his name. He called himself John. He's a Chinese guy but—"

"Chinese-Chinese or Chinese-American?"

"I don't know. He doesn't have an accent."

"Not good enough," Kay said, and again aimed the gun at his right knee.

"Hold it! I know where he lives. I did another job for him once and I had Billy follow him after we got paid. I wanted to know more about him. He lives on the corner of Utah and Tennyson in the District. I looked at property records, but the house is owned by a property management company."

"What's the address?"

"I don't remember. It was two years ago."

Kay believed that the house belonged to a company. If "John" worked for the Chinese government, the house wouldn't be in his name. And it was fairly close to the Chinese embassy.

Now what? What should she do with Otis?

Kay had killed nine men in her life: four drug dealers in Miami; three men who'd been involved in Callahan's disastrous Afghanistan operation; and Quinn and Billy. She'd also caused the deaths of two other men in Mexico, the cartel men who'd kidnapped her daughter. But each time she'd killed, it had been an act of self-defense. She wasn't an executioner. She believed that capital punishment should be carried out by the state, not vigilantes. But she couldn't allow Otis to be arrested and tried, because he might expose the Callahan Group. She also couldn't let Otis live, because he would probably call John and warn him that she was coming for him.

She didn't see that she had a choice. Whether she wanted to be an executioner or not, she was going to become one.

She aimed the gun at Otis's head, but before she could pull the trigger, she heard a motorcycle coming fast down the road. Who the hell was it? Whoever it was, she was going to have to deal with him as well.

A moment later, Kay heard the back door open—apparently nobody knocked when visiting Billy—and a man called out, "Hey, Billy!" Kay was ready to shoot, but Otis screamed, "Simpson. She's got a gun. Don't come in here. Kill her."

"Shit!" Kay muttered. She thought about killing Otis right then, but he had already given her the location of the guy who'd planned the attack, and she didn't see the point of getting into a gunfight with Simpson, whoever the hell he was. Then a man stepped partway out of the kitchen with a gun in his hand. Before he could shoot, Kay fired off a shot to keep him pinned down, then sprinted for the front door.

As she was leaving, she heard Otis yell, "Get her, Simpson, get her!"

Kay's last thought as she went through the door was: *Left my finger-prints on the doorknob.*

As Kay had expected, the front of Billy's house faced the Occoquan River, which was about seventy feet away. The front yard was only about a hundred feet wide, and on both sides of the house was untended forest, the trees fairly close together. Kay ran for the woods. With only the moonlight to guide her, she could barely see where she was running. She made it to the tree line and looked back at the house.

A man holding a gun stepped into the front yard—Simpson, she presumed. She realized that he must have been the driver of the U-Haul because the rest of Otis's crew was dead.

She couldn't see Simpson's features, just that he was another big guy, like Otis, who appeared to be in good shape. She thought about shooting him but knew she wasn't likely to fatally hit him from sixty or seventy feet. In fact, she might not hit him at all, and if she missed, he'd see the muzzle flash from her weapon and know where she was. So she wouldn't take the shot, but if he followed her into the woods, she'd kill him.

Simpson stood there looking around for a couple of minutes, then went back into the house. He knew she was armed and was probably afraid to hunt for her in the dark. He wasn't a total idiot.

Kay started walking back toward her car, moving as quickly as she could in the darkness. She wanted to get to Utah and Tennyson as soon as possible. Then she stopped. She could see Otis's pickup parked in Billy's backyard and had an idea. She sneaked over to it, keeping her eye on the back door in case Simpson came out, opened the passenger-side door, and placed her cell phone under the seat. Now Prescott's technicians would be able to track Otis using the phone. It occurred to her then that Prescott could have been using the iPhone to track her movements, but if she had done that, Kay didn't see that it mattered. Later, she realized it mattered very much.

Ten minutes later, Kay was back in her car, headed toward Washington. It was time to get John, whoever he was.

PRESCOTT COULDN'T HEAR ANYTHING. She'd heard one shot after Simpson arrived and wondered if he'd killed Hamilton. But she doubted that. Hamilton was just too damn good—or too damn lucky.

23

H ow bad are you hit?" Simpson asked Otis.

"Bad. She blew out my knee. Go into the bathroom and see if you can find something to stop the bleeding."

"We gotta get moving," Simpson said, "before the cops get here. I'll help you—"

"She's not going to call the cops. She's going after the guy who hired us."

"Are you sure?" Simpson asked.

"Yeah. Go find a first aid kit."

Otis thought briefly about calling John to warn him that Hamilton was coming for him, but decided not to, at least not now. He was in too much pain and needed to focus on his own situation. John could look out for himself—plus he suspected that John had lied to him about who he worked for.

Simpson came back holding a white box with a red cross on it. He cut Otis's jeans with a jackknife and placed two big Band-Aids over the entry wound—there was no exit wound—then wrapped tape around the knee to make sure the Band-Aids stayed in place.

"Where were you when I called you," Otis said. He'd been pissed that Simpson hadn't answered when he'd called him earlier, but now he was glad. If Simpson hadn't arrived when he did, Otis was sure that Hamilton would have killed him.

"After the job, I went to see my mom and I forgot to take the damn burner phone into the house with me. Stupid, I know, but I'm not used to having a second phone. Anyway, when I got your message I headed over here as soon as I could. Sorry."

"Well, I'm not. You saved my life."

"Where's Billy?" Simpson asked.

"That woman killed him, or so she said. Take a look outside and see if you can find him."

"What if she's still out there?"

"Be careful," Otis said—and Simpson laughed.

Simpson came back a couple of minutes later. "Billy's dead. She shot him. And it looks like she beat the hell out of him first. Who was that woman?"

"Her name's Hamilton. She's the murderous bitch who killed Quinn."

Otis pointed at the piles of cash and gold bars sitting on the coffee table. "Put all that back into the big gym bag and bring Billy's body inside. He doesn't have many friends, so it could be weeks before any-one figures out he's dead. Then put your Harley in the back of my pickup. Billy's got some ramps outside that he uses to get his ATV onto a trailer."

"Okay," Simpson said, "but why?"

"Did you see the Prius?" Otis asked.

"Yeah."

"It belongs to Ray's sister, so we need to get it out of here. It's too long a story to go into, but I took Shirley to a motel in Lorton, where she's probably passed out. Anyway, we gotta get the Prius out of here and we can't leave your bike here for somebody to find."

"Are you going to be able to drive?" Simpson asked.

"Yeah. My truck's an automatic, so I can drive just using my right leg. Anyway, we'll drop off Shirley's car, and then you and I . . . Simpson, we're going to have to run. We're up against some really bad people, and we need to find a place to hide where they can't find us."

PRESCOTT STILL COULDN'T HEAR ANYTHING, but the GPS monitor showed that Hamilton's phone was still near the Occoquan River. What was she doing?

AFTER DOING EVERYTHING Otis had told him to do, Simpson asked, "We ready to go?"

"No. One more thing. Find a rag or something and get rid of prints. Doorknobs, these chairs, the bathroom. Then find some bleach and slop it everywhere you see blood."

Five minutes later, Simpson helped Otis out to the pickup, then he got into Shirley Brown's Prius and followed Otis to Lorton.

PRESCOTT HEARD A CAR DOOR SLAM and saw Hamilton's phone begin to move. The only thing she could hear was a man who sounded like he was groaning in pain. It was probably Otis. But if Hamilton's cell phone was with Otis, where was Hamilton?

Hamilton's phone was now moving toward Lorton, and fifteen minutes later it stopped near a motel. Prescott heard a man say, "Help me out of the truck. I need to talk to Shirley."

Fifteen minutes later, Hamilton's phone was moving south. There were now two men in the vehicle, and they were going on and on about Otis's knee and the trouble they were in. At one point Otis asked, "Are you sure this guy's all right?"

"Yeah, Younger's a good guy. He'll let us stay at his place," Simpson said.

Prescott drummed her fingers on the desk. It was obvious that Hamilton wasn't following Otis and Simpson. She was going after the man who lived on the corner of Utah and Tennyson.

Prescott no longer wanted to listen to Otis and Simpson whine, but decided it might be prudent to keep tabs on them. She called an agent named Beckman. The fact that it was now after one in the morning didn't bother Prescott at all.

Prescott liked Beckman. She was a young, attractive woman and reminded Prescott in some ways of Kay Hamilton: gutsy and smart, but a bit too mouthy for Prescott's taste.

Prescott told Beckman about the cell phone in Otis's truck and told her to use portable monitoring equipment to follow Otis and Simpson and report back. If the men split up, she was to stick with Otis. She said Beckman could get a mug shot of Otis from Brookes but it would be several years old. "By the way," Prescott said, "Otis and Simpson are armed, so try not to get killed."

Prescott called Brookes and told him to begin monitoring Hamilton's personal cell phone, then called two other agents, a couple of reliable old warhorses named Tate and Towers. She described Hamilton and told them to head down to the corner of Utah and Tennyson immediately and watch for Hamilton, making damn sure that Hamilton didn't catch them. If she did, Prescott wouldn't fire them; she would send them to an NSA listening post off North Korea, where they would remain until the end of their careers.

24

F orty minutes after leaving Billy's house on the Occoquan River, Kay was parked on the corner of Utah and Tennyson. She didn't know which of the four corner houses belonged to the man whom Otis called John. There were no lights on in any of them, which was what you'd expect at this time of night.

Three and a half hours later, the sun rose and Kay could see the houses more clearly. One of them had a kid's big-wheel tricycle in the front yard, turned over on its side. Another was a mess: the yard untended, the siding in need of a coat of paint. There was no way to tell which house belonged to John, so Kay hoped that the occupants would venture outside soon so that she could see if one of them was Asian.

She thought about calling Prescott with an update but decided not to. She didn't want to get into an argument with her about what she was doing or give Prescott the chance to stop her. Which made her think about the call Prescott had made to her while she'd been sneaking toward Billy's house. She sure as hell hoped that Prescott didn't call again, not with the phone, even though the ringer was off, sitting under the passenger's seat of Otis's truck. In any case, she wasn't going to talk to Prescott until after she'd identified John.

Two hours later, at seven a.m., while Kay was fighting to stay awake and dying for a cup of coffee, a woman came out of the house with the big-wheel trike, tugging on the arm of a truculent boy. They got into a car parked in front of the house and drove away. At seven thirty, an overweight woman in her fifties came out of another house, carrying a briefcase, and trudged slowly down the street, most likely toward a bus or Metro stop. She moved like she was walking to her own execution.

At eight a.m., a taxi pulled up in front of the third house, and a moment later, a tall, very striking Asian man dressed in an expensive suit came out. The guy looked like a damn movie star. She didn't know for sure if this was the man she was looking for, but he had the same height and build of the man she had seen at the high school in Falls Church.

The man got into the cab and Kay followed. When the cab pulled up in front of the gates of the Chinese embassy, she was sure she was following the man Otis called John.

Kay thought about going back to his house and breaking in so she could ID him, but then thought, why take the risk? She no longer had the NSA phone but she still had her personal cell. If she could get the guy's picture, Prescott could probably identify him.

She parked across from the embassy in a No Parking zone. She needed John to leave so she could snap a headshot, and wondered how long she'd have to wait. She would have killed for a cup of coffee and a donut. Having nothing better to do, she called Eli.

"How's Callahan doing?" she asked.

"Better. The nurses told Henry that the antibiotics are beating back the infection and the pneumonia. He's still not out of the woods, but things are looking up."

"You still have Henry watching him?"

"Yeah. What have you been doing?"

She hesitated. "I don't want to say too much over the phone, but I found the guys who put Callahan in the hospital. I took care of one of them but couldn't finish the job. I'll explain everything the next time I see you. Right now I'm waiting for the guy who was behind the whole operation."

"Jesus, Kay. Are you by yourself?"

"Yeah, but I'm safe."

"Where are you? I'll meet you."

"No. I just want to ID this guy. Look, I gotta go now. I think I see him coming."

She didn't see anyone coming. She just didn't want to argue with Eli.

AT TWELVE THIRTY—about lunchtime—John did come out of the embassy. He was with a short, plump Chinese woman. They were chatting; John seemed completely relaxed. They stood on the curb, apparently wait-ing for a cab. John glanced over at Kay but she wasn't concerned. As far as Kay knew, John had never seen her before. She was just a woman parked in a car looking at her cell phone.

She rolled down the driver's-side window and snapped John's pic-ture when he wasn't looking in her direction. It was a profile shot but good enough for facial recognition. She had what she wanted. Now it was just a matter of making Prescott tell her who this guy really was.

FANG ZHOU WAS with the ambassador's secretary. He suspected the woman was in love with him. She bored him to tears and she was unbe-lievably homely, but he took her to lunch periodically, sent her small gifts and flowers occasionally, and once took her to a show at the Ken-nedy Center. He tolerated her company because she kept him informed of things the ambassador was doing, including anything the ambassador said about him. He knew the ambassador was not his friend, and Fang was glad he had someone to watch him.

As Fang and the secretary passed through the embassy gate, he glanced across the street and saw an attractive blonde parked in a No Parking zone.

"So where would you like to go for lunch today?" Fang asked the ambassador's secretary, and she named a place they'd been to before, a place that served oversized portions the woman clearly didn't need.

As they waited for a cab, the secretary began to prattle on about something the ambassador's wife had said to her, apparently something rude, but Fang wasn't listening. He was thinking about the operation. As best he could tell, the bold actions he'd taken had succeeded. At least there'd been no reports of a Chinese spy being arrested at Zytek. He looked over to see if the pretty blonde was still parked across the street, but she was gone.

PRESCOTT WAS EXHAUSTED. She'd spent the entire night in her office and had only caught a brief nap on her couch. She wondered if anyone would notice she was wearing the same clothes she'd been wearing yesterday.

Tate and Towers—the team she'd assigned to watch Hamilton— had been giving her periodic updates. They'd caught up with Hamilton at about two in the morning. She was sitting in her car on the corner of Utah and Tennyson. At eight a.m., Tate had called again and said that Hamilton had followed an Asian man to the Chinese embassy.

Shit, Prescott thought, but she didn't think Hamilton would be insane enough to go after a Chinese diplomat. She asked Tate if he got a picture of the man and he said yes and e-mailed it to Prescott. The NSA had files on everyone at the embassy—including cooks and gardeners—and ten minutes later Prescott knew that the man in the photograph was a cultural attaché named Fang Zhou.

At twelve thirty p.m., Tate reported that Fang had left the embassy accompanied by a Chinese woman, and right after that, Hamilton had driven to M Street in Georgetown.

Thank God, Prescott thought. At least Hamilton wasn't following Fang any longer. But what the hell was she doing on M Street?

NOW THAT KAY HAD JOHN'S PICTURE, she decided it was time to call Prescott. She also decided it was time for lunch and drove to Georgetown, miraculously finding a parking spot.

She couldn't remember Prescott's private number—that had been in the contacts directory in the NSA iPhone now in Otis's truck—so she once again called the NSA operator, said that her name was Kay Hamilton, and she needed to speak to Olivia Prescott.

Prescott came on the line snarling. "Why in the hell do you keep calling me through the operator? What do you want?"

"I've got a picture of the guy who ordered the attack on Callahan's office. Give me your e-mail address and I'll send it to you. I need you to identify him."

"No!" Prescott screamed. "You have no idea what's going on right now and how much damage you can cause, and I mean damage to the United States. We need to talk, but not on a phone."

"Then why did you call me last night?" Kay asked.

"I didn't call you. I don't know what you're talking about."

Kay suspected Prescott was lying about not calling last night as she was approaching Billy's house, but before she could say so, Prescott said, "I want you to come to Fort Meade. Immediately."

"I don't think so," Kay said. She could see herself leaving Fort Meade in the back of a windowless van with a black hood over her head. She would meet Prescott someplace public. "I'm at Clyde's in Georgetown, in the back room where they have all the hanging ferns. I'll give you an hour to get here."

She hung up before Prescott could scream at her again.

PRESCOTT WALKED INTO THE RESTAURANT, looking mad enough to kill. Kay had just finished a steak lunch and was now having a glass of iced tea. She'd felt like having a martini to celebrate, but it was too early in the day for a cocktail, and considering that she hadn't slept in over thirty hours, a martini might put her right to sleep.

Prescott sat across from her and immediately said, "Tell me what you've been doing."

Kay almost said, "You first," but decided not to.

"I found out that a guy named Dylan Otis was in charge of the crew who attacked Callahan's office."

"Yes, go on," Prescott said, which surprised Kay. She'd expected Prescott to ask how she found Otis, but she didn't, and Kay got the impression that Prescott already knew about him. But how could that be?

"Otis told me that he did the job for a Chinese guy named John. He didn't know John's real name, but he had John's address."

"Then what?" Prescott said—which again struck Kay as odd.

"I went to the address Otis gave me and followed a man to the Chinese embassy. About an hour ago I took his picture."

Kay took out her phone and showed Prescott the picture. "Do you know who this guy is?"

Prescott glanced at the picture. "Yes."

"Well, what's his name?" Kay said.

"You don't need to know that."

"Olivia, I know where he lives and where he works. So you might as well tell me."

Prescott glared at her, then finally said, "His name is Fang Zhou and he's supposedly a cultural attaché at the embassy. We suspect he's part of the Chinese intelligence apparatus in this country, but we've never caught him actually engaged in an operation."

"Fang Zhou," Kay repeated.

"Yes, and the only reason I gave you his name is that I can't afford to have you stumbling around like a bull in a china shop, killing more people."

"*More* people?" Kay said. "What do you mean by that?" Prescott knew Kay had killed Otis's guy, Quinn, on K Street but how would she have known that she'd killed Billy?

Prescott ignored the question. "Okay, Hamilton, I'm about to tell you something, even though you don't have the clearance. This information is so sensitive and so vital to national security that you won't be given a trial if you ever tell anyone. You'll be tossed into a cell and placed in total isolation. You won't be freed until we've achieved world peace."

"Yeah, yeah, enough with the threats. Talk," Kay said.

"My people identified the man at Zytek who sent the e-mail attachment that was in Callahan's safe. I'm not going to tell you his name. We also figured out that the e-mail was sent to the Chinese. Normally we'd have the FBI arrest the spy at Zytek, but instead, we're going to use him to feed information to the Chinese that could give the United States a significant military advantage."

"Gee, could you be any more vague, Olivia?"

"Don't get smart with me. I'm not in the mood. But now do you understand why you need to stop pursuing Fang? We don't want the Chinese to know that we've identified their spy. We want to let them think that no one ever saw the attachment, and that we would never be able to identify the sender or the recipient. Do you understand?"

"Yeah, I understand. But this guy killed two of Callahan's people and almost killed Callahan. He killed Danzinger and her secretary. He may not have done it personally, but he hired the people who did."

"Well, that's the way these things go sometimes," Prescott said.

"What the fuck does that mean?" Kay asked.

"Lower your voice! It means, that sometimes there are casualties in intelligence operations." Before Kay could go ballistic, Prescott said, "What do you think we could do to Fang? Even if we wanted to arrest him, we can't prove that he had anything to do with the attack, and he has diplomatic immunity. We could invent some reason to expel him from the country, but then the Chinese would retaliate by expelling some of our people from China."

"Okay," Kay said. "I'll leave Fang alone. For now. But I want you to locate Otis for me."

"And how am I supposed to do that?" Prescott asked.

"I put the cell phone you gave me in his truck, so I know you can find him."

"I'll think about it. I'm not sure I want to do anything about Otis at this point."

"Goddamnit, he killed two of Callahan's people and I'm not going to let him get away with that. And if we're not going to do anything about Fang, we can at least make Otis pay."

"I said, I'll think about it," Prescott said. She rose from her chair. "I'm leaving. But I want you to know that I'll be watching you, Hamilton. And I think you're bright enough to understand that I'm not just talking about having a guy in a trench coat follow you around."

25

While Kay was parked on the corner of Utah and Tennyson, Otis and Simpson left Billy's place. They stopped at the motel in Lorton where Otis had stashed Shirley, and Simpson had to help Otis get out of the truck and walk to Shirley's room. Shirley didn't answer the door when he knocked, and Otis figured she was probably passed out. Since he didn't want the motel staff to see him—his ripped jeans, and the big bandage on his left knee—he had Simpson get a screwdriver from his truck and forced open the cheap motel room door.

Shirley was on the bed fully clothed, dead to the world, snoring and stinking of booze, and Otis wasn't able to revive her—which was probably just as well. He wrote a note saying her Prius was in the parking lot and that he'd call her later. He placed the note, her car keys, and her cell phone on the toilet seat, figuring that was the first place she'd stumble to when she woke up. He thought for a moment about leaving her brother's share of the money but decided not to. Things had changed now that he was on the run.

With Simpson driving Otis's pickup, they left Lorton and headed for North Carolina. Simpson knew a guy there, an older guy he'd met in prison, named Younger. Younger had been a good friend to Simpson when he was inside and Simpson, in turn, made sure the hard-core cons didn't take advantage of the old man.

Simpson said Younger would let them hide out at his place until they could figure out what to do next.

Younger was about seventy, and he'd spent the last twenty-two years in a cell for shooting a woman when he was holding up a liquor store. At the time, he'd been so drunk he didn't remember pulling the trigger. He now lived in a little cabin on the edge of Nantahala National Forest. He lived alone, hunted and fished, made his own whiskey, and grew a little pot. The pot, in fact, was his only source of income, and he sold it to a few folks in the small town of Franklin, North Carolina.

By the time they got to Younger's, it was ten in the morning—nine hours after leaving Billy's place. Otis's knee was killing him, and he had a fever. He had to do something about his knee soon or he might lose his leg.

EVA BECKMAN WAS STILL MONITORING Otis and Simpson, and it looked as if they'd finally stopped driving for the day.

When Prescott had called her at one in the morning and told her to start bird-dogging Otis, Beckman had to go to Fort Meade to get a briefing from Brookes and pick up the equipment she would need. By the time she was ready to leave, Otis and Simpson (per the cell phone in Otis's truck) were past Richmond and on I-85 headed toward North Carolina—but that didn't pose a problem for Beckman, because she had access to an NSA helicopter.

Beckman boarded the chopper and caught up with Otis, then called back to headquarters and told Brookes to have a car waiting for her in Greensboro, something fast with four-wheel drive.

At six a.m., Beckman was parked on I-85 and was watching Otis approach her on the GPS monitor mounted on her car's dashboard. She let him pass and then fell in behind his black Toyota Tundra.

At nine a.m., Otis's truck had passed through Asheville, got onto US Route 23, and headed toward the small town of Franklin. After Otis passed through Franklin, however, following him became problematic. He headed into the Nantahala National Forest and began taking unmarked, unpaved roads and Beckman had been forced to stay well behind.

Finally, an hour after Otis left Franklin, Otis's pickup stopped. Half an hour later, the pickup was still in the same position, and Beckman wondered if Otis had finally reached his destination. There wasn't an address corresponding to his location, so he was definitely out in the boondocks, in fuckin' *Deliverance* country. Beckman could envision a small cabin sitting in a dark clearing, surrounded by tall trees.

Beckman decided that if Otis's pickup was still in the same spot when it turned dark, she'd creep up closer to see what Otis and Simpson were doing.

Beckman smiled. She *loved* her job.

Beckman was twenty-seven, had spent four years in the army—two tours in Afghanistan—and had worked for the NSA for four years. Her civil service job title was "security specialist"—which could mean almost anything: a uniformed guard at Fort Meade, a geek involved in IT security, or a person who did background checks on NSA employees. Or it could mean that she was a field agent who was dispatched when a situation required someone in the field. Beckman didn't know why she was following Otis—but that wasn't all that unusual. It was the principle of "need to know," and apparently Prescott didn't feel that a lowly agent like Eva Beckman needed to know much of anything.

WHEN ROY YOUNGER HEARD A VEHICLE pull up to his cabin, he looked through a fly-specked window and saw a big black Toyota pickup with two men in it park in front of his porch. No one ever visited him and he couldn't figure out who the men could be. He grabbed a shotgun that he kept near the door and stepped out onto the porch, trying to look tough, knowing he didn't. He hoped the shotgun would scare these two guys off, whoever they were.

Then the driver stepped out of the pickup and he recognized Simpson, whom he hadn't seen in two years, and he let out a whoop of joy. He didn't know what the hell Simpson was doing here, but Younger was glad he'd come. He didn't have many friends and the only time he ever talked to anyone was when he went into Franklin to sell his pot.

The guy with Simpson stepped out of the pickup next: a big, hard-looking guy, older than Simpson, who had a bloody bandage on one knee. Simpson went over to the injured guy and helped him walk to the porch.

"Roy," Simpson said, "this is my friend Otis. We need to stay here for a bit."

And Roy Younger thought, *Uh-oh.*

YOUNGER WAS SCRAWNY, with wispy white hair and white whiskers he hadn't shaved in a week. He still had about half his teeth. He was wearing bib overalls without a shirt, and his feet were bare and dirty. Otis could tell Younger was pleased to see Simpson but he was leery about them staying with him. His attitude changed when Simpson said they'd pay him five grand for the privilege of sleeping on the floor of his shack.

"The thing is," Simpson said, "I've got to get a doctor for my buddy, one that will keep his mouth shut. He's got a bullet in his knee, and if he doesn't get it out, he could lose his leg."

"I don't know any doctors," Younger said. "But I know this woman. She's a nurse, worked at a VA hospital in Asheville for years. She lost her license, some kind of malpractice thing, and now she calls herself a midwife and does abortions and helps folks who don't have insurance. I went to see her once when I had a bug bite that got in-fected. She's a mean bitch, but if you pay her enough, she'll help and she won't talk."

Otis thought about having Younger bring the nurse to him, but he didn't want anyone to know where he was staying, so they all piled into Otis's truck and took off for the nurse's place in Franklin. They needed Younger to introduce them to the nurse and to find her place. They'd make sure they weren't followed returning to Younger's cabin, but they were just going to have to take Younger's word that the nurse wouldn't say anything.

BECKMAN COULDN'T FIGURE OUT what was going on. The GPS monitor showed that Otis's pickup had started moving again, and it was headed right toward her. She was on a narrow, unpaved road, and there wasn't room to turn her car around. She backed up fast and spotted an area where there was a bunch of tall bushes but no trees. She was driving a four-wheel-drive SUV, so she stepped on the gas and crashed through the brush until the SUV was almost invisible. If Otis looked closely, he might see her as he passed—but he didn't. Beckman waited five min-utes, then took off after him.

An hour later, Otis was parked in front of a small clapboard house in Franklin with a front lawn that was completely covered with dande-lions. Beckman parked so she could see the house. While she waited, she learned that the house belonged to a Viola Patterson and that Pat-terson was a nurse; it said so right on her Facebook page.

THE NURSE IN FRANKLIN turned out to be a fat woman with dyed black hair and the mean black eyes of a snapping turtle. The only anesthetic she had was a bottle of Gordon's gin, so all Otis could do was grit his teeth as she probed his knee with a dental pick to locate the slug. Then she shoved a handkerchief in his mouth so the neighbors wouldn't hear him scream as she dug out the slug with a pair of needle-nosed pliers.

After she removed the bullet, the nurse poked around in the wound some more, removing remnants of clothing and bits of bone. He passed out when she poured what felt like gasoline into the wound to clean it out before she bandaged it. Otis figured she'd probably destroyed his knee beyond repair, but at least he wasn't going to lose his leg to gangrene.

By the time she finished, Otis's clothes were soaked with sweat and he felt as weak as a kitten. He asked how much he owed her, and when she hesitated, he said, "How 'bout two grand."

She nodded and he could tell she would have settled for less, but Otis could afford to be generous. She gave him a pair of old crutches and an aluminum cane for when he didn't need the crutches. She also tossed in a bottle of antibiotic pills to fight off infection and, even better, gave him a dozen OxyContin for the pain.

As they were leaving, Otis said, "You talk to anyone about me, I'll come back here and kill you."

"Get the fuck out of here," the nurse said. Florence Nightingale she was not.

BECKMAN WATCHED as Otis, Simpson, and an old man in overalls emerged from the nurse's house. Otis was now on crutches, his left pant leg was split from crotch to ankle, and there was a large clean bandage on his knee. Simpson was twirling a cane in one hand. Beckman didn't know who the old man was but guessed he probably owned the place in the forest. The three men got back into Otis's pickup, and headed back to the woods.

When it was almost dark, Beckman took a knapsack from her SUV, tossed in two bottles of water, three protein bars, a flashlight, a Glock, night-vision binoculars, and a switchblade knife. Holding the GPS monitor in her hand, she made her way through the woods to Otis's pickup.

The pickup was in front of a small shack. The lights were on—she could hear a generator running—and through a window, she could see Otis, Simpson, and the old man at a table, eating. Beckman was going to have to spend the night watching the cabin. She just hoped the fucking bugs didn't eat her alive.

26

When Otis woke up the next morning, he felt fairly good. He hadn't slept well and his knee hurt like a bastard, but his fever was gone and he could think again. He borrowed a pair of overalls from Younger to replace his jeans that had been destroyed by the nurse; the overalls were two inches too short and smelled as if they hadn't been washed in a month.

He needed to call Ginnie. She had no idea what had happened to him and was probably going out of her mind. But he doubted that he'd be able to get a cell phone signal out in the middle of nowhere. Using the crutches, he hobbled out to the front porch, where Simpson and Younger were sitting on folding lawn chairs, drinking coffee, bullshitting about the bad old days they'd spent in prison together. He noticed that Simpson had somehow gotten his Harley out of the back of his pickup.

"Would you mind getting my phone out of the truck," Otis said to Simpson.

Simpson collected Otis's phone and Otis was surprised to see a couple of bars of service. He also noticed he'd missed three calls from

Shirley. He went back inside the cabin so Younger and Simpson wouldn't hear him and punched in Ginnie's cell phone number.

"It's me," he said when Ginnie answered.

"Thank God! Where the hell are you? Are you all right?" she asked.

"I'm fine—well, not exactly fine—but I'm alive. I don't want to say much, but I'm going to have to lay low for a while. Maybe quite a while. This last job, Ginnie, I stepped into some serious shit."

They'd talked about this before, that if he had to run, he'd run. South America, Mexico, Canada, wherever he'd be safe. Then somehow he'd find a way for Ginnie and the kids to join him.

"You have enough money," Otis said, "that you and the kids should be okay for a long time, and I'll send you some more when I can. I'm not going to be calling very often, because the people that are after me might use my phone to locate me. I love you, babe," he said, and hung up.

He thought about calling Shirley next—then he thought, what was the point? Shirley was going to get screwed. She wasn't going to get Ray's share, not the way things stood now.

But he would do one thing for Shirley: He would make sure that John followed through on his promise to pay off her mortgage and unfreeze her bank accounts.

He called John next, and the first words out of John's mouth were, "What time is it? And why are you calling me?" It sounded as if he'd woken John up.

"It's eight in the morning, and I'm calling because that woman who killed one of my guys tracked me down and killed another one."

"What?" John said.

"She also shot me. I'm lucky I'm still alive. She doesn't know your name but she knows where you live."

"How could she know where I live?" John said, for the first time losing the *I'm so cool nothing gets to me* attitude.

"I don't know," Otis lied. "But she does. And she's coming after you. Her name's Hamilton."

"But how would she know where I—"

"Look, I'm leaving the country," Otis said, "but you better keep your promise. You said you'd pay off Shirley Brown's mortgage and unfreeze her accounts, and if you don't, I know people who can get to you. I know where you live, too."

John—or whoever the fuck he was—laughed. "Mr. Otis, I am the last person on earth you want to threaten. But don't worry. I'll do what I said. I want to preserve our relationship. You can never tell what the future might bring."

"You better," Otis said and hung up, thinking, *Sorry, Shirley, but that's the best I can do for you.* Otis was willing to bet, however, that Shirley was never going to get over the loss of her brother, and he was pretty sure that she would end up killing herself with booze before long.

BECKMAN WONDERED HOW much longer she should watch the cabin. It was light out now, and although she was well hidden behind a couple of thick bushes, she was still at risk of being seen. She should go back to her car and update Prescott. She'd been up all night and it had been impossible to sleep even if she'd wanted to, and there were lumps all over her face and arms from insect bites.

She'd give it a few more minutes, then she was splitting.

AFTER OTIS HUNG UP WITH JOHN, he sat for a moment, reluctant to do what he needed to do next.

He walked over to the door, leaned his crutches against the wall, and picked up the shotgun that was next to the doorframe. It was an old double-barreled Winchester with two triggers. He broke the shotgun open, verified it was loaded, and flipped off the safety. He pushed open the door, and braced himself against the doorframe so he wouldn't fall.

Simpson and Younger were still on the porch, and Simpson, who was seated closest to the door, turned toward him. When he saw Otis holding the shotgun, he looked puzzled, but before he could ask why Otis had the gun, Otis pulled the trigger and blew Simpson's head apart. Younger, who'd been whooping with laughter at something Simpson had just said, stopped whooping. But he didn't do anything. He just sat there in shock with Simpson's blood all over his face, looking at the gory mess that was Simpson's head. Then Otis pulled the second trigger and shot Younger.

Otis didn't want to leave the dead men on the front porch, but with his leg fucked up the way it was, he didn't have a choice. Fortunately, the cabin was so isolated that it would probably be months—maybe even years—before anyone found the two rotting corpses.

He went back into the cabin and did his best to wipe his fingerprints off any place he'd touched, including the shotgun. He thought briefly about searching for the five thousand he'd given Younger, but decided not to bother. Then he picked up the bag containing all the gold and cash and headed for the door. The bag was heavy and it was hard to hold it while walking with the crutches, but he took his time and headed carefully down the steps.

He felt bad that he'd had to kill Simpson. He hadn't known him long, but he'd seemed like a good guy. But what choice did he have? He needed all the money so he could hide out for a while—and with the shape he was in, he wouldn't be pulling another job anytime soon. And the money wasn't just for him; it was for Ginnie and the kids.

HOLY SHIT! HOLY SHIT! Beckman couldn't believe it when Otis stepped out of the cabin and blew the two men's heads apart. He'd just *executed* his two friends. As Otis gimped down the steps toward his truck,

Beckman backed out of the bushes where she'd been hiding, staying low for about fifty yards, and when she was sure Otis wouldn't be able to see her, she sprinted for her car.

Jesus! He just blew their fuckin' heads off.

OTIS FIGURED IT would take him about eleven hours to get to Miami if he really pushed it hard, which he would do. He knew a guy there who could turn the gold into cash, but more important, his Miami connection knew people who could make him a passport. After he'd taken care of the gold and had a new ID, then he'd decide where he wanted to go, but first he had to reach Miami without getting caught. Someplace along the way he'd steal license plates off a truck or a van and replace the plates on his pickup. He'd also dump his cell phone so it couldn't be used to track him; he'd pick up another one later.

He swallowed one of the OxyContin the nurse in Franklin had given him, and as he drove he cursed his luck. He hadn't had a job go this bad since the first time he'd been arrested when he was seventeen, the bank job he'd pulled with his old man. And that damn Hamilton, she was like the Bitch from Hell. He still couldn't believe that a woman had taken down half his crew and turned him into a cripple. He was also pissed that John had given him gold, because the guy in Miami was going to charge him a bundle to turn it into dollars.

But he was alive. He needed to start getting his head around the future rather than spending time stewing over the past. But he still felt bad about Simpson. It was really a shame he had to kill him.

BECKMAN WAS ABOUT A MILE behind Otis as he drove toward Franklin. She had no idea where he was going, but she doubted Franklin was his destination.

Beckman had been keeping Prescott informed via text messages, but she wasn't going to send a text to tell Prescott what had just happened.

She called Prescott and said, "Otis just killed Simpson and the old man. I mean, he took a shotgun and blew their heads off!"

"Calm down," Prescott said, and Beckman was embarrassed to realize she was practically screaming into the phone and sounded hysterical.

"I'm sorry," she said, "but I couldn't believe—"

"What's Otis doing now?"

"He's back in his truck, driving. I don't know where he's going. What do you want me to do?"

There was a brief pause, then Prescott said, "You do what I told you to do. Stick with Otis and keep me informed." Prescott disconnected the call.

Jesus, what a cold-blooded, scary old bitch.

27

When Otis had called Fang Zhou, Fang had been lying in bed next to a lovely redheaded Russian. Last night he'd gone to a party at the British embassy. Attending the party was part of his job, but he'd also been celebrating. The redhead worked at the Russian embassy and claimed to be a secretary, but Fang suspected she was Russian intelligence and thought that she might be able to use her beautiful body to recruit him. She was the bait in a classic honey trap—but Fang hadn't been the least concerned. She would never recruit him, but he might end up recruiting her—and even if he didn't, he would at least enjoy her favors in bed.

Now, however, after speaking to Otis, all the good feelings he'd had the night before had been shattered and he felt like a fool. He'd known that Hamilton was more than a lowly security guard but he'd failed to deal with her.

Fang looked in on the Russian lying in his bed. She was lying face-down and he was treated to the sight of a marvelous derriere, long shapely legs, and a mass of flaming red hair fanned out over a pillow.

He thought about waking her up and telling her to leave—she was a distraction he didn't need right now—but decided to let her sleep. He made a pot of coffee and, wrapped in a lightweight robe, took a cup out to his backyard patio.

What should he do about Hamilton? He was a Chinese diplomat, so the most the American government could do was expel him from the country. But Hamilton was obviously not a government agent; if she had been one, she wouldn't have gone after Otis on her own and would have involved the police or the FBI. She clearly wasn't interested in merely arresting the people who'd attacked Callahan. She was killing them—and now it appeared that she was coming for him.

He needed to take Hamilton off the board, but how should he remove her? He certainly wasn't going to kill her himself. So who could he use?

The answer was obvious: his young friend Jamal.

He glanced at his watch. Eight twenty a.m. He doubted Jamal was an early riser—he imagined the young man didn't rise before noon—but disturbing Jamal's slumber was the least of his concerns.

He called Jamal using the same phone he'd used to communicate with Otis, a prepaid cell phone that couldn't be traced to him or the Chinese embassy. As expected, he woke Jamal up.

Jamal answered his phone saying, "Who the fuck is this?"

"It's your friend John. I have another job for you, one that will pay very well."

"What time is it?"

"Wake up! Do you remember the tavern where we met one time?"

"No."

"We've only met in a tavern once. Think about it."

"Shit. Hold on a minute."

Fang heard what sounded like a cigarette lighter clicking.

"Yeah," Jamal said, "I know where you mean."

"Good. I'll meet you there at eleven."

"Well, shit. Then why didn't you wait until ten thirty before you called me?"

Fang didn't bother to tell Jamal that he didn't want to meet until eleven because he needed to obtain some information before the meeting.

He called his contact at the D.C. Metro Police Department and told him that he needed everything they had on Hamilton. He knew the police would have some information because she had been questioned after the attack. When the detective asked him why, Fang evaded the question and said that he could have his Redskins seats for every game this coming season. Ten minutes later, he had the information he wanted.

Fang realized that if Hamilton was killed, the detective would immediately suspect that Fang had something to do with her death. But so what? The man could hardly tell people he was providing information to a member of the Chinese embassy in return for football tickets.

Fang's next call was to his researcher. He gave her the information he'd just obtained from the police and told her to find a picture of Hamilton. He had a description of her—in her early thirties, tall, blond, very good-looking—but he wanted to give Jamal more than a description. Ten minutes later his researcher called him back. She had found photos of Hamilton in articles about two DEA operations—one in Miami and one in San Diego. Hamilton was ex-DEA, the researcher said—and she'd killed four men in Miami.

The researcher e-mailed him the photos and Fang printed out the most recent one. It was a photo of Hamilton at a press conference after she arrested a drug dealer named Tito Olivera in San Diego. Fang was impressed by her beauty. She had an incredible body. In the photo, she was wearing a skirt and he could appreciate her long legs. Then it occurred to him that maybe he *had* seen Hamilton before: Could she have been the blonde parked in the No Parking zone in front of the embassy?

Fang had more than two hours before he had to meet Jamal, but it was going to take him a long time to get to the meeting place because he would need to take precautions to make sure he wasn't being followed. But first, he needed to get the Russian out of his bed and out of his house. He wasn't about to leave her alone so she could search his house after he left.

FANG DRESSED IN CASUAL CLOTHES: a white polo shirt, jeans, and tennis shoes. Over his arm he carried a lightweight windbreaker that was reversible—blue on one side, red on the other—and in a pocket of the windbreaker was a red Washington Nationals baseball cap. He headed for the door, then stopped and returned to his bedroom and removed a small .380 automatic he kept in the nightstand next to his bed. With a maniac like Hamilton stalking him, he needed to take precautions.

He looked carefully up and down the street. He didn't see Hamilton or anyone else watching him. Nonetheless, he spent the next hour doing everything he could to make sure he wasn't being tailed. He took a taxi to a Metro station, got on a train and got off abruptly at a random stop, waiting until the train was just about to depart the station before he exited. He walked rapidly, turning corners for no reason. He went into a restaurant, left by the back exit wearing the windbreaker, blue side out, no cap on his head. He took another Metro ride—one that would take him closer to his final destination—walked about some more, checking constantly behind him, entered another restaurant, and this time left wearing a red jacket and a baseball cap.

Satisfied that he wasn't being followed, he took a seat in a bar called Tunnicliff's Tavern. Fifteen minutes later, at exactly eleven a.m., Jamal Howard entered the bar. He was a punctual gangster.

Jamal was hardly inconspicuous. He had a heavy gold medallion two inches in diameter on a gold chain around his neck. He was wearing a gaudy blue silk sweatshirt that had a logo on it that Fang didn't recognize, and those baggy jeans young people seemed to favor. On his feet were Timberland boots of a yellowish color.

Jamal took a seat across from Fang. "My man, John," Jamal said.

Fang didn't appreciate his flippancy. Nonetheless, he said, "Would you like a drink, a beer?"

"I don't drink," Jamal said.

That surprised Fang. It also pleased him.

"So wuzz up?" Jamal asked. "Why did you want to meet? What's the big fuckin' deal?"

Fang removed a folded piece of paper from the back pocket of his pants—the photo of Hamilton. He unfolded it and slid it across the table to Jamal. Written on the bottom of the photo was Hamilton's address on Connecticut Avenue.

"Whoa!" Jamal said when he looked at the photo. "She's hot."

"I want her dead," Fang said. From another pocket he pulled out an envelope and slid it across the table to Jamal. Jamal opened the envelope and without removing the money, counted the bills inside, which were all hundreds. The money had come from Callahan's safe. Fang thought it somewhat ironic that Callahan's money would be used to kill another of his employees.

28

When Otis called Fang Zhou to warn him about Hamilton, Kay was just getting out of bed. Yesterday, after she met with Prescott at the restaurant in Georgetown, she'd gone home. She didn't know what to do about Fang. She was forced to admit that Prescott was most likely correct and that she should leave him alone so she didn't screw up whatever Spy-vs-Spy operation the NSA was running. She knew what to do about Dylan Otis, but she didn't know how to force Prescott to tell her where he was.

She'd also gone home because she needed to sleep. She hadn't gone to bed immediately, however, because she knew that if she crawled into bed at three in the afternoon, she'd most likely wake up at three in the morning. So she'd washed a load of clothes, cleaned up her apartment, paid a few bills she'd been neglecting, then took a long shower before lying down. She slept for twelve hours and woke up feeling rested and restless.

The first thing she did was call her daughter, hoping to catch Jessica before she headed off to a class. She hadn't spoken to Jessica since before the attack. But Jessica didn't have time to chat; she was just leaving her dorm. She'd been able to talk her way into observing a heart transplant, and she could hardly wait. Kay's reaction was: *Yuck!* Who'd want to watch someone's chest cracked open and heart yanked out like some kind of Aztec sacrifice? But all she said was, "Hey, well, that's great."

"Yeah," Jessica said. "The things they're doing with organ transplants these days are just amazing."

Then she hung up before Kay could ask the important questions, like, are you getting enough to eat, do you have enough money, and—the biggie—are you seeing anyone?

She called Henry next and asked how Callahan was doing.

"Better," Henry said. "They finally beat back that infection and he's recovering from the pneumonia. He's not strong enough to leave the hospital but he's able to talk when he's not sleeping." Henry laughed. "He keeps pestering me to sneak him in a pack of smokes and some booze."

"Sounds like he's recovering," Kay said. "Oh, one more thing, Henry. I need a favor."

AFTER SPEAKING TO HENRY, Kay decided to go see Callahan. She needed his advice.

She drove to the hospital, but before she entered Callahan's room, she asked Henry, "Did you talk to your guy?"

"Yeah, he's expecting a call from you."

"Thanks, Henry."

She walked into Callahan's room, and the first thing he said to her was, "Go get me a pack of Marlboros."

He didn't look good—although he looked better than the last time she'd seen him. There was a little color in his face, but he looked weak and he'd lost quite a bit of weight—but then, Lord knows, he needed to shed a few pounds. Kay knew that as soon as he got out of the hospital, he'd start stuffing his face and drinking again. A near-death experience would not be a life-changing experience for Callahan; it would instead be an excuse to do everything he liked to do in excess before the next bullet actually killed him.

Callahan also didn't have any answers for her. He told her the same thing Prescott had said about their relationship: that they knew each other from his days at the CIA.

"Then why did you give me Prescott's name?" Kay asked.

"I didn't know I did. In fact, I don't even remember talking to you."

Kay figured he might be telling the truth about that. He'd just come out of surgery, was still groggy from the meds he'd been given and in pain, and he might not have known what he was doing.

"I know Prescott's one of the people running you, Callahan," Kay said.

"I don't know what you're talking about," Callahan said, his blue eyes doing their best to look innocent—which wasn't possible.

"You're lying," Kay said.

"So tell me what you've been doing," Callahan said, not the least perturbed that she'd called him a liar.

She told Callahan the whole story; she didn't see any reason not to. He was shocked to hear that the technician at the NSA and Danzinger had both been killed. She also told him that Prescott had determined who the spy was at Zytek and was now planning to turn the spy into a double agent to use against the Chinese.

"That's smart," Callahan said.

"Yeah, I guess," Kay said.

She went on to say that she'd tracked down Otis and shot him in the knee and killed another one of his men. Then she identified the Chinese operative who hired Otis—a so-called cultural attaché at the Chinese embassy named Fang Zhou.

"Wow," Callahan said when she finished. "You've been a busy little bee."

As she'd been telling him what she'd done, Kay had the sense—just like she'd had with Prescott—that Callahan already knew some of the things she was saying. She didn't know how he knew, but he didn't ask the type of questions she thought he would have asked if he'd been hearing the story for the first time.

"Have you ever heard of Fang Zhou?"

"No," Callahan said.

"Prescott doesn't want me to touch him because she's afraid that will screw up this double-agent operation she's planning."

"Well, it sounds to me like Olivia's right. You need to leave Fang alone."

"But he killed Danzinger, tortured and killed her secretary, and killed Norton and Klein—two guys who worked for you."

"I know, and I'm not happy about that, but you gotta keep your eye on the big picture."

"Fuck the big picture," Kay said.

"No, Hamilton, you can't do that. You gotta leave Fang alone, like Prescott told you."

"But there's no reason to leave Otis alone. Right now Otis has a ton of money, and he's going to get away with killing our people unless we do something. And we can't turn him over to the cops, because if they link him to Fang Zhou, all this shit could end up in the papers."

"Do you know where Otis is?" Callahan asked.

"No, but Prescott does. I planted a cell phone in Otis's truck and I know Prescott can track him with it, but she won't tell me where he is. That's one of the reasons I came here today. Can you think of some way to persuade Prescott to tell me?"

Callahan closed his eyes. "You know, I'm not feeling so hot," he said. "Maybe we can talk about this later. And stop at the nurses' station when you leave and tell them I need something more for the pain."

Kay had to admit that he didn't look good. Talking to her for just twenty minutes appeared to have exhausted him. On the other hand, the duplicitous bastard could be using his condition so he wouldn't have to talk to her any longer. But all she said was, "Okay, but I'll be back." She hoped he realized that that was a threat.

As she was leaving, Callahan said, his voice weak, "Leave Fang alone, Hamilton. I'm serious about that."

"I'll think about it," Kay said.

Outside Callahan's room, she asked Henry, "Has anyone been to see him? I mean, other than doctors and nurses."

"Just you and Eli," Henry said. "Why are you asking?"

"Just curious," Kay said. To change the subject she said, "You must be getting pretty tired of sitting outside this hospital room."

"I'm not leaving Callahan's side until he's well enough to take care of himself." And again Kay wondered about Henry and Callahan's history.

WHAT KAY DIDN'T KNOW was that Prescott had seen Callahan two hours before Kay arrived at the hospital.

Prescott had entered the hospital wearing blue scrubs, large-framed glasses, and a badge that identified her as Dr. Harriet Sheppard, Internal Medicine. She wore a surgical cap to hide her platinum blond hair. When Henry saw her, he made no attempt to stop her or question her. And she barely glanced at Henry as she pulled a mask up to cover her mouth and nose and entered the room; she acted as if Henry had as much significance as the furniture in the hallway.

Once inside, she gave Callahan a briefing on all that had transpired since he'd been shot, including all that Hamilton had done. She even told him about Admiral Kincaid's plan to use Winston to feed the Chinese information that might allow the U.S. Navy to track their attack submarines.

Her last words to him were: "You get that goddamn woman under control, Callahan, because if you don't, I will have to deal with her."

Prescott currently had an electronic and physical net around

Hamilton; she still had Tate and Towers following her, and Brookes was still monitoring Hamilton's cell phone calls, her landline calls, and her e-mails.

But Prescott wasn't satisfied. All she was doing was *monitoring* Hamilton—which wasn't the same thing as *controlling* Hamilton. She was beginning to think that maybe she should give Otis to Hamilton— rather like giving a feral kitten a mouse to play with. She needed to keep the kitten occupied, and maybe if Hamilton was allowed to take care of Otis, she'd be content and leave Fang alone.

There was also another reason for letting Hamilton reacquire Otis—although Prescott hadn't decided if she was ready to go there yet.

THE FAVOR THAT KAY had asked of Henry was if he could put her in touch with someone who could get her a couple of weapons. The D.C. cops still had her Glock—the one she'd used to kill Otis's guy at the building on K Street—and Kay no longer had Eloise Voss's Beretta.

Kay had hated to do it, but after she'd killed Otis's pal, Billy, she'd tossed Eloise's Beretta into the Potomac River. She thought it pretty unlikely that the police would ever match the slug in Billy's body with Eloise's gun, but for Eloise's sake, she didn't want to take the chance. So into the river it went. Kay had always thought that if they ever drained the Potomac, it would look like that famous fountain in Rome—except that the riverbed would be littered with weapons, not coins.

When Kay had called Detective Mary Platt and said she wanted her gun back, Platt had told her no. She said the Glock was evidence in a multiple homicide and until the case was closed, it was going to remain with the police.

"But you might never close the case," Kay complained.

"That's right, and one reason why is that no one who works for Callahan is cooperating," Platt had said. Platt said the few employees she'd been able to talk to all claimed to have no idea why a group of masked men armed with machine guns would want to steal Callahan's safe. Platt had yet to talk to Callahan; whenever she tried, she was informed he was too sick to talk. She was pissed.

"There's something screwy about that company," Platt said to Kay. "I'm starting to think it's some kind of front for laundering money and that's why the robbers hit the place."

Kay laughed. "You've been watching too many movies, Mary. And by now you've processed my Glock, so I don't understand why I can't have it back."

"Because I don't want you to have it back," Platt said and hung up.

Which was why Kay had asked Henry if he knew where she could get two weapons: one to replace her Glock and one to replace Eloise's Beretta. She told him she didn't have the time—or the inclination—to fill out a lot of paperwork and wait for whatever background checks were required. Kay was actually a big believer in background checks for people purchasing handguns—she just didn't think the rules should apply to her, at least not when she was in a hurry. She figured that Henry—being a hometown boy with connections—might know a guy. And he did. Henry gave her a number to call and said he would call the guy first to vouch for Kay.

Kay called the gun dealer and told him she wanted a .40 Glock and Beretta 92. Not a problem, the man said. He told her to meet him in the mall near Metro Center at eleven a.m.—which, coincidentally, was the same time Fang Zhou was meeting Jamal at Tunnicliff's Tavern. On the way to the mall, Kay stopped at her bank to get cash.

THE GUN DEALER was sitting at a table in the mall's food court. He'd told Kay that he would be wearing a black beret so she'd recognize him. He was in his sixties, with a neatly trimmed white beard and wire-rimmed glasses. He looked more like a guy who might teach at Howard University than an urban guerilla. He was reading a book by Barbara Kingsolver, and when he saw Kay glance at the title as she sat down, he said, "For my book club. It's quite good. You should try it."

Kay handed the man a Walgreens bag containing thirty-two hundred dollars.

He passed her a Gap bag containing one used Glock, one brand-new Beretta, and two fully loaded clips for each gun. He wasn't cheap, but he delivered.

She thanked the gun dealer and returned to her car.

Kay thought about calling Eli to discuss the situation, then decided not to. All Eli would do is tell her the same thing Callahan and Prescott had, which was to leave Fang alone.

Kay had lunch at a McDonald's—a double cheeseburger, fries, and a chocolate shake—then because she'd stuffed herself, she decided to go to the gym and burn off all the calories she'd just consumed. She was also feeling edgy and pissed off, and needed to release some of her restless energy and simmering anger.

Her gym was near the office on K Street and she kept shorts, a tank top, and tennis shoes there. Ten minutes after she arrived, she was riding a stationary bike, pedaling like she was racing in the Tour de France.

AS KAY WAS PEDALING TO NOWHERE, Jamal Howard parked his car a block from her apartment building.

29

Jamal Howard stood across the street from Hamilton's building, wondering why John would want such a fine-looking woman killed—but it didn't really matter. All that mattered was the thirty Gs that John was paying.

Jamal was dressed in what he thought of as his Joe Citizen clothes: khaki pants, a white button-down short-sleeved shirt, and plain white tennis shoes. He was young enough that people who saw him might think he was a student. He left the shirt untucked so the tails covered the Glock that was slipped into the back of his pants.

Jamal crossed the street toward Hamilton's building. John had told him that she lived in apartment 812, but Jamal didn't know if she was home or not. The building didn't have a doorman—Hamilton must not be rich—but the front door was locked. Next to it were four rows of doorbell buttons with the tenant's name beside each one. Jamal pushed the one labeled K. HAMILTON. No one answered.

Jamal crossed the street again and leaned against the building across from Hamilton's. There wasn't any shade and he didn't know how long he would have to stand there. It was the middle of the day and if the woman worked, he could be waiting around all afternoon—and it was hotter than a bitch. Nothing to be done about that, though. It was the price a professional like himself had to pay.

ELOISE VOSS DECIDED it was time to go for her walk. She walked every day for at least a mile, rain or shine, hot or cold. Today was hot, so she put a bottle of water in her fanny pack and donned a pink breast cancer fun run baseball cap.

As she left the building, she noticed the young man across the street. She couldn't help it. After thirty years protecting presidents, their wives, and their children, she was always aware of the people around her. The young man didn't seem threatening. He was good-looking and clean-cut. She found it odd, though, that he'd be standing there with the sun beating down on his head instead of finding some-place shady to wait for whomever he was apparently waiting for.

When she came back from her walk thirty-five minutes later, he was still standing there. *Hmm*, she thought.

JAMAL HAD BEEN hoping that he might get lucky and see Hamilton enter her building, follow her inside, and shoot her in the elevator, but after waiting outside for an hour, he decided to give up on that dumb-ass plan. There had to be a restaurant or a coffee shop somewhere close by. He'd sit and drink sweet iced tea and come back every hour or so and ring Hamilton's buzzer.

FEELING BETTER AFTER HER WORKOUT, Kay drove back home and parked in the garage under her building. She opened the trunk and removed the Gap bag containing the weapons she'd purchased.

As soon as she was inside her apartment, she called Eloise Voss.

"Hi," she said, "it's Kay Hamilton. I've got a present for you. I could bring it down to your place, but why don't you come up here. I know it's a bit early in the day, but I thought I could make us a pitcher of martinis and you could tell me what it was like working for the Secret Service."

"What a delightful proposal!" Eloise said. "I'll be there in five minutes."

Exactly five minutes later, Eloise knocked on Kay's door and Kay poured them each a martini in the fancy glasses she used when she had guests.

"I've got some good news and some bad news," Kay said. "The bad news is I had to throw the Beretta you loaned me into a river."

"What? Why?"

"Sorry, I can't tell you."

"Okay. What's the good news?"

Kay handed Eloise a box wrapped with Christmas paper, the paper depicting fat, laughing Santas. It was the only wrapping paper Kay had available. Eloise carefully took the wrapping paper off, making sure she didn't tear it, which was something Kay never understood. Whenever she was given a present, she just ripped the paper off.

When Eloise opened the box and saw the Beretta, she said, "How sweet of you"—like Kay had given her a box of chocolates. "Are you sure you can't tell me why you had to toss my gun? I can keep a secret, you know."

"I wish I could," Kay said. "But I can tell you I didn't do anything illegal." That was sort of true. Killing Billy had been an act of self-defense, but some nitpickers might think that shooting Otis in the knee was illegal.

Eloise Voss turned out to be a hoot, especially after her first martini. She'd joined the Secret Service in 1964, at the age of twenty-four, the year after Kennedy was assassinated. She served under every president from Lyndon Johnson to Bill Clinton, retiring in 1995, in the second year of Clinton's first term. Most often, she was responsible for protecting the First Lady and the presidents' children. The stories she told about the presidents' wives—particularly Barbara Bush and Hillary Clinton—were hilarious. And Kay was sure Eloise wasn't telling her the *really* good stories—the ones she'd take to her grave.

Kay could see a lot of herself in Voss—a tough lady still going strong at seventy-six—and Kay could imagine herself being like her when she was older. The only difference was that Kay would never be able to share her experiences working for Thomas Callahan.

About an hour after Eloise arrived, the buzzer sounded. Kay punched the intercom button and said, "Yes? Who is it?"

"FedEx. Delivery for Zimmerman."

"You buzzed the wrong apartment," Kay said.

From the couch, Eloise said, "Tell him the Zimmermans live in 912."

"The Zimmermans live in 912," Kay repeated.

Kay sat back down and said to Eloise, "Sorry about that. Now finish the story about Nancy Reagan. I can't believe she did that."

"But she did," Eloise said. "Nobody pushed Nancy around."

FINALLY, SHE WAS HOME, Jamal thought. But he needed to wait awhile. Hamilton might get suspicious about someone knocking on her door right after she got a wrong apartment buzz.

Twenty minutes later, Jamal saw a pizza guy coming down the street in his direction. The guy nodded to Jamal as he walked by him. He was probably going into the apartment building that Jamal was leaning against.

Jamal let him pass and then said, "Hey, pizza boy."

The guy turned around and said, "What?"

Jamal didn't take out his gun. He knew he didn't need it. "Give me the pizza. And that stupid fuckin' hat."

The pizza guy just stood there—he was about Jamal's height and outweighed him by about twenty pounds—but Jamal knew the guy was a sheep and the guy knew Jamal was a wolf.

"Look, I don't want any trouble," he said.

"Then give me the pizza and that stupid hat, and get the fuck out of here." The guy took off his hat, handed it to Jamal, and handed him the pizza, insulated bag and all, then he took a breath and walked away. That is, he walked for about twenty feet, before he started running.

Jamal laughed. He put on the Domino's hat and walked across the street to Hamilton's building. He hit about a dozen doorbells, said "Delivery" when someone answered, and finally some trusting fool buzzed him in. He walked over to the elevator and hit the Up button. The smell of the pizza was driving him crazy.

He planned to knock on her door, and he figured that even though she hadn't ordered a pizza, she'd still open the door. He'd go into the apartment, use a sofa cushion or a pillow or some fuckin' thing to muffle the sound of the shot, and kill her. Then he'd eat the pizza.

The elevator stopped on the eighth floor and he got off—and that's when he saw the old lady walking down the hall, holding a box in her hands. He hesitated for just a second, then kept going. The lady was older than dirt, probably couldn't see for shit, and all she'd remember seeing was a guy with a red Domino's hat, carrying a pizza box.

ELOISE WAS FEELING GOOD, a pleasant buzz from two martinis. She really liked Hamilton. She assumed Hamilton worked for one of the intelligence agencies. A couple of times during the course of her Secret Service career Eloise had thought about transferring to the CIA—when she was mad at her boss or bored with an assignment—but she never did. Although a job with one of the spy shops would have been fun. She heard the elevator ding and saw a man step into the hallway. Red hat, pizza box in his hand. Pizza sounded good. Hamilton made a great martini but she wasn't much of a hostess and hadn't offered Eloise any-thing to eat.

As she got closer to the pizza guy, she realized it was the same young man she'd seen standing across the street. She had no doubt it was the same guy. She smiled at him as they passed each other in the hall, then turned her head to look at him. She could see what she was sure was the outline of a pistol under his shirt; the way he was holding the pizza box pulled the material of his shirt tight around the weapon.

Eloise took the Beretta out of the box and placed the box on the floor. She'd already loaded a magazine into the Beretta when she'd been fiddling with it earlier. She jacked a bullet into the firing cham-ber, clicked off the safety, and turned around—and as she turned she put the Beretta behind her back.

The pizza guy—who she was certain wasn't a pizza guy—had stopped and was about to knock on a door. Hamilton's door.

JAMAL WAS ABOUT TO KNOCK, then noticed the old lady he'd just passed coming down the hall toward him. *Son of a bitch.* Why was she coming back? And if he didn't knock on the door, she'd wonder what he was doing. Then he thought he'd pretend he'd just gotten a phone call, take out his phone, and talk on it until she passed.

When she was about twenty feet from him, she smiled at him and said, "I forgot my umbrella."

Jamal thought: *Your umbrella? It's ninety fuckin' degrees outside and there's not a cloud in the sky.*

When she was about ten feet from him, she pointed a gun at his face. "If you reach for your gun, I'm going to put a bullet through your head."

For just a second, Jamal thought about rushing the woman and tak-ing the weapon from her, but then he saw the look in her eyes. The old bitch wasn't kidding. He could tell. Without a doubt, she'd kill him if he made a move.

ELOISE MADE JAMAL lie down on the hallway floor and, while holding the muzzle of the Beretta against the back of his head, removed the Glock he was carrying. She knocked on Hamilton's door, and when Kay answered, Eloise said, "I think pizza boy here was planning to kill you."

30

Kay was furious. She didn't know who had sent Jamal Howard to kill her and Jamal wasn't talking. If he had actually taken a shot at her—or if he'd even drawn his gun—he could have been arrested for attempted murder and might have given up whoever had hired him in exchange for a reduced sentence. And she had no doubt he'd been hired; he hadn't acted on his own. Unfortunately, the only crimes Jamal had committed were possessing an unregistered weapon and stealing a pizza.

After the cops hauled Jamal off, Kay called Eagleton and asked him—no, she *told* him—to keep her updated on Jamal's case. She also told him to have someone check if the gun in Jamal's possession had been used to kill Danzinger.

An hour later, Eagleton reported that Jamal's gun was not the weapon used to kill Danzinger. He also said that Jamal would be arraigned the next day, and if he didn't plead guilty, he'd be released on bail and his trial wouldn't be for months.

But who had sent Jamal? There were only three possibilities Kay could think of.

One was Prescott. Prescott might want her dead because Kay knew—even if she couldn't prove it—that Prescott was one of the people controlling the Callahan Group. But Kay seriously doubted that Prescott would have her killed, and if she had decided to, she wouldn't have sent a twenty-something D.C. gangbanger. A woman in her position would certainly have access to a more qualified assassin.

Which left two logical suspects: Dylan Otis and Fang Zhou. Otis knew Kay's name, and she figured that Otis had told Fang who she was. So she guessed that one of them had sent Jamal, but she didn't know which one—but she knew someone who might be able to tell her.

Kay called Prescott again, but she was unavailable, so Kay told the NSA operator to tell Prescott to call her as soon as possible, that the matter was urgent. Ten minutes later, she received a text message from a blocked number, telling her to go immediately to a café in Greenbelt, Maryland. Greenbelt was the last Metro stop on the line going to Maryland. It was also the closest stop to Fort Meade.

THE FIRST THING Prescott said to her at the café was: "This has to stop. You have to quit calling me. Our business is finished."

"Well, it might have been," Kay said, "but somebody tried to kill me today."

"What?" Prescott said. "Who?"

It appeared that even the see-everything, hear-everything NSA didn't know about Jamal Howard's arrest. Or maybe Prescott did know and was just pretending she didn't. With Prescott, it was impossible to know when she was telling the truth.

Kay told Prescott how Howard had shown up on her doorstep, armed, and that if it hadn't been for a neighbor, she could have been killed.

"How do you know he planned to kill you?" Prescott said.

"Why else would a kid armed with a Glock show up at my apartment pretending to be a pizza delivery guy? And I'm guessing that Fang Zhou was the one who sent him."

"Fang wouldn't do that," Prescott said.

"Why wouldn't he? He must know that I know he was the one responsible for the attack on K Street. Maybe he thinks that by eliminating me, he's protecting himself."

When Prescott didn't respond, Kay said, "If you think I'm going to sit around and be a target, you don't know me at all."

"All right," Prescott said. "I'll find out more about this man Howard. I can dig deeper into his background than the cops can, and I'll see who he's been talking to."

"And if you find out he was working for Fang?" Kay said. "What will you do then?"

"I don't know. In the meantime, I can offer you some protection. I'll assign some of my people to watch over you."

Kay didn't like the sound of that. Kay didn't want the NSA watching every move she made—but the NSA was probably *already* watching every move she made. She also realized that Prescott's team could be used to shuttle her off to wherever the NSA put problematic people.

She was in way over her head.

"I don't need protection," Kay said. "I can protect myself. And I'll give you a few hours to investigate Howard, but if—"

"Don't try dictating terms to me," Prescott said.

Kay stood up. "I'll give you a few hours to get some answers," she repeated, "but if you don't find anything, I'll deal with this on my own. And in my own way."

She could feel Prescott's eyes boring holes into her back like laser beams as she left the café.

31

The long drive from North Carolina to Miami had practically killed Otis, his knee in agony the whole way.

He wanted to sleep and rest his leg, but he couldn't. He needed to meet his connection tonight to get things moving, and there were a couple of things he needed to do first. He drove to a drugstore and found a knee brace. The brace didn't allow his knee to bend, and provided enough support so that he could walk with only a cane. He hated the crutches; they made him appear helpless, and it wouldn't be smart to let the man in Miami think he'd be an easy target. His next stop was a Kmart next door to the drugstore, where he bought some new clothes. He was still wearing the smelly overalls he'd borrowed from Younger and wanted to be shed of them. He changed clothes inside the Kmart, which was tricky with the brace. Lastly, he bought a gym bag, and when he returned to his truck, he transferred the cash from the old bag to the new bag, leaving only the gold in the old bag.

Now feeling more presentable, he drove to a pawnshop in South Miami. He knew it would still be open because the guy who owned it also lived there, and he didn't close until he went to bed. Otis removed

234 | M. A. LAWSON

the heavy bag containing the gold from his truck and walked toward the door on his cane. It was a bitch trying to open the door balanced on the cane, holding the gym bag, but the Hispanic kid sitting behind the counter just watched him, making no attempt to help. Little shit.

The pawnshop was filled with the usual collection of crap—musical instruments, bicycles, jewelry, watches, knives—and most of the stuff was covered with a thick layer of dust. This particular pawnshop didn't make its money by selling the items in the shop. The Hispanic kid had suspicious eyes, and one of his hands was out of sight, under the counter, probably gripping a sawed-off shotgun. One thing Otis didn't see were surveillance cameras, which was expected considering Sol Goldman's clientele.

"Is Sol here?" Otis asked the kid.

"Who are you?"

"Tell Sol it's Otis."

The kid hesitated for a second, then picked up a phone on the counter, punched a button, and said, "There's a guy named Otis here." He heard the kid describe him to Sol. He hung up the phone and said, "He's in his office," and pointed to an unmarked door. "Knock before you go in."

Otis walked over to the door and knocked as instructed. A voice called out, "Come in." He entered, and once Goldman saw it really was Otis, he placed the .45 he'd been holding on top of the desk and said, "Otis, it's good to see you. What's with the cane?"

"Motorcycle accident," Otis said.

"Those damn bikes will kill you," Goldman said. Otis could tell that Goldman didn't believe his story, but who cared?

Goldman was in his seventies, tall and skinny. He was wearing a Hawaiian shirt and his thinning gray hair was tied in a ponytail, which Otis thought looked absurd. He had small blue eyes that glittered like the cheap costume jewelry in his shop.

Otis dropped the gym bag on Goldman's desk.

"What have you got?" Goldman said.

"Gold. A million."

Goldman nodded. A million was a lot to process, but he'd handled more in the past.

"How much can I get for it?" Otis asked.

Goldman shrugged. "After my cut, probably seventy cents on the dollar."

Otis grimaced but he didn't doubt Goldman. He'd used him before when he had jewelry, artwork, or bearer bonds to unload and he trusted him. Goldman's business was turning stolen goods into spendable cash, and he wouldn't have stayed in business for thirty years if he ripped people off.

"It'll take a day or two," Goldman said.

"Yeah, I figured that," Otis said. "I also need two IDs. How much will that run me?"

"If you want good quality, about ten. If you want flawless, twenty-five."

"I want flawless."

"Okay, that'll take a few days, maybe longer than it'll take to deal with the gold."

"Just do the best you can. I'm in a hurry."

"A job go bad on you?"

"You could say that. But you don't need to worry. Nobody knows I'm here."

Before he left the pawnshop, the Hispanic kid took Otis's picture with a digital camera for his new identity documents.

Thankful he could now get some sleep, Otis checked into one of the first motels he saw, a low-budget place called the Starlight. The Starlight was in a pink-painted building constructed out of cinder blocks and had two floors, maybe forty units total, and a pool at one end. He told the clerk he wanted a room on the first floor because he had a bad leg—which the clerk could clearly see when Otis limped into the lobby on his cane. He paid for the room for a week in cash.

EVA BECKMAN WAS WATCHING when Otis left the pawnshop, and she followed him to a motel. She had been following him ever since he left North Carolina, and had been texting Prescott periodically with updates. She texted Prescott now, reporting that Otis had visited a pawnshop in South Miami called Mercury Pawn and had just checked into a place called the Starlight Motel.

32

Prescott returned to Fort Meade after her meeting with Hamilton and told Brookes to see if he could find a link between Jamal Howard and Fang Zhou or Dylan Otis. While still sitting at her desk, she closed her eyes. She'd nap until Brookes reported back. An hour later she was awakened when her cell phone vibrated with a text message from Beckman. Beckman said that Otis had visited a place called Mercury Pawn owned by a man named Solomon Goldman. She had no idea why Otis would be visiting a pawnshop; she doubted he was trying to turn his wristwatch into cash.

Prescott called a man she worked with frequently at the FBI and asked him to find out what he could about Goldman. The only criminal record Prescott had been able to find was for forging signatures on other people's checks, and that arrest was decades old.

The FBI man asked, "Is this terrorism related?"

"What do you think?" Prescott replied. "And I need to hear back from you tonight. This can't wait until tomorrow."

Half an hour later, the FBI man called her back and said, "According to our field office in Miami, Goldman's a fence. He's the guy you go to when you have jewelry or art to unload. He also knows the right people if you need a new ID or a way out of the country."

Now Prescott understood why Otis had visited Goldman.

At that moment, Brookes walked into her office—the man looked exhausted—and said, "An unregistered cell phone called Jamal Howard once. That phone is currently located in the Chinese embassy. I can't find any link between Dylan Otis and Howard."

"Very good, Brookes. Now try to get some sleep, but stick around in case I need you."

So Fang had sent Howard. Who else in the Chinese embassy would have called him? But Prescott couldn't allow Hamilton to go after Fang, which Hamilton would certainly do if she found out he had hired Howard to kill her. She could not, under any circumstances, for any reason, permit Hamilton to ruin the operation involving the Zytek spy.

She needed to *end* this—but she knew that Hamilton wasn't going to stop. Hamilton was the type who would never stop.

She rose from her chair and walked over to a window and looked down at the massive parking lot seven floors below her. Even though it was after eight, it was mostly full. The NSA never slept. She touched the leaves of her terminally ill ficus plant as she thought about Hamilton. Finally, she decided there was only one thing to do. Hamilton wasn't giving her a choice.

She called Brookes—she'd forgotten she'd told him to get some sleep—and told him to bring her another secure phone for Hamilton.

"Do you want me to monitor the phone?" Brookes said.

"Yes, but don't start monitoring for two hours. Oh, and go see Ackerman. I'll bet he has some pills that will help you stay awake."

She texted Hamilton next, telling her to meet her at the same café in Greenbelt where they'd met earlier. The text said: *I have the information you want.*

.   .   .

PRESCOTT WAS ALREADY in the café when Kay arrived, sitting at a table, ignoring the cup of coffee in front of her. Kay sat across from her and said, "Well?"

"My people found several phone calls between Dylan Otis and Jamal Howard. We don't have recordings, but we know that the calls were made. We couldn't find any link between Fang and Howard, so it appears that Otis may have sent Howard to kill you."

"Thanks," Kay said. "Now will you tell me where Otis is?"

"He's at a place called the Starlight Motel in Miami."

"Miami?"

"Yes."

"What's he doing there?"

"I'm not sure, but he visited a man named Solomon Goldman, who owns a pawnshop there. According to the FBI, Goldman's a well-connected guy, someone who can turn Otis's gold into cash and get him a new ID. So my guess is that Otis is planning to get out of the country and Goldman is helping him."

Kay looked away to hide her reaction to the bombshell that Prescott had just dropped. She wasn't shocked that Otis was trying to flee the country; it was something else that Prescott had said.

"Is there anything else?" Kay said.

Prescott rose. "I don't care what you do, Hamilton, as long as Otis isn't arrested." She turned to leave, then said, "Oh, I almost forgot." She took a cell phone out of her purse and put it on the table in front of Kay. "That's to replace the phone you put in Otis's truck. Use it to call me, but only if you feel it's absolutely necessary."

Prescott left the café—but this time it was Kay's eyes boring holes into Prescott's back.

. . .

KAY LOOKED DOWN at the phone and thought, *You treacherous cunt.*

How had Prescott known that Otis had gold? She hadn't told Prescott about it.

She must have heard them talking about it through the fucking iPhone she'd given her. Cell phones these days made it possible to not only track people but also to eavesdrop easily.

And that's what Prescott must have done. When Kay caught up with Otis at Billy's place, Kay remembered saying to Otis: *I don't care about you—you're just hired help—and I don't care about all that gold and cash on the coffee table.*

So that must be how Prescott had known about the gold, but Kay suddenly had a bigger revelation: Prescott had been willing to let Otis and Billy kill her. Prescott must have known that she was in trouble, but instead of sending in the cops or the NSA to help her, she'd been willing to let her die.

PRESCOTT RETURNED to Fort Meade and called Beckman. "I'm e-mailing you a picture of a woman. She'll show up at the motel where Otis is staying in the next few hours. Call me when you see her."

"Yes, ma'am."

Prescott glanced at her watch. Even though it was almost ten p.m., she decided that now would be a good time to update her partners. She knew they wouldn't care about the hour any more than she did, not when it came to Hamilton.

33

Kay needed to get to Miami before Otis left the country, but she didn't want her name on a flight manifest, and she knew that she couldn't take a commercial flight with what she was planning to bring with her.

She left her cell phone and the NSA phone that Prescott had given her in her apartment, and took the stairs down to Eloise Voss's place. Eloise would still be up; she was a night owl. She smiled when she saw Kay, then seeing the tense expression on Kay's face, said, "You're not here to borrow my new Beretta, are you?"

"No. I just need to use your phone."

"Okay," Eloise said. "I assume you can't tell me why you can't use your own phone."

"I'm sorry," Kay said, "but I can't."

"Okay," Eloise said. "Do you need privacy?"

"Do you mind?" Kay asked.

Kay called Eli and told him what she needed: a charter flight to Miami that night. Callahan had a couple of charter outfits he used, but Kay didn't know how to get hold of them. Eli would.

"What are you doing, Kay?" he asked.

"Eli, I don't have time to tell you right now and I'm not using a secure phone."

Her statement was greeted with silence.

"Eli, please. Just get me a plane."

"Okay. But it may take a while at this time of night. I'll call you when I've got something."

"Don't call my cell phone, Eli. Call me at this number." She gave him Eloise's number and hung up before he could ask more questions or change his mind.

She called out to Eloise that she was off the phone, and told her that she had to wait for a call back.

"Would you like a drink while you're waiting?" Eloise said.

"Maybe some coffee," Kay said. "No booze."

"You lead an interesting life, young lady."

Eloise made her a cup of coffee using one of those fancy machines that makes a single cup at a time, and poured a brandy for herself. Knowing Kay wouldn't tell her what she was doing, Eloise said, "So how's your daughter doing? I haven't seen her in a while."

"Eloise," Kay said, "I swear when this is all over with I'm going to treat you to the best steak dinner in Washington."

Forty minutes later, Eli called back and told her a charter flight was waiting for her at National.

Eli concluded the call by saying, "Be careful, Kay."

Kay returned to her apartment and packed a knapsack. She tossed in enough clothes for a couple of days, but before she placed the clothes inside, she checked every item to make sure there weren't listening or tracking devices sewn into a lining or disguised to look like a button. She also packed a wig with short dark hair, followed by her new Glock, a Taser, night-vision binoculars, and a jackknife with a four-inch blade. It was a good thing she was taking a charter flight.

The last things she tossed into the knapsack were a driver's license and a few credit cards that belonged to a woman named Elle McDonald. Considering what she was planning to do, she didn't want to use her real name or allow anyone to be able to prove she'd been in Miami. She had several sets of false identities from Callahan, but she also still had an alias from her time in the DEA. She'd gone undercover for a long period in Miami and still had the IDs she'd used, which were made out to one Elle McDonald. Although Prescott might know about her aliases from her time at the Callahan Group, Kay doubted that she would know about McDonald.

One thing she did not pack was her cell phone, and she certainly had no intention of taking the cell phone that Prescott had given her. She took the NSA iPhone and placed it in front of the clock radio beside her bed and tuned the radio so that the only sound coming out of the speaker was irritating static. She was hoping that the NSA would think that the iPhone had malfunctioned—and if not, she would at least drive whoever was monitoring her insane.

She took a cab to National Airport, and the plane took off twenty minutes later. The only people on board were Kay and two handsome young pilots. No one searched her before she boarded.

34

Prescott once again arrived first at the room in the Key Bridge Marriott.

Lincoln arrived next. He was dressed in a suit and tie, which made Prescott wonder if there was some CIA op happening that required him to burn the midnight oil at Langley. Grayson arrived five minutes later, dressed casually in jeans and a T-shirt, both spattered with paint.

"Okay," she said. "It appears that Callahan is going to make it. I had one of our doctors take a look at his electronic medical records, and he says Callahan's improving and he'll recover completely unless something drastic happens."

"Thank God," Grayson said.

"How long will that take?" Lincoln asked.

Prescott shrugged. "Probably a month before he's able to function normally, but since all he does is sit at a desk, he may be able to come back to work sooner than that."

"What about Hamilton?" Lincoln asked.

"She's the reason I called this meeting. Hamilton has tracked down the people who stole the safe from Callahan's office. She's killed a second one."

"Jesus," Grayson muttered.

"She's also identified the leader of the group, a bank robber named Dylan Otis. She planted a cell phone in Otis's vehicle, and we've tracked him to Miami. Hamilton also knows that Fang Zhou was the one who hired Otis."

"For God's sake, Olivia," Lincoln said.

"Hey! Don't you dare take that tone with me. You wouldn't have been able to control that woman either."

Lincoln made an expression that Prescott interpreted as: *Well, I don't know about that*—and she felt like hitting him.

"I've told Hamilton that she has to leave Fang Zhou alone," Prescott said.

"Do you think she will?" Grayson said.

"Yes," Prescott said. "I think she understands the importance of not exposing the operation involving Winston. The problem, however, is that Hamilton wants . . . Hell, I guess she wants *justice*. She wants someone to pay for killing the innocents, people like Sally Ann Danzinger and the men who worked for Callahan."

"So what are you going to do?" Lincoln asked.

"I gave her Otis's location."

"She'll kill him," Grayson said.

"Yes, Grayson, she'll kill him. And who cares if she does? At least this way she's less likely to go after Fang."

"But then what?" Lincoln said. "We still have the problem that Hamilton knows—or thinks she knows—that you're controlling Callahan."

"I think," Prescott said, "that what Grayson said the last time we met was correct, that Hamilton won't expose me and she'll never talk about the Callahan Group."

"Well, I'm really glad to hear you say that," Grayson said.

"I'll have to admit that I've come to admire Hamilton," Prescott said with a straight face. "It would be a shame to lose her." She rose, signaling an end to the meeting. "So, gentlemen, we'll soon be back to business as usual."

Olivia Prescott was an excellent liar. She had no intention of telling Lincoln and Grayson what she had planned for Hamilton. What they didn't seem to understand—particularly Grayson—was that Hamilton posed a threat to her personally that she couldn't allow to stand.

35

s Kay was wending her way toward Miami, and while Olivia Prescott was meeting with her partners, Fang Zhou was speaking with his wife in Beijing, where it was eleven in the morning. His wife said, as she always did, that she missed him terribly and wanted to know when he'd be home again. He, in turn, said he missed her, too, and that he wasn't sure when his horrible boss would permit him to return. She then told him he needed to speak to his son.

His son was permitted to play his video games for one hour a day but had been violating this rule and had been disrespectful toward his mother when she scolded him. Fang told her to put the boy on the phone. He said stern, fatherly things to him—how his studies came first and that disrespecting his mother was not to be tolerated—but his heart wasn't in it. They then talked about his son's performance on his soccer team; he was an excellent player and might one day be good enough for the national team.

After he'd spoken to his family, he checked the Internet again for news of Kay Hamilton. He'd been hoping to find confirmation of her death, but so far there hadn't been a report of a murder at her address. Ten minutes later, he found out why.

"It's me," Jamal said when Fang answered his phone. Fang recognized Jamal's voice.

"What can I do for you?" Fang said.

"We need to meet again. My ass is in a crack."

"Does that mean you failed to complete the job I paid you for?"

"We need to meet," Jamal said, evading the question.

"All right," Fang said.

"Where?" Jamal said.

"Let me think." He paused and then said, "Do you remember the park where we met once, the one by the river." Fang meant the same dilapidated park where he'd killed James Parker.

"Yeah, I remember. How soon can you get there?"

"I can leave immediately," Fang said.

AT MIDNIGHT, Fang pulled into the parking lot of the park near the Anacostia River. He saw only one other car: a black Honda with shiny hubcaps and one of those absurd spoilers on the trunk, like the Honda was an Indy racer. His headlights revealed Jamal in the driver's seat. Fang parked and joined Jamal in the Honda.

"What's the problem?" he asked.

"I fucked up," Jamal said. "I went to take care of that bitch, but I was arrested inside her apartment building."

"Arrested for what? Attempted murder?"

"No. For carrying an unregistered weapon. This old lady saw me and . . . Never mind the fuckin' details."

Jamal was too embarrassed to admit that a woman in her seventies had gotten the drop on him. He still couldn't believe the old woman had been packing a gun.

"I see," Fang said. "Do the police know why you were carrying a gun?"

"Shit no. I didn't tell them anything. I sure as shit didn't tell them you sent me."

"Good," Fang said. He believed him. Jamal was too street savvy to tell the police anything. On the other hand, what if the police connected him to Danzinger's murder? Would Jamal give him up then?

Jamal had suddenly become a liability.

"There's no way I'm doing time, so I'm going to skip town before the trial. The D.C. cops won't try that hard to find me. It's just a fuckin' gun charge."

"Then what's the problem?"

"The problem is the bondsman. My bail was set at fifty grand, and if I skip, he'll come after me. He's a tough motherfucker and he's smart, so he might find me. I need to give him fifty Gs to keep him from coming after me, which is pretty much all the cash I got. So I need money. Enough to take off for a while, enough to live on until things cool down."

"I see," Fang said again. He wondered what Jamal had done with all the money he'd already paid him. Fang reached into one of his jacket pockets, and Jamal stiffened and reached toward his waist.

Fang pulled out a pack of cigarettes, and Jamal relaxed and said, "Aw, man, please don't smoke in my ride."

"Okay," Fang said, and he put the cigarette pack back in his pocket and when his hand came back out it was holding the small .380 he'd been carrying. He pulled the trigger once, shooting Jamal in the side, then pulled it three more times. The last shot he fired was into Jamal's head.

Jamal had become a complication he didn't need.

36

Kay's charter flight had landed in Miami at about five a.m. She rented a car using the Elle McDonald ID and drove straight to the Starlight Motel. She didn't know which room Otis was in, but saw a black Toyota Tundra with a crew cab in the parking lot. She was certain it was Otis's truck, even though it had Florida license plates. She thought about finding out Otis's room number, then decided not to. It was too risky to approach him in a crowded motel. She'd have to wait for him to leave.

She didn't know if Otis was an early riser or not, but she decided to take the chance that he wasn't. She drove to a nearby 7-Eleven, ate a hot breakfast sandwich, and stocked up on water, Coke, and a couple of sandwiches. She had no idea how long she'd be watching Otis. She also bought a Miami Heat baseball cap and a pair of sunglasses with large black frames.

She drove back to the Starlight Motel wearing the black wig she'd brought with her and the Miami Heat ball cap and sunglasses. From her parking spot she could see Otis's Tundra, half the rooms in the motel, and a gated area around a small swimming pool. She hoped that Otis would leave the motel soon and drive to some isolated place where she could deal with him.

Later, she thought, *Be careful what you wish for.*

OTIS WOKE UP AT NINE, feeling fairly good. His knee still ached, but it wasn't as bad as it had been. He peeled off the bandage the fat nurse had applied; the wound looked awful—the crude stiches, the swelling, an actual divot where part of his knee was missing—but it wasn't bleeding and it wasn't oozing pus. He rebandaged it to keep it clean and so he wouldn't have to look at it.

He dressed in some of the new clothes he'd gotten the day before. Since it was Florida in July, he chose a sleeveless T-shirt, cargo shorts, and flip-flops. He left the motel, leaning on the cane; he wasn't able to run or even walk very far, but at least he could get around. There was a diner only a block from the motel and he decided to walk there. That turned out to be a huge mistake. It took him fifteen minutes to get there, and by the time he arrived he was drenched with sweat and his knee felt like it was on fire.

After breakfast, he'd go back to the motel and wait. That's all he could do. Wait for his new ID and for the cash from Goldman. That almost made him smile: Goldman the gold man.

KAY WATCHED OTIS hobble toward a diner using a cane. He was obviously in pain, and that made her smile. Even better, the knee injury made Otis less mobile and gave her an advantage when it came to a fight. And there was going to be a fight.

. . .

BECKMAN CALLED PRESCOTT.

"I think she's here," Beckman said. "The woman whose picture you sent me."

"What do you mean, you *think*?" Prescott said.

"I mean it's hard to be sure. She's wearing big sunglasses and a base-ball cap, and her hair's black and not blond like it is in the picture. But it looks like her. She's parked in a car about half a block from the motel, and she's been there since about seven this morning."

"Where's Otis?"

"He went to breakfast, then came back to the motel and went out to sit by the pool. When he left for breakfast, the woman in the car got out and watched him walk to the diner, then got back into her car. What do you want me to do?"

"Nothing. Just keep watching them. If Otis leaves, stay with the woman not him, although I'll bet she follows him. And be careful she doesn't spot you. You're a very capable, well-trained agent, but she's better than you."

"Is that right?" Beckman said.

"Yes. And it would be good for you to remember that."

OTIS WAS NOW behind the low concrete wall that partially hid the motel swimming pool. Kay guessed that he was waiting for something or someone. He sure as hell wasn't working on his tan.

She wondered what had happened to Simpson. She assumed that he had taken his share of the money and split for greener pastures, but she didn't really care.

BECKMAN WAS STAYING in a room at the Starlight Motel as well. Otis didn't know who she was, so why not? She'd gotten a room on the second floor and it was pure, dumb luck that she could see the woman sitting in her car from her room. Unfortunately, she couldn't see Otis by the pool unless she stood on the walkway outside her room, so to have an excuse for standing on the walkway, she'd taken up smoking, which she hated. Her hair smelled like she'd brushed it with an ashtray. But every twenty minutes or so, she'd step out of the room, have a cigarette or pretend to blab on her cell phone, and check on Otis.

OTIS WAS RECLINING IN A LOUNGE CHAIR, reading the ads in the *Miami Herald*, looking at the classic cars that were for sale—the kind of cars he refurbished. He couldn't help but think about the Thunderbird sitting in his shop back home. The way things were looking, that Thunderbird might be sitting there for a long time.

The gate to the pool area opened and the skinny Hispanic kid who worked for Goldman walked toward him carrying a cloth shopping bag.

"Here's your money," the kid said.

"How much?"

"Seven fifty."

Shit. It had cost him two hundred and fifty thousand to convert the gold. "When will the IDs be ready?"

"At least two more days," the kid said. "It's the passport. They got so much electronic shit in 'em these days to prevent forgeries, you gotta steal a real one and modify it, and it ain't easy."

"Yeah, I understand," Otis said—no point taking out his frustration on the kid. "What about the boat?" Otis asked. One of the things he'd asked Goldman to do was arrange for a boat to take him to Costa Rica. It would drop him off at a marina where he wouldn't have to deal with customs.

"All set. You can take off as soon as the ID is ready."

When he reached Costa Rica, the first thing he'd do was find a competent doctor to fix his knee. Then he'd decide if he wanted to stay there or move on to someplace else.

He didn't know how long he'd have to wait before it would be safe to come back to the States. He'd have to wait for the cops to give up on their investigation into the K Street job. Then he should probably get new IDs for his whole family and move them out of Virginia. Then he'd form a new crew; other than restoring old cars, being a thief was the only thing he knew how to do.

"Sol will let you know when the IDs are ready," the kid said. The kid turned and walked away, and, as he did, Otis looked up at the good-looking young redhead smoking on the second-floor landing, which made him wonder if his daughter had stopped smoking after Ginnie's "intervention."

KAY SAW THE Hispanic kid walk into the pool area carrying a shopping bag. He was good-looking, tall, lithe, and graceful. He stopped and she could see him look down at someone, talking. The wall surrounding the pool prevented her from seeing who the kid was talking to, but she guessed it was Otis. Ten minutes later, the kid left and he was no longer holding the shopping bag.

BECKMAN SAW THE Hispanic kid—he was actually kinda hot—hand a shopping bag to Otis. She had no idea what the kid could be bringing Otis, but she went back inside to update Prescott anyway.

PRESCOTT FIGURED THAT the Hispanic kid worked for Sol Goldman and was bringing Otis either cash or new identity documents. But it didn't matter.

"Where's the woman?" Prescott asked.

"Still sitting in her car. Every once in a while, she leaves and walks around a bit. It's hot here and she's gotta be baking inside that car. She's not running the engine, so she doesn't have the air conditioner on."

Prescott couldn't care less about Kay Hamilton's discomfort—but it was time to move this drama forward.

"What kind of car is she driving?"

"A silver Ford Fusion," Beckman said.

"Okay, here's what I want you to do," Prescott said.

KAY SAW THE young redhead from the second floor enter the pool area. She could see her upper body over the top of the low wall, but then the woman sat down and disappeared.

OTIS WATCHED THE redhead walk toward him. She was a looker, and he was hoping she'd take off her shorts and T-shirt and strip down to a tiny bikini. He was surprised—and pleased—when the woman sat in the lounge chair nearest to his, and then scooted her chair over so she was closer to him.

Otis had committed many sins in his life, but adultery wasn't one of them. But he could still flirt with the redhead.

As soon as the woman sat down, she stuck out a hand holding a cell phone.

"Take the phone, Mr. Otis," she said. "There's someone who needs to speak to you." And Otis thought: *What the fuck is going on? How does she know my name?*

"Who are you?" Otis said.

She was still holding the phone, her slim arm stretched out so he could reach it. "Mr. Otis," she said, "take the phone."

Otis took the phone and held it up to his ear. "Hello?" he said. He sounded scared—and he was.

"Listen carefully, Mr. Otis."

It was a woman speaking, and she sounded older. He didn't recognize her voice.

"I'm an associate of the man you know as John," the woman said. "Kay Hamilton is parked across the street from your motel. She's driving a silver Ford Fusion and she's wearing a black wig, sunglasses, and a Miami Heat baseball cap. She's there to kill you."

"Who are you?" Otis said again.

"I told you. I'm a friend of John's. Now, you don't have to take my advice, but I'd suggest that you kill her before she kills you. What you could do is drive to somewhere remote—she'll follow you—and take her out before she takes you out. Good luck, Mr. Otis."

The woman hung up. Otis didn't know what to do, and while he was thinking, the redhead took the phone from his hand and left the pool area.

What the fuck was going on? How did John know where he was? And how had Hamilton found him? And how did the mysterious caller know where he was? In spite of all the precautions he'd taken, *everyone* seemed to know where he was.

But he didn't have time to worry about it. What he needed to do now was clear. He needed to take care of Hamilton.

BECKMAN RETURNED TO HER MOTEL ROOM, and her phone rang. It was Prescott.

"I want you to return to headquarters," Prescott said.

"What? You mean I'm finished here?"

"Exactly. You did your job, you did it well, and now I want you to return to base. Immediately."

37

Otis packed his clothes and cash into the gym bag he'd bought when he purchased his clothes. He had over one point seven million dollars—which wasn't going to do him much good if Hamilton killed him. He needed to do something with the money before he dealt with Hamilton.

KAY WATCHED OTIS LEAVE HIS ROOM. Thank God! He was finally going somewhere, maybe someplace where he'd be alone. She was surprised when he drove to a FedEx store. He entered the store, and a couple of minutes later, he came back out carrying a shipping box. What was he shipping and who was he shipping it to? He opened the back door of his pickup, but Kay couldn't see what he was doing.

OTIS COUNTED OUT A MILLION DOLLARS and placed the money in the FedEx box. He sealed it and took it to the clerk at the desk. When the kid asked if he wanted to insure the package, Otis almost laughed and said, "Yeah, for a million fuckin' bucks."

The kid gave him his copy of the shipping papers; if he was still alive tomorrow, he'd check to make sure the package had made it to Ginnie. He still had seven fifty for himself, which should be enough to hold him over.

Now he needed to find the right spot to take care of Hamilton.

KAY WAS PRACTICALLY TINGLING WITH EXCITEMENT.

Otis drove the streets of Miami for a while and eventually got on Highway 27, going past Hialeah. He stayed on 27 until he was going due north, passing along the eastern edge of the Everglades Wildlife area.

When 27 intersected I-75, he got onto 75. Interstate 75, known as Alligator Alley, runs due west across Florida, terminating on the west coast near the city of Naples. The highway was as flat as a pancake passing through the Everglades, the view consisting mostly of swampy saw grass and cypress trees. It was called Alligator Alley for a reason. All along the road, behind cyclone fences, were gators, their heads barely visible above the water. They gave Kay the creeps. But the fences didn't always contain the critters and they often ended up on the highway, scaring or thrilling tourists. Where was Otis going?

OTIS WAS JUST DRIVING, looking for the right place. And then he saw it: a rest area on I-75. He slowed down a little, but not too much. He glanced into his rearview mirror for the thousandth time: Hamilton in the silver Fusion was still behind him. Good.

He pulled off at the next exit and headed back to Miami. Now it was just a matter of waiting until nightfall.

38

As the light was fading from the sky, Kay watched Otis leave his room, again carrying the gym bag. He obviously wanted to keep it close to him. He pulled out of the motel parking lot and Kay gave him a one block lead.

This time, Otis didn't drive aimlessly around the city. He drove directly to Highway 27, then merged onto I-75.

Otis could only see headlights behind him, but he knew Hamilton was there. Forty minutes after he left the motel, he came to the rest area on I-75.

The rest area consisted of a grass strip with a few picnic tables and a small cinder-block building. It was dark; the lights illuminating the parking lot and the restrooms had been turned off because it was temporarily closed to the public. It was undergoing some sort of renovation or repair. When he'd driven past the place earlier in the day, he'd seen stacks of cinder blocks, lumber, and plastic pipe enclosed in a small fenced-in area with a locked gate. He'd also seen a large backhoe. There was a large wooden sign in the middle of the access road stating the rest area was closed, but Otis just drove around it, the Tundra's big tires biting into the shoulder of the road.

He parked and got out of his car as fast as he could and stepped behind the big backhoe; there was no way Hamilton would be able to see him.

KAY SAW THE TUNDRA'S TAILLIGHTS leave the highway. She slowed down, and when the Tundra stopped moving, Kay immediately pulled to the side of the road, parking on the narrow shoulder of I-75. She reached into the bag she'd brought with her and pulled out the night-vision binoculars.

Otis had driven around the sign blocking the access road. She trained the binoculars on the Tundra, but couldn't see him. He must have gotten out of the truck. She scanned the rest area more closely and could see a backhoe, a small enclosure containing a bundle of plastic pipe, and the low concrete building. Why had he pulled into this place?

She was almost positive—*almost* being the operative word—that Otis didn't know she was following him. There was no way he could have known that she'd placed the cell phone in his truck. But why had he stopped at the closed rest area? Was he planning to bury the gold she had seen at Billy's place on the river? No, that didn't make much sense.

Whatever the case, if she wanted to make Otis pay for killing Callahan's people, this was the time and place to do it.

She removed the black wig and the Miami Heat ball cap—she didn't need a disguise anymore—jacked a round into her Glock, and stepped out of her car. She left her car on the shoulder of 75 and walked in. Carefully.

ENTERING THE REST AREA was like entering a box canyon. There were a few trees near the picnic benches but there was no place to hide along the access road. The only advantage Kay had was the darkness, and the best thing she could do was move quickly.

It was about two hundred yards from the highway to Otis's truck, which was parked near a large backhoe. When she reached it, she stayed behind the truck, breathing harder than she liked.

The only way Kay could get behind the restroom building—which is where she suspected Otis was—was to take the rough, muddy path between it and the backhoe. She looked through the night-vision binoculars again, but she didn't see anything except the big machine. She started forward and accidently kicked a small rock. *Shit!* She immediately stopped.

HAMILTON WAS THERE; Otis heard her. She was near his truck, probably waiting for him to show himself. Then he had an idea: one of the oldest tricks in the book.

Very carefully, and very quietly, he searched the ground until he found a good-sized rock, a bit larger than a baseball. He transferred his gun to his left hand, and threw the rock over the building. It was perfect: You could hear it hit the vegetation behind the building but it was just a slight noise, like something moving through the brush.

KAY HEARD A NOISE from behind the building, which is where she'd thought Otis might be. She started to move forward, then stopped and looked through the night-vision binoculars again—and smiled.

OTIS WAS WAITING, the .45 in his right hand, the cane in his left. He knew that Hamilton would have to walk right past him, and when she did, he'd shoot her. He wondered what the hell was taking her so long. Then he found out.

262 | M. A. LAWSON

"Otis, drop the gun."

Shit! Instead of walking past the backhoe, she had sneaked around it and come up behind him. Without turning to look at her, Otis asked, "How'd you know where I was?"

"Night-vision binoculars. I saw your feet under the backhoe. Now drop the gun."

Fucking night vision. It had never occurred to him that she'd have that sort of equipment.

He lowered the gun so that it was beside his leg, but he didn't drop it. He turned slowly.

"Drop the gun!" she said.

He didn't drop the gun. He completed the turn so that he was facing her; her blond hair almost created a halo around her head in the darkness. But she was definitely no angel.

"Goddamnit, Otis, drop the gun!"

He wasn't going to let her take him. He wasn't going to spend the rest of his life in a cage. He had quick hands; all he had to do was flex his wrist and fire. And he remembered the way she'd hesitated when she should have shot Shirley. All he needed was a millisecond of hesitation.

Otis must have done something—but all he knew was that he'd barely moved his hand when she shot him.

"DAMN IT," KAY SAID SOFTLY. "Why didn't you just drop the gun, Otis?" She hadn't wanted to kill him before she had a chance to question him.

She kicked the .45 out of his right hand and knelt down beside him. She'd hit him in the middle of the chest. She knew he was going to die, but there was one thing she needed to know.

"Who told you I was coming for you, Otis? Who told you?"

Otis didn't answer.

Otis was dead.

Kay needed to get moving. With the night-vision goggles, she found the shell casing ejected from her Glock. She picked up the .45 that Otis had been holding and put it in her back pocket. She searched his pockets and removed his wallet and cell phone. She walked back to Otis's truck and grabbed the gym bag from the front seat. She also removed the NSA phone she'd planted. She'd toss it into the Everglades later. She opened the glove box and removed the registration and insurance information. That would slow the cops down a little. Lastly, she used the bottom of her T-shirt to wipe her fingerprints off the truck.

She walked quickly back to her car. She wasn't worried about being arrested for Otis's murder. The police would have a hard time proving she'd ever been in Miami, and she was sure that nobody had seen her shoot him. There weren't any houses around, just cars zooming down Alligator Alley.

When she reached her car, she finally looked inside the gym bag. Just as she'd expected, there was a shitload of cash, but it didn't look like as much as she'd seen on the coffee table at Billy's place. Maybe Simpson had the rest. Whatever the case, it was still a lot.

She started to head back to the airport where the charter plane was still waiting for her. In an hour, she'd be out of Florida. As she was driving, she thought about the question she'd asked Otis: *Who told you I was coming for you?* The answer was obvious. Other than Eli, the only one who could have known she would go to Florida was Olivia Prescott.

THE OLD BULL ALLIGATOR smelled blood and he crept forward on his clawed, webbed feet. The thing that bled wasn't moving. He grabbed it by one of its limbs and began pulling it toward the swamp. He had some difficulty getting it through the gap in the fence, but he was strong and kept tugging and tugging until it was through the gap. The old bull would shove it under the water, beneath a fallen cypress log, and when it was nice and ripe in a few days, he'd gorge himself.

39

Prescott had told Brookes to look for reports in the Miami area of young women being killed within the last twenty-four hours. Brookes reported back that the only female homicide victim had been a woman named Maria Gomez, and she'd been killed by her husband.

"Where are Hamilton's cell phones?" she asked Brookes. Brookes reported that Hamilton's personal cell and the NSA iPhone were both in her apartment. Neither phone had moved in the last twenty-four hours and no calls had been made. The NSA cell continued to broadcast static, which made Brookes want to jam toothpicks into his eardrums.

THE REST AREA construction workers found an abandoned black Toyota Tundra pickup. They also found a cane. They called the sheriff in Collier County, who sent a deputy. He didn't find any paperwork in the glove box of the Tundra to identify the owner. He called in the license plate number, but the plates belonged to a Mazda minivan owned by a man from Jacksonville.

Then the deputy got called away to a three-car pileup farther west on I-75. On the way, he told the dispatcher to send a tow truck to the rest area to haul away an abandoned vehicle. He told himself he would run the VIN number later—but he never did.

PRESCOTT HAD MADE a mistake by calling Beckman back to D.C. too soon. She should have kept her watching Hamilton. She figured that Hamilton was most likely dead, but she couldn't be sure. Frustrated, she decided to try calling her. She was shocked when Hamilton answered.

"Hello," Hamilton said.

"Where are you?" Prescott said.

"My apartment. Why?"

"What did you do about Otis?"

"Nothing," Hamilton said.

"You're lying," Prescott said. But she couldn't tell Hamilton that the reason she knew she was lying was because Beckman had seen her in Miami.

"Hey, believe what you want, Olivia. But I'm done with you and Callahan and this whole mess," Hamilton said, and hung up.

BUT KAY WASN'T FINISHED. Not yet.

Fang Zhou still had to pay for what he'd done.

40

Kay tucked her hair under a baseball cap, put on shorts, a sleeveless T-shirt, and running shoes. In her fanny pack she put ten thousand dollars in cash—money she'd taken from Otis. She'd been pleased to find seven hundred and fifty thousand in the gym bag she'd removed from Otis's truck. She'd use some of the money to deal with Fang; the remainder she considered her severance pay for leaving Callahan's employment. She wasn't about to return the money to its rightful owner: the Chinese.

She didn't take her cell phone. She left the building and, while stretching, looked around to see if she could spot anyone watching her. Then she started running—fast. She figured if Prescott had anyone following her, they were going to either have to run to keep up with her or they'd have to tail her in a car, which would be moving slowly and she'd spot it. She constantly switched directions, and an hour later, sweating like crazy, she figured that she'd lost a tail if there'd ever been one. She entered an office building on New York Avenue and took the elevator to the fifth floor to the office of the Goreman Agency.

She didn't know anything about Frank Goreman other than what she'd read in the *Washington Post*. He was a private investigator, and a couple of days ago he caught a rapist the police hadn't been able to catch. The paper said that Goreman had been a decorated detective when he was on the force, and although he was usually a one-man shop, he used other retired cops whenever he needed extra hands. But the information in the article was all Kay really knew. She'd been hesitant to research detective agencies online because she feared that Prescott's elves would be able to see what she was doing.

Goreman looked surprised to see a tall, striking blonde enter his office, albeit a sweaty blonde. To make sure she had Goreman's undivided attention, Kay took the ten grand in cash from her fanny pack and plopped it on his desk. Goreman was short for an ex-cop—only about five-foot-eight—but he was strongly built. He had a forgettable face and was neatly attired in a white short-sleeved shirt and tie, and Kay thought that he'd fit right in with the sales reps at Sears.

Kay told him she wanted Fang Zhou followed for the next five days. Five days should be long enough for her to learn about his routine.

"You want me to follow a Chinese diplomat? I'm not sure I want to do that," Goreman said.

"This isn't about Fang's position at the Chinese embassy," Kay said. "It's personal. And all I want you to do is follow him and report back to me. I want to get a sense of his habits, where he goes after work, what he likes to do, where he likes to eat, and so forth."

She would have followed him herself, but she was afraid Prescott's people were watching her.

"Am I going to have a bunch of FBI agents crawling up my ass if they see me tailing this guy?" Goreman asked.

"No," Kay said. "I'm telling you this doesn't have anything to do with the U.S. government, and I'm not asking you to do anything illegal."

"Okay. My rates are—"

"That's ten thousand dollars," Kay said, pointing to the stack of bills on Goreman's desk. "That should be enough to cover five days. If it's more than enough, you can keep what's left over."

"How do I get hold of you?" Goreman asked.

"You don't. I'll come back in five days."

FOR THE NEXT FIVE DAYS Kay did nothing that might alarm Prescott.

She went for her morning jog.

She went shopping, and with Otis's money, bought herself an absurdly expensive pair of Jimmy Choos. She was sort of a shoe freak.

She called her daughter and had to listen to her describe, in graphic detail, the heart transplant she had seen. She couldn't believe how excited Jessica was about it. When she asked if Jessica was dating anyone, she said she didn't have time for boys. Her daughter was wonderful, but weird.

She also spoke to Eli. The last time they'd spoken was when she'd asked him to line up the charter flight to Miami. He had called her cell phone while she was in Miami, but her phone was in her apartment, and his call went to voice mail. After she returned to D.C., he had called her a couple more times, but each time she ignored his calls. So, when she finally called him back, he was mightily pissed.

She called him on her personal cell phone, and the first thing he said when he answered was, "Why in hell haven't you returned my calls? I've been worried about you."

"I'm sorry, and you have every right to be angry with me, but I can't talk about this over the phone."

"Then let's meet. Now."

"We can't. Not today."

"Why not?"

"Because I have to go down to Duke to see Jessica. She's sick. She has the flu and just needs a little TLC."

Instead of saying he was sorry to hear her daughter was ill, Eli said, "Are you telling me the truth?"

"Of course. Why would I lie about something like that? But as soon as I get back, we'll get together and talk. I promise. I can tell you right now that it's all over with and that I'm safe and I don't plan to do anything else." She said this mostly to make Prescott, who she was certain was listening in, think that she was going to leave Fang alone.

When he didn't respond, she said, "Please, Eli, just give me a few days."

He hung up. Oh, boy. But she was doing the right thing. She didn't want to see Eli and possibly put him at risk until everything with Fang was settled.

FIVE DAYS AFTER her initial meeting with Goreman, Kay returned to his office, once again sweating after her run. Goreman offered her a bottle of water, which she accepted. She took a long drink, then said, "Well? What did you find out?"

"I don't know what this guy does all day inside the embassy, but when he's not working, he chases tail. I'm sorry, I mean women. The first night, he went to a party at the French embassy and took this stunning black woman back to his place. The gal looked like a model, but I didn't get her name or attempt to follow her when she left. The next night, he went to a pricey bar in Georgetown and picked up a woman about his age, a good-looking professional type, like maybe a lawyer or a government executive. The third night he just went home after work and stayed in. The fourth night, he met with a guy in a bar in Alexandria. The guy looked familiar, like maybe I'd seen him on the news, but I don't know who he was. Anyway, after he met with the guy in Alexandria, he stopped off at a bar in Georgetown and tried to pick up some girl who looked like a college kid, but she brushed him off. Last night, he went to another party, this one at the Venezuelan embassy, then went back to his place by himself. So as near as I can tell, the guy's just a hound."

"Did he take drugs?"

"Not that I saw."

"How much did he drink?"

"Not much. He drinks, but he's not a drunk."

THE FOLLOWING DAY, Kay went for her morning run and used a pay phone to call a DEA agent she'd worked with in Miami who was now stationed in D.C. He was delighted to hear from her—until she told him what she wanted.

That night she took several cabs to a club in the Adams Morgan district of D.C., which was packed with young people, all dancing and drunk or high, and found the man she wanted—the man the DEA agent had told her about.

THE NEXT MORNING, Kay left her apartment at ten and again took several cabs to reach her destination, which was only a few miles from her apartment: a Hertz rental agency. She didn't want to drive her own car in case Prescott had installed a tracking device.

She drove to Philadelphia, two hours away. She could have found what she needed in D.C. or Baltimore, but figured it might be safer to use someone who didn't live too close to D.C. Safer for the person she planned to hire, that is, not safer for her. She checked into the Sheraton on North 17th Street and used the hotel's Internet to find what she wanted: escort services. The websites all had the escorts' pictures and disclaimers that said the women did nothing illegal and simply offered wholesome companionship.

She made appointments with three escorts, all stunning young women in their twenties.

The first escort turned her down. The second one—a busty, long-legged, dark-haired beauty—didn't. The escort, who claimed her name was Heather, was a bit surprised to see that her date was a woman—

but not too surprised. Heather smiled at Kay and asked, "Would you like me to get undressed?"

"No," Kay said. "Just sit down. Would you like a drink?"

"Sure. Champagne if you have it."

Kay took a bottle from the minibar and poured a glass for her.

"How many dates do you have in a day?" Kay asked.

Heather shrugged. "Two, sometimes three."

"Which means you make about three to five grand a day. I'm willing to pay you fifty thousand dollars for a job that will take no more than two or three days," Kay said.

"Fifty thousand?"

"Yes," Kay said. It wasn't like she was spending her own money.

"Is it something illegal?" Heather asked.

"Definitely," Kay said. "Why else would I be paying you so much?"

Heather hesitated, but then asked, "What's the job?"

And Kay knew she'd found the right girl. "You'll go to D.C., check into the Four Seasons in Georgetown, pick up a man in a bar, and take him back to your room. You can say you work for an ad agency in New York, or you're a model from California on the East Coast for a fashion shoot. Whatever. Anything that makes you comfortable."

"Then what? What happens after I pick up the guy?"

Before Heather left, Kay gave her a prepaid cell phone. She'd also bought one for herself.

After they were finished, Kay called Goreman. "I want you to follow Fang for the next two nights. I'll send another five grand. When he arrives at a bar, immediately call a woman named Heather and tell her where he is. I'll give you her number. Do you have a pen?"

THE NEXT NIGHT, Fang ended up at the Café Milano on Prospect Street in Georgetown, one of the more expensive watering holes in the

District. He'd only been there fifteen minutes—the service was so slow he hadn't even been served a drink—when a stunning brunette walked into the bar. She was wearing a black suit—the skirt ending about three inches above her knees—and a white blouse with enough buttons undone to show a remarkable bit of cleavage. She saw him and smiled, and Fang thought that it was going to be a wonderful night.

Two hours later, after a delightful dinner, Heather and Fang left the Café Milano and they drove to the Four Seasons, only a few blocks away. As soon as they arrived in Heather's suite, after a few passionate kisses, Heather took a bottle of Dom Pérignon from the small refrigerator and poured glasses for her and Fang.

Half an hour later, Fang was lying on the bed. Unconscious. Heather had placed a roofie in Fang's drink—Kay had bought it at the club in Adams Morgan from a dealer the DEA agent had told her about. As soon as Fang was out cold, Heather called Kay. Kay was already checked into the Four Seasons, and she pushed a wheelchair to Heather's room.

Kay and Heather undressed Fang, and Kay took several salacious photos of him with Heather. In some of them she was nude; in others she wore a black thong, a garter belt holding up black stockings, and stilettos with four-inch heels. In all the photos—some with Heather on top of Fang simulating sex, some with Fang tied to the headboard with white silk scarves—Heather's face was covered by her long dark hair and Kay made sure the butterfly tattoo on her ass wasn't visible.

Heather then helped Kay dress Fang, which wasn't easy, and they put him in the wheelchair. Kay pushed it to the nearest elevator and descended to the garage. They made sure they were alone, and quickly dumped Fang into the trunk of his Jaguar. Kay had gotten the keys before they'd left the room. She slid into the driver's seat and placed a brown paper bag containing twenty-five thousand dollars in the glove box—money Fang had given to Otis.

Heather, to Kay's delight, stayed cool throughout the operation. She didn't babble or act frightened; she did what she was told and moved quickly and efficiently. Kay knew nothing about Heather's past but she got the impression that the young woman had been in dicey situations before.

They drove toward Fang's house on Utah Avenue. It was close to midnight so the streets weren't filled with people. A block from Fang's place, she ran the Jaguar up over the curb and placed the nose of the car against a fire hydrant. She would have rammed the Jag into the hydrant but she didn't want the air bags to deploy because it would be harder to get Fang into the driver's seat. She and Heather got out of the car and transferred Fang from the trunk to the driver's seat and strapped him in. The last thing Kay did was slip a small clear plastic envelope into the right-hand pocket of Fang's suit coat, and got a surprise—a small .380 caliber automatic. She and Heather had been in such a hurry that they hadn't noticed the gun when they dressed Fang back at the Four Seasons. She left the gun in his pocket.

She and Heather walked away quickly, not running, but walking fast. At the first pay phone she saw, Kay called 911, saying that she'd just seen a drunk run his car into a fire hydrant and the guy appeared to be unconscious. A few blocks later, Kay thanked Heather for her help, and Heather caught a cab back to the Four Seasons. She would drive back to Philadelphia that night, tired, but fifty grand richer. Kay caught the next cab she saw and headed home, tired but satisfied.

41

The day after Fang's "accident," Olivia Prescott was sitting at her desk, having a cup of coffee, thinking that maybe everything would be okay. She'd thought about having Tate and Towers watch Hamilton after she returned from Miami but then decided she didn't need to. What she needed to do was watch Fang to make sure Hamilton wasn't stalking him. So she had assigned Tate and Towers to follow him, and told them that if they spotted Hamilton, they were to call her immediately.

After three days, Prescott decided to stop the surveillance on Fang. It appeared that Hamilton wasn't a total maniac.

She'd also spoken to Admiral Kincaid, who said the technical modification he was working on—the one he intended to embed in Chinese sonar systems—was proceeding well. She loved it when a plan came together.

Prescott turned on her computer, glanced at her schedule for the day, then went to the *Washington Post*'s website. She'd just taken a sip of coffee when a short article caught her eye—and caused her to choke on her coffee.

The article said that a Chinese diplomat named Fang Zhou had been found in his car last night, passed out but uninjured after running into a fire hydrant. The police had also found two grams of cocaine in Fang's pocket and an unregistered pistol. Prescott immediately called Eagleton at D.C. Metro and told him to find out if there was anything else about Fang's accident that hadn't been reported in the *Post*.

Half an hour later, Eagleton said that, yes, there was much more.

"They found twenty-five grand in cash in the glove box," Eagleton said, "but the weird part was that Fang said the money didn't belong to him. When we tried to give it back to him after he was released, he refused to take it. But that's not the big news. The gun Fang had was a .380, which he claimed had been planted on him. Well, a .380 isn't a common weapon, and about a week ago, a gangbanger named Jamal Howard was killed with one. They found Howard's body in a park in Anacostia, and Homicide figured that he was probably whacked by some other gangbanger, but gangbangers don't usually use .380s. They like 9s in general. So ballistics did a check and it looks like Fang's gun was used to kill this moke, Howard."

"Where's Fang now?"

"We released him. He's a diplomat. Right now the big boys upstairs and the State Department are trying to figure out what to do about him. We're not going to just send a couple of uniforms over to the embassy and arrest him."

The only thing Prescott cared about was that nobody had connected Fang to Winston or K Street or Danziger or Parker. She also knew that Fang would never be arrested for killing Jamal Howard; the Chinese would whisk him out of the country while the State Department tried to make up its mind.

But Prescott could not believe that Fang had had such a string of bad luck—not unless Kay Hamilton was the one dealing the cards.

. . .

DAO YUNYI, ambassador to the United States from the People's Republic of China, had a small smile on his face as he looked at the photos that had been e-mailed to the embassy that morning—photos of Fang Zhou in bed with an American whore. The photos had not been sent directly to Dao, but to the embassy's general e-mail address, which meant that half the people in the embassy had probably seen them.

Last night, Dao had to send a lawyer to a police station to pick Fang up after he was detained. Fang insisted that he'd been set up, that he'd been drugged by a woman he'd met in a bar—which Dao found laughable. When Dao asked *who* had set him up, Fang said it must have been the CIA, but that made no sense.

But it was worse than simply being arrested for driving under the influence. Much worse. The lawyer said that the police seemed to be particularly interested in a weapon they'd found on Fang's person.

Fang finally admitted to Dao that he'd used the gun to kill the young gangster who'd assisted in the operation to save Winston. This meant that Dao needed to get Fang out of the United States immediately, before the police could build a case against him.

Fang's biggest problem, however, wasn't being arrested by the American police for murder. His biggest problem was the money found in his car. The cash was evidence of a crime against the People's Republic. Every penny Fang had spent to save Winston had been carefully documented: the gold and cash he'd paid Otis and his men to steal the safe; the cash he'd paid Jamal Howard; even the money spent to pay off some woman's mortgage. Fang's superiors didn't care that he'd spent the money, but where had the twenty-five thousand dollars come from? It made them wonder if Fang had lied and kept some of the money for himself. A bullet in the back of the head was well within the realm of possibility.

It was possible that Fang might survive this debacle. He'd performed superbly on past assignments, and his incompetence in this case might eventually be forgiven. But ultimately, his fate hinged on his father-in-law, a man who sat on the Politburo Standing Committee—and a man known to be very protective of his daughter. He certainly wouldn't use his influence to help Fang if he found out about the photos with the whore. His daughter would be humiliated, and Fang would be finished.

A few minutes later, using his secretary's computer, Dao forwarded the photos to Fang's wife. Fang had been a rising star, but that star was about to experience a rapid, painful descent.

42

Prescott couldn't focus. She'd been in her office since six looking at a transcript of another phone call between the retired Russian colonel and the Saudi prince. The two men were speaking in code, pretending to talk about a trip the prince was planning to make to the Caspian Sea with all his wives, but they were actually discussing transporting ten kilograms of plutonium. Still, Prescott's mind kept wandering back to Hamilton. There wasn't anything left for Hamilton to do to avenge the attack on the Callahan Group, and if she was the least bit rational, she *must* realize this. But Hamilton wasn't rational.

Prescott was worried that Hamilton might have figured out she'd warned Otis that Hamilton had gone to Miami to kill him and now might come after her. No, she wasn't worried. That wasn't the correct word at all. She felt *vulnerable*—and she'd never, ever felt vulnerable before. It would be prudent to begin watching Hamilton again.

KAY WOKE UP AT SEVEN, feeling great. The only way she might have felt better was if Eli Dolan had been lying in bed next to her.

Today she was going to go see Callahan. He was finally out of the hospital and back in his crummy apartment. It was time to tell him that she was quitting the Group and would be looking for other employment. She was thinking about either the CIA or the Joint Terrorism Task Force in D.C. The task force included a gaggle of federal agencies—CIA, Homeland Security, ICE, Secret Service—as well as the local cops, and she figured she'd fit right in. And she knew how she was going to get a leg up on the competition: She was going to force Thomas Callahan to use his connections to help her.

She took a shower and instead of dressing in jeans and a T-shirt as she usually did, she put on a sleeveless blouse that matched her eyes, a tight skirt that showed off her legs, and her expensive new Jimmy Choos.

But she wasn't dressing for Callahan. Her first visit was going to be with Eli—which was why she'd picked a skirt that showed off her legs. She knew he was still annoyed with her for not keeping him in the loop, and she wanted to give him a reason to be less angry.

She called him. "Hi," she said, "would you like to meet for lunch?"

Eli didn't answer.

"Come on, Eli, I know you're pissed at me, but after you hear what I have to say, you'll understand why I didn't tell you everything I was doing."

"All right, fine," he said. What a grump.

"Do you remember where we went to brunch for your birthday? Let's meet there."

"Okay."

"Oh, and don't bring your cell phone."

"Why not?" he said.

"Just trust me. Don't bring it."

Kay didn't know if Prescott was still monitoring her or if she was monitoring Eli, but she decided not to take the chance of Prescott eavesdropping on their lunch.

. . .

AS KAY WAITED for a cab to arrive, she noticed a young woman walking on the other side of the street. The woman was wearing a cute pink baseball cap, sunglasses, and had on a snug-fitting white T-shirt and blue jeans. She was slim and moved athletically. There was something familiar about her but Kay couldn't say what; she was fairly sure she didn't know her and didn't recall ever seeing her in the neighborhood before. The woman never looked at her as she walked and then she turned into the doorway of the apartment building across the street and rang one of the doorbell buttons just as the cab stopped and picked Kay up.

SHIT! **BECKMAN HADN'T** expected Hamilton to take a cab. Beckman's car was parked near the garage exit so that if Hamilton took her car, Beckman would be able to follow. If Hamilton decided to walk, she'd follow on foot. When she saw Hamilton exit her apartment building, Beckman started walking because she didn't want Hamilton to see her just standing there. She let the cab drive half a block, then sprinted back to her car and took off after it.

She didn't know why she was following Hamilton. Prescott had called this morning and told her to tail Hamilton, report what she was doing and whom she was seeing. Then Prescott told her for the second time that Hamilton was better than her so she needed to be really cautious, but so far Beckman wasn't all that impressed. Hamilton appeared to have no idea that she was being tailed.

The cab dropped Hamilton off at a restaurant in Georgetown called the Café Deluxe. After Beckman finally found a place to park—the lack of parking probably being why Hamilton had taken a cab—she reached into the bag on the backseat of her car and put a short-sleeved blue blouse over her white T-shirt, took off the pink baseball cap, and put on a drab brown wig. She walked past the restaurant and looked into the window and saw Hamilton. She was sitting across from an absolute stud and Beckman wondered who he was.

KAY TOLD ELI EVERYTHING. As she was talking, she could see that he was about to explode, but not because of what she'd done but because of the risks she'd taken. She was glad she'd chosen someplace public for their meeting.

"I didn't tell you what I was doing," she said, "because Prescott was monitoring me around the clock. If I'd told you anything earlier, she might have gone after you, too."

"What are you talking about?" he said, and that's when she told him how she discovered Prescott was monitoring her conversations and tracking her movements.

"But that's not the worst thing she did. She told Otis I was coming after him in Miami. She must have been hoping he'd kill me so I'd never be able to reveal her connection to Callahan."

"You're being paranoid," he said.

"No, Eli, I'm not paranoid. I've seen what this woman can and will do. I told you everything so you'd know the kind of person that Callahan is working for. That *you're* working for."

"But *why* would Prescott want you dead?"

"Because she's the one who's paranoid. She's afraid I'm going to talk about her connection to Callahan."

Eli didn't say anything for a moment, then he said, "So what are you going to do?"

"I'm quitting. I was actually planning to quit before this all happened. I've had enough of Callahan's lies. And Prescott may not be the only one working with Callahan. There may be other people in the intelligence community involved and they're probably as ruthless as she is."

"What are you going to do about Prescott?"

"Nothing. I'm walking away, and I'm hoping that when I do, she and whoever else she works with will just leave me alone."

"But what will you do after you quit?" he asked.

"I have no idea. But I'm going to force Callahan to help me find a legitimate job."

Eli smiled. "Have you considered making Callahan get you a job in New York?"

At that moment, Kay knew she'd been forgiven.

SHE AND ELI left the restaurant together. She gave him a soft kiss on the lips and suggested that they meet that night for dinner. She thought she might stop by Victoria's Secret later and buy something to make the night memorable.

Callahan's apartment was about a mile from the Café Deluxe, so she decided to walk, even though the Jimmy Choos—as gorgeous as they were—weren't designed for it. As she was crossing the street, she looked both ways to make sure some idiot wasn't about to mow her down, and she noticed a woman with short dark hair coming toward her. There was something about the way the woman moved—the long, athletic strides—that was familiar.

She crossed another street, which gave her another opportunity to look around, and this time Kay was certain the woman with the short dark hair was the same woman she'd seen near her apartment. It was the woman's shoes—gray running shoes—that gave her away.

CALLAHAN LIVED IN A ONE-BEDROOM DUMP. He had a generous civil service pension, but after four divorces, it was the only place near his office that he could afford.

He was also a slob. Three weeks' worth of mail was scattered on the floor; clothes littered his couch. Kay didn't know if the unwashed dishes in his sink had been there before he'd been shot or if they'd accumulated in the short time he'd been home. Without a doubt, a mop had never been introduced to Callahan's kitchen floor.

He was sitting in a red leather recliner in front of a television that was probably a decade old, watching the Nats lose to the Mets. He didn't look too bad. When he'd answered the door he'd moved stiffly, as if he was still in some pain, but at least he was mobile. The docs had done a good job of patching him up, but now he was doing his best to undo the work they'd done. The ashtray next to the recliner was over-flowing with cigarette butts and he was drinking some amber-colored liquid.

Kay didn't see any point in beating around the bush. "I'm quitting, Callahan."

Instead of responding to what she'd just said, Callahan said, "There's an Italian place just a block from here and they don't deliver. Go pick up an order of clam linguini and a couple bottles of red wine. Oh, and the calamari appetizer. Get that, too. I've been eating nothing but fuck-ing Jell-O and soup for almost a month. I need something substantial."

"Did you hear what I just said?"

"Yeah, I heard, but we can talk about that while I eat."

Kay couldn't help but smile. "Okay, Callahan. I'll buy. My treat to celebrate your homecoming and my departure. Do you want a salad, too?"

"Hell no. I want real food. And get some garlic bread, too."

Kay walked to the restaurant and spotted the woman tailing her again. She'd ditched the blue blouse and the dark-colored wig and was once again dressed in a white T-shirt. Her hair was short and red—and now Kay remembered where she'd seen her before: in Miami, at the Starlight Motel.

Half an hour later, Callahan was stuffing his face. With his mouth full, he said, "You can't quit. Not now. You see, there's this Russian—"

"Callahan, your pal Prescott tried to kill me."

"What?"

She then told Callahan everything she'd told Eli about what had happened. She once again had the impression that he already knew most of what she was saying.

"Your ego is driving you to the wrong conclusion," Callahan said. "I mean, I haven't worked with Olivia since I left the CIA . . ."

More bullshit.

". . . but I'm telling you she would never have done what you're saying."

"She did, Callahan, but I'm not going to debate it with you anymore. I'm done. I can't work with people I don't trust. And that includes you."

Callahan shook his head, but he surprised her by saying, "Hamilton, somebody has to make the hard decisions. Now let me tell you about this Russian colonel. He's selling plutonium for a suitcase nuke to a nut in Saudi Arabia. In fact, as near as we can tell—"

"Who's we?"

"—as near as we can tell, the sale's already been made. We don't know where the material is right now—only the Russian does—but we have to find it before it ends up in Grand Central station. *Somebody* needs to deal with this, because the administration isn't."

Kay stood up. "Sorry, Callahan, not my problem."

"Hamilton, what are you going to do if you quit? What kind of job are you going to get that's as much fun as this one? Admit it. You *love* the kind of stuff you do for me and you're doing work that makes a difference. Can you really see yourself back in law enforcement? They got cops wearing body cameras now, so they can catch 'em if they break the rules, and pretty soon DEA and FBI agents will be wearing them, too. Can you see yourself in a job where you're *not* breaking rules?"

"I don't know what I'm going to do," Kay said, "but when I figure it out, you're going to help me. I have to go now but—"

"Hold on. We're not through talking."

"For now we are. I need to deliver a parting gift to Prescott."

. . .

PRESCOTT HADN'T HEARD from Beckman in five hours, and wondered why.

The last update from Beckman was a text message saying that Hamilton was meeting with Callahan, which wasn't totally unexpected. She'd contact Callahan later and find out what they had discussed. Right now, though, she just wanted to go home and get some sleep. She felt bone tired from everything that had happened in the last three weeks.

When she opened her apartment door, the first thing she noticed was that the alarm didn't start beeping. She stood in the doorway, listening, then she reached into her purse and pulled out a small .32 automatic. She'd never carried a weapon before; she didn't even own one. But with Hamilton out there, and not knowing what she might do, she'd decided it might be prudent to arm herself. She'd borrowed the gun from one of the security guards, saying only that there'd been a rash of burglaries in her neighborhood.

The smart thing to do would be to leave and call the police. Then she looked at the door; it didn't appear as if anyone had forced it open. Maybe, as tired as she was, she'd simply forgot to set the alarm that morning.

Holding the gun in front of her, ready to shoot—she wouldn't hesitate to kill an intruder—she moved into the apartment. She checked the closet nearest the door, making sure no one was hiding in it, feeling a bit silly as she did. She could see part of the living room from where she was standing. There was no evidence that it had been ransacked. She moved forward cautiously until she was standing in the living room. And there was Beckman, gagged and bound to a chair with duct tape.

On the white wall behind Beckman, in red spray paint, were the words:

LEAVE ME ALONE, OLIVIA.

ACKNOWLEDGMENTS

I would like to thank the people at Blue Rider Press for working so hard to publish this book. In particular, David Rosenthal, Katie Zaborsky, Vanessa Kehren, and Dorian Hastings. And, as always, thanks to my agent, David Gernert.

ABOUT THE AUTHOR

M. A. Lawson is a pen name for award-winning novelist Mike Lawson, author of *Rosarito Beach*, *Viking Bay*, and the eleven novels in the Joe DeMarco series. Lawson is a former senior civilian executive for the U.S. Navy.